A DARK SEPTEMBER NIGHT

A DARK SEPTEMBER NIGHT

A JUSTICE BAY MYSTERY

PATRICIA SMILEY

LEVEL
BEST BOOKS

Author Photo Credit: Guy Viau Photography

First edition

ISBN: 978-1-68512-994-1

Cover art by Level Best Designs

This book was professionally typeset on Reedsy.
Find out more at reedsy.com

For Bill—Always

Praise for A Dark September Night

"Longtime mystery novelist Patricia Smiley is on her way with a new series featuring businesswoman-turned-sleuth Emmaline McCoy and a sparkling location called Justice Bay. It's all here: Smiley's trademark humor, her witty observations, her memorable characters, her spot-on descriptions of places and people. Her observations about love, grief, and somehow getting on with life are tender and deep. *A Dark September Night* is a great start to a series that promises to be both memorable and great fun."—*New York Times* bestselling author Elizabeth George

"*A Dark September Night* is a superb read, with everything you want in a mystery—relatable characters, a setting that draws you in, a plausible plot, and a satisfying resolution. I read it in one day! Couldn't put it down."—Terry Shames, author of the Samuel Craddock series

"*A Dark September Night* is the perfect book to cozy up with on a rainy day. Welcome to Justice Bay, a sweet small town full of romance, spies, a touch of the supernatural, and of course, murder. Emma McCoy is a feisty, funny heroine you'll love rooting for."—Matt Witten, bestselling author of *Killer Story*

Chapter One

T he early Monday morning telephone call jarred me out of a sound sleep and into a nightmare, threatening my day and perhaps my career. A prominent tour group had canceled their ship reservations just before the no-refund policy kicked in. As Marketing Director for Fortuna Cruise Lines, my boss expected me to fill those empty cabins immediately, if not sooner. I raced to work, hoping to outrun an erupting volcano.

Pre-dawn light cloaked the city when I arrived at our corporate headquarters. As I dashed down the hallway toward my office to begin panic calling, I glanced out the window at the downtown Los Angeles skyline. I'd seen this view hundreds of times, at all hours of the day, but today, it seemed different. Across the street, the first ray of morning sun reflected off the skyscraper's glass windows. The bright beam caught me unawares as it burned into my retinas with the intensity of halogen headlights.

My eyelids slammed shut. Lightning flashes pierced the darkness. My world began to spin, and the smell of cinnamon overwhelmed me. I flattened my palms against the window until the dizziness receded, and I could steady myself enough to reopen my eyes.

I had no idea what had just happened, only that the burning headlights had disappeared, but the aroma of cinnamon, oddly enough, remained.

Cinnamon?

Giving myself a mental headshake, I detoured into the lunchroom to investigate the source of the scent.

"Hey, babe. What's up?"

1

Tall, blond, and lean Brad Gerber sat at a table, hunched over a cappuccino and *The Wall Street Journal*. Brad and I had been "work" friends for years until four months ago when we had a short fling. No company policy barred employees from dating, so during those first three months, we enjoyed day-sailing a rented 32-foot sloop on Santa Monica Bay, watched the latest art films, and ate at our favorite mom-and-pop Mexican restaurants.

There were many reasons for our breakup, including the challenges of being together all day at work and during our off hours. But a month ago, Brad landed in my should-have-known-better file after breaking the cardinal rule of office boyfriends. He shared intimate details of our relationship with co-workers, even exaggerating them for laughs. For the record, I rarely sing show tunes in the shower, and certainly not off-key. I'd devoted ten years of my life to this job, and with rumors of a possible promotion to vice president floating in the ether, I couldn't bear the thought of office gossip derailing all my hard work.

"Please don't call me babe," I said.

He looked around the room. "What's the big deal? Nobody is in here except us."

Brad had his charms, but that babe comment had passed its sell-by date. "We agreed to keep our relationship professional, remember?"

His smile ratcheted up to eleven. "Sorry, Ms. McCoy. Ms. Emmaline McCoy. Emma. Em. Emma-Emma-bo-bema, banana-fana-fo-fema. Fee-fi-fo-femma. Emma."

I rolled my eyes and changed the subject to avoid saying anything I'd regret later. "The Ladies-Who-Read book club canceled their Cabo Fiesta cruise."

Brad dropped the newspaper and bolted upright in the chair. He assigned passenger cabins on Fortuna's cruises, so it didn't surprise me that the news elevated his stress-o-meter. The Neptune was our smallest ship. We had others in the fleet, but the company operated on a narrow profit margin, and we couldn't afford the lost revenue.

"The Tuscaloosa Library group? When?"

"The coordinator left a message shortly before midnight," I said.

"Did she give a reason?"

"The group read *Call of the Wild* and decided a Rocky Mountains bus tour provided more of an action-adventure wilderness experience than Cabo San Lucas."

Some might disagree, I thought.

"Eighteen empty cabins," Brad said. "That's almost a quarter of Neptune's capacity. What are you going to do?"

My stomach flip-flopped, but my tone remained calm. "I'll do what I always do, Brad. Hustle. Make some calls. Find another group to fill the space." My gaze swept the counter near the refrigerator as I sniffed the air. "Did somebody bring in cinnamon rolls?"

He shrugged. "Nope. There are a couple of stale bagels in the fridge, though."

That didn't make sense. The fragrance was pungent. If the odor hadn't come from here, it must have drifted into the hallway from another office.

I turned to leave.

"Just so you know," Brad said, "even though we broke up, I still think you're hot."

Brad's cheeky come-on signaled an intentional effort to provoke me. I ignored it for now because payback delayed wasn't necessarily payback denied.

On entering my office, my desk phone rang. I hesitated before answering, fearing more bad news. When I finally picked up, a woman identified herself as Helen Marché, my aunt Lydie Halstad's Justice Bay attorney. A feeling of foreboding rattled my bones. An attorney had called me instead of my aunt.

"I'm sorry to inform you," she said, "that your aunt died last night."

Her words sucked the air from my lungs. There must be some mistake. Lydie couldn't be gone. She was only in her early sixties, physically and mentally fit, a world traveler, a brilliant and engaging human being, and most importantly, a second mother to me.

I sank into the desk chair, barely able to speak. "What happened?"

"A car hit her as she walked along the road near her home."

My fingernails bit into my palms as crushing images bounced through my head. Had she died instantly or lay in pain on the cold ground, calling for help as her life slipped away?

"Was the driver drunk?" I asked. "Speeding?"

"Whoever hit her didn't stop."

My muscles tensed. "So, the driver hit my aunt, and instead of calling 911, they left her there to die."

"She had on dark clothing. The police think the driver may not have seen her."

An angry knot formed in my stomach. "The driver must have felt the impact. Any decent human being would stop to see what happened. They could have saved her life."

Marché sounded nervous as she cleared her throat. "Yes, well—"

"Somebody killed my aunt." The moment the words left my mouth, I felt light-headed, wondering if someone had targeted her. That seemed far-fetched, but I had to know the truth. "What are the police doing to find the driver?"

"They're looking into it," Marché said. "I'm sure they'll figure it out. I called to remind you that you're the executor of Lydie's will. As her sole heir, you inherit everything, including the house and some money. Not a fortune, but a modest nest egg."

Lydie had no children. She'd married once, but it didn't last long enough for me to meet the husband. A year ago, my aunt had given me a key to her house and asked me to handle her estate—just in case, she'd said.

"Your aunt wanted to be cremated," Marché continued. "Instructions were set out in her will, including a pre-purchased columbarium niche at the cemetery for her ashes. Per your aunt's wishes, I notified the funeral home to start the process."

I'd seen those niches before. They reminded me of rows of rental mailboxes at the post office. Given Lydie's passion for travel, it seemed more appropriate to scatter her ashes from Mount Kilimanjaro or an outrigger canoe in the balmy waters off Waikiki.

"You'll have to make other decisions," the attorney said. "How soon can you come to Justice Bay?"

"I'll leave as soon as possible," I said, ending the call with faux confidence.

News of my aunt's death left me shattered, but I had work to do. I took a deep breath and swallowed my grief before leaving a message for Reggie Press, Fortuna's district sales rep for Alabama, asking if he could persuade the library ladies to reconsider their canceled booking. While waiting for his callback, I contacted travel agents who'd previously organized groups with us. It took all my strength to strip misery and desperation from my voice while pitching the wonders of our Cabo Fiesta cruise. A few agents promised to call their clients and get back to me.

Getting time off work would be challenging. The company had bereavement leave, but with the library group cancellation, my ordinarily reasonable boss, Mike Woods, wouldn't be happy about any time-off request. It took until late afternoon before I'd summoned the courage to meet with him.

Mike's office smelled of stale coffee and despair. The fading light from the large windows in his executive suite stood in contrast to the dark mood of the man hunched over the spreadsheets on his desk. I suspected the stress of this job didn't suit him well.

"Mike, you know how much I love Fortuna," I said, "but Lydie meant everything to me. I'm her only living relative, so I need time off to settle her estate."

Mike didn't speak until my pleading and cajoling ended. "Company policy obligates me to give you two weeks, but your absence presents a problem."

"I've already made oodles of calls," I said, "and promise to keep working from Justice Bay. Don't worry, I'll fill those cabins. You'll see. You'll hardly know I'm gone."

"Okay," he said, returning to his spreadsheets without so much as a "sorry for your loss."

That night, I packed a few necessities in a duffle bag, including my running gear, laptop, and a spy novel I plucked from my to-be-read pile. Before dawn the following day, I left my West L.A. apartment and headed to Northern California.

* * *

Gravel crunched beneath the tires of my ten-year-old Audi as I turned off the main road leading to Justice Bay and drove the final two hundred feet down the driveway to Lydie's waterfront cottage. She had owned the place for years, using it as a weekend getaway from her hectic life in San Francisco and, later, as her retirement home. I called it a cottage because of its quaint appeal, but in truth, it was a two-story house with three bedrooms on the second floor—the main suite, the guestroom, and a third bedroom she used as a library/office. It also had a turret, which, as a child, I'd dubbed the Rapunzel Tower after the Grimm brothers' fairy tale.

Sunny L.A. had been replaced by Northern California fog, snaking in from the bay, casting eerie shadows on the gables of the stone and clapboard siding. All the house's charm had been rendered invisible by an opaque gray haze that muted the setting sun.

I parked near the garage. Before entering the house, I grabbed my cell to let Brad know I'd arrived safely. Then I realized we weren't a couple anymore, so I called Helen Marché instead. I'd hoped to reach Justice Bay in time to meet with her, but road construction had upended my plans. Despite the late hour, I wanted to tell her I'd arrived in town. A recorded message advised me that the office had closed for the day. There appeared to be no option to leave a message.

The outside lights were off, but the fog lifted enough for the moon to expose the mullioned windows of the front entrance. I grabbed my backpack from the front seat and my duffle bag and laptop from the trunk and walked toward the door, devastated that my brilliant, funny, unconventional Aunt Lydie wouldn't be opening the door to greet me. Life without her seemed unimaginable.

When I slipped the key into the lock, I experienced an unexpected shiver, which I brushed off as fatigue and grief. Inside the house, I flipped on the lights and inhaled the aroma of verbena from the scented candle by the door.

A framed snapshot of Lydie and me sat near the candle. A neighbor had taken it on my first visit to Justice Bay without my parents. I'd just turned eight but had grown tall and gangly, with skinny legs and strings of hair escaping from my thick honey-colored ponytail. I had on my usual summer uniform—shorts and a ratty T-shirt. Lydie's hair had always been blonde, medium length, blunt cut, and parted on the right side. In the photo, she wore a flowing linen outfit as if she'd just stepped off some African Savannah. We'd wrapped our arms around each other and were both grinning.

I walked down the hallway and into the kitchen. A cup of what looked like tea and a plate with a half-eaten pastry sat on the breakfast nook table. When I got closer, I saw it was a cinnamon roll. *How odd*, I thought. Lydie died at night, so that was likely the last thing she ate. Pastries weren't a conventional evening meal, but people living alone don't always follow standard food choices. I considered popcorn a perfectly acceptable dinner option.

Those rolls were one of Lydie's favorites, but the longer I stared at the pastry, the more abnormal it seemed. She'd always been a stickler about cleaning up the kitchen because of the occasional mouse that wandered in the house from the nearby woods, so leaving food out challenged her tidiness gene.

My muscles tensed as I caught the aroma of cinnamon. I flashed back to yesterday morning at the office. I'd experienced an unexpected dizzy spell and a disturbing vision of headlights bearing down on me, accompanied by that same potent scent of the spice.

I wondered if that strange episode foreshadowed the news of Lydie's death, especially now that I knew she'd been eating a cinnamon roll shortly before she died. The theory was dubious at best. I acknowledged I had people skills. You might even call them insights that I'd honed from years of hiring and managing employees and smoothing the ruffled feathers of Fortuna cruise passengers. However, I shared those talents with millions of others, which hardly qualified me for a booth at a psychic convention. Nothing like that vision had happened to me before. There was no connection. It was simply a weird coincidence. All I knew was that something or someone had forced my aunt out of her house, where she died alone on a dark rural road. I had to find the truth.

I moved my travel bags to the bottom of the staircase, gazing at the familiar curios, antiques, and souvenirs from Lydie's travels. Each one had a story, and I recalled most of them—the brown gourd mate cup with the metal straw given to her by a gaucho from the pampas of Argentina, with whom she'd had a short fling. The yellow and orange Tahitian pareo she'd worn to dance the Tamouré on the island of Moorea and later transformed into pillows for the breakfast nook. She bought the four-color knitted alpaca hat in Cusco, Peru, on her way to spiritual enlightenment at Machu Picchu. It now served as a tea cozy to remind her of the Peruvian coca tea she drank to banish altitude sickness.

In the living room, I glanced out the French doors. Through the fog, I glimpsed the arcing light of an anchored sailboat and, across the bay, streetlamps lining the main drag of Justice Bay.

As I headed upstairs to the guest bedroom, a knock on the front door startled me. A muffled voice called my name. I tiptoed to the window, wondering who knew I'd just rolled into town.

Chapter Two

A fit man with thick white hair stood under the porchlight. He looked to be in his mid-sixties. Cradled in his arms loomed a large, charcoal and tan cat. Older man. Chubby cat. Dangerous? Probably not. I put aside my L.A. wariness and opened the door.

"Sorry if I startled you," he said with a low, gravelly voice. "The lights were on. I figured it must be you."

"How do you know my name? Who are you?"

"I'm Lydie's neighbor. Walter Kestrel. My place is five hundred feet up the road, or as city slickers might say, a couple of blocks. She told me all about you. Claimed you'd be moving back here to live."

I motioned him inside. "I'm not sure where Lydie got that idea. I live in Los Angeles—"

He cut me off mid-sentence. "—I hear you, but Lydie had a knack for knowing things that turned out to be true. I never understood how or why. She just did. Some people called her a telepathic empath. I just called her an Intuitive with a capital 'I.' I'm surprised you didn't know."

The term telepathic empath sounded vaguely familiar, but I couldn't remember its meaning. Perhaps it had something to do with tarot cards and channeling the dead. That certainly didn't sound like my aunt. Lydie was astute. I'd even acknowledge her generic intuitiveness, but not with a capital "I," unless I'd been missing something all these years.

Walter scratched the cat's head, but his focus remained on me. "Your aunt thought you shared the gift."

My eyes widened at the thought. Lydie sometimes called me an old

9

soul because I loved boomer music artists like Jim Croce and Bill Withers. However, I was confident that spooky headlight vision and cinnamon smell were one-offs. The notion that I'd inherited some kind of woo-woo superpower was absurd.

"Trust me," I said. "There is no shared capital 'I' gift. I don't have a psychic bone in my body."

Walter shrugged. "Okay. Anyway, I'm sorry for your loss. I thought kindly of Lydie. I'll miss her."

Grief squeezed my chest, so I changed the subject from feelings to felines. "Beautiful cat. He looks exotic."

Walter glanced at the furball in his arms. "He's a she, and she's not mine. She's Lydie's Siberian Forest cat. I took care of her while your aunt traveled in Tibet."

I'd spoken with Lydie shortly before she left on that trip. She'd called to wish me a happy birthday because I'd just turned an ancient thirty-one. I expressed concern about her traveling to a place with such highly charged political and cultural history, but she assured me she'd be safe with her government-approved guide. By the time we hung up, she had me laughing at myself. Now she was gone, and nothing would ever be the same.

"Technically," he continued, "the cat is yours now."

My first thought almost erupted as, no, no, no, I can't have a cat. I don't know anything about cats. I'm probably allergic, but cats aren't allowed in my L.A. apartment, even if I'm not. Instead, I said, "What's her name?"

"Cassandra, but Lydie called her Cassie, Cass, Cass-boo, Boo-kitty, and Sweet Baby Girl, sometimes in the same sentence. I call her Boo because, frankly, she scares me. Take your pick. If she trusts you, she'll come when you call her, no matter what name you use."

The string of monikers reminded me of Brad's name game song. I almost warbled Cassie Cassie Bo-bassy, banana fanna fo-fassy, but I held back because I didn't want Walter to think I'd become unglued.

I stared uncomfortably at Cassandra, worrying about the added responsibility of finding her a new home. "Lydie never mentioned a cat."

"Boo's new to the area," he said. "One day, Lydie opened the French doors and found her sleeping on the porch swing. Boo invited herself in and never left. Lydie posted signs, but nobody claimed her." He paused to run his hand through the cat's fur. "Like I always say, family isn't always the one you're born to. It's the one you choose, right, Boo?"

"I've never owned a cat."

Walter chuckled. "You don't own cats. They own you. You'll see. Anyway, this is her home, and I don't think we should uproot her so soon after losing her human, do you?"

"No, of course not." My tone sounded more defensive than I'd intended.

The cat squirmed out of Walter's arms and jumped to the floor with the grace of an Olympic gymnast. She appraised me with her pea-green eyes as if to say—I'll train you later. Then she strolled toward two ceramic bowls near the pantry, one filled with water and the other with kibble.

"How long are you staying?" Walter raised his hands in mock surrender. "I know. I know. Not forever."

"My boss only gave me two weeks off, and only if I continued working from here."

Walter brushed cat hair from his black sweater. "I'm guessing you'll need more time than that."

I picked up the dishes from the table. The cinnamon roll had become dry and crusty, which made sense. It had been two days since Lydie died. Before dumping it into the garbage, I paused momentarily to inhale the fragrance. As a kid, I loved sitting on the porch swing, eating Lydie's homemade cinnamon rolls, and listening to stories of her exotic travels.

Walter interrupted my reverie. "Anyway, let me know if there's anything I can do to help."

"I need a real estate agent. I adore the cottage, but my life is in L.A. I can't afford a vacation house, so I'll have to sell it."

Walter nodded. "There's only one agent in town. She's not the sharpest knife in the drawer, so don't count on getting rid of the place in two weeks. I'm guessing it'll take more time than that." He nodded toward the collectibles in the kitchen. "What are you going to do with all her stuff?"

"Not sure." I washed the plate and teacup and set them in the dish rack.

"Right now, it's too painful to part with anything she loved. I may rent a storage unit for those things. I'll have a yard sale for stuff I don't want, like pots and pans."

He shook his head. "You'll have trouble getting people out this far, especially tourists."

"In L.A., I have to drive forty-five minutes to work. Lydie's house is only a few miles from the town center."

"Justice Bay isn't Los Angeles. It's two miles and a long gravel driveway, which isn't easy to find. Besides, do you want strangers snooping through the house?"

"Do you have a better idea?"

"Maybe. You L.A. hipsters invented the so-called pop-up store, right? It seems like a good way to sell some of Lydie's collectibles. There's a vacant shop for rent on the main street downtown. I bet you can get it for cheap."

"How do you know that?"

He grinned. "Because I own the building. Check it out." He rattled off the address.

I paused for a moment to consider the idea. My main interests included the three Rs: reading, running, and roaming through gift and collectible stores. The quirkier, the better. One of my favorite side hustles at Fortuna included scouring trade shows for items to sell in our onboard gift shops. I'd even nursed the fantasy of one day owning a store. A pop-up shop might be a lot of work for only two weeks, but it could be fun.

"I'll think about it," I said. "How long have you known my aunt?"

He picked up a seashell from the counter and stared at its pearly interior. "A while."

His answer sounded evasive. "I'm just curious because Lydie never mentioned you."

He set the shell down. "I'm guessing there's a lot your aunt never told you."

His comment took me aback. My aunt and I had been close, which struck me as unlikely. On the other hand, I had secrets I'd never shared with anybody.

"Lydie warned me about walking on that road after dark. There are no street lights, and people drive fast, often crossing the center line to 'straighten the curve,' as she called it. My aunt also encouraged me to question things I didn't understand. And right now, I don't understand why she broke her own rule. Why did she go out there that night? Why didn't she see the headlights and move out of the way?"

Walter stared at the floor, unwilling to meet my gaze. "I couldn't tell you. I wasn't there." He pulled a key from his pocket and set it on the counter. "Lydie gave me a spare key to the house. I won't need it anymore."

His expression seemed pained when he finally looked up at me. Without another word, he walked out the door, disappearing into the night.

Chapter Three

I awoke the following day to a low rattle and a vibrating pillow. Boo lay beside me, purring in the decibel red zone. I pulled my hand from beneath the covers to pet her. Just as I trusted that effective cat-sitting was within reach, Boo darted off the bed and ran toward the door. I found her in the kitchen next to her empty food dish.

Once I'd filled the cat's food bowl and refreshed her water, I put on my running gear. My muscles became stiff and creaky during the long drive the day before. I had to shake off the road tension before visiting the police station to learn more about Lydie's death.

My father ran to relieve stress because he had the soul of a poet and the ulcer of a trial attorney. In addition to all his work responsibilities, he taught me the art of shoelace knots by allowing me to tie his, over and over, as he sat patiently in his big chair watching the TV news. He showed me how to make change from coins he pulled from his pocket, occasionally cheating to test my math. He played catch with me in the backyard, taught me how to shoot pool, and told me I could do anything if I set my mind to it.

No long illness prepared my mother and me for his death if anyone could ever be ready for such a thing. He'd died of a heart attack at work at the ripe old age of forty-three. I was thirteen. I started running after that. At first, I hoped to merely catch a whiff of his aftershave still floating in the breeze. Later, I ran to be alone with my thoughts. He and Lydie were siblings, and now they were both gone, which made me feel hollowed out and alone.

After about three miles, I headed home to shower and pull my shoulder-length hair into a ponytail. I dressed in denim jeans and a honey-colored sweater that matched my hair.

Before leaving the house, I called Helen Marché to arrange a meeting and a second call to the real estate agent Walter had recommended. As it turned out, Pearl Potts had visited Lydie's place. She promised to start pitching it to buyers.

I kept thinking about Walter Kestrel's abrupt departure the night before. Maybe rudeness replaced sympathy as his way of confronting grief. If so, I understood the sadness but sensed he hadn't told me everything about Lydie's death. I wanted to know what and why.

His claims about my aunt's so-called intuitive abilities still troubled me because she'd never discussed it with me, and I hadn't figured it out on my own. Lydie oozed intelligence and competency. She'd traveled the world and encountered all kinds of people and situations. Maybe all those skills and experiences made adding two and two together easier for her. My eyes grew moist when I realized her talents hadn't warned her away from a dark road in the dead of night.

My aunt's vintage Schwinn was still in the garage, propped against the wall near her lime green VW Beetle convertible. The bike's frame had a few rust spots, but when I pinched the tires, they were full of air.

During my summer visits to Justice Bay, I spent many happy days peddling around town on that bicycle. Lydie would borrow a bike from a friend, and we'd ride together. After I got older, she'd let me go into town alone to buy ice cream.

I didn't have a bicycle back in L.A. Maybe I'd take the Schwinn home. For now, I savored the fresh morning air as I rode into town.

Downtown Justice Bay hadn't lost any of its charms since I'd last visited. Wednesday found only a few tourists in the commercial area, wearing sensible shoes and snapping selfies by the iconic dolphin fountain in the town square. Creative city planners had built the library on prime waterfront property. Several new businesses had opened since I'd last visited, including a bakery called Tarts & Bars and C'est Shells, a picturesque seafood café overlooking the bay.

I arrived a few minutes early for my appointment with Helen Marché, so I rode over to look at Walter Kestrel's rental storefront. It stood mid-block in the center of the town's Main Street shopping area. The small space included a large front window and built-in shelves, perfect for displaying collectibles. In my head, I'd already created a marketing plan to attract tourists from the sensible shoe and selfie crowd, coincidentally, Fortuna Cruise Line's target audience.

Helen Marché's office was nestled above Bay Threadz, a small boutique featuring upscale women's clothing. The bike had no lock, so I propped it against the building and hoped it would still be there when I returned. A narrow staircase led to the second floor, where I found Marché's name on one of the doors. A vintage brass shopkeeper's bell dinged as I stepped into a small anteroom with a desk and telephone but no receptionist.

From the interior office, the wheels of a chair rolled across a hardwood floor. A moment later, a woman in her late thirties wearing a business suit appeared, trailed by the scent of orange blossoms and cedar.

"Ms. McCoy, I assume."

I nodded and settled into the chair across the desk from hers.

She put on a pair of black-rimmed glasses before opening the top file from a neat stack on her desk. "I ordered a half dozen death certificates. You'll need at least one for the bank. Some financial institutions will accept a copy, but it's always wise to have extra originals. I also copied Lydie's will, designating you as her rightful heir. The bank's address is on the statements. Removing her name from the accounts and adding yours shouldn't take long."

I half expected her to commiserate with me about Lydie's death, but she didn't appear in the mood for heartfelt memories or even friendly banter. I accepted the paperwork without comment, including a life insurance policy from my aunt's former employer with instructions on how to claim death benefits.

Spellman Polk & Kimble was a consulting firm in San Francisco whose clients included defense contractors and the U.S. military. Before she retired, Lydie worked as their human resources director. Because of her proximity to sensitive material, she rarely talked about her nine-to-five life.

I glanced at the insurance payout—a hundred grand. "That's a lot of money," I said because stating the obvious was one of my superpowers.

"There are some outstanding bills," she said, ignoring my comment, "including expenses associated with her trip to Tibet. Ask the bank for generic checks until they print your name on a new supply."

"Thanks." I paused for a moment before continuing. "Walter Kestrel dropped by the house last night. Do you know him?"

Marché tidied the already neat files on her desk. "Slightly. I only moved to Justice Bay six months ago when I bought this practice."

I sensed a friendly chit-chat opportunity and took it. "How do you like living here?"

She shrugged and checked her watch. "It's like a lot of small towns, I presume. It's hard to break into social cliques. Your aunt introduced me to a few people, and that helped. I know Mr. Kestrel because Lydie gave me his number in case of emergencies. She told me he'd owned the vacation house on the bay next to hers for about seven years. A year ago, he retired and moved there permanently. Maybe that's how they got to know each other and why she trusted him to care for her cat."

"It must be comforting to have a cat sitter living next door," I said. "Just curious, when Lydie gave you Walter's number, did she seem worried about any particular emergency?"

A chill crept into her tone. "You mean more important than her cat? I guess you've never had a pet. They're family. Before Benjy crossed the rainbow bridge, I had Save-My-Dog instructions in my wallet, on all the doors of my house, and in the glove compartment of my car."

I gave her a closed-lip smile. "Of course, that's exactly the right thing to do. Walter's been very kind. He gave me the name of a real estate agent."

She swiveled toward me and frowned. "You're selling the house?"

I nodded, wondering why she sounded upset. "Is that a problem?"

"Of course not," she said. "The property belongs to you. It's just that your aunt told me you loved the place."

Her words ignited feelings of guilt. I loved the house, but had my own financial and work obligations. "Walter offered to rent me a shop down the street to sell some of Lydie's collectibles."

When she rechecked her watch, I realized my charm offensive had failed. Still, I persisted. "Can you tell me anything about the investigation into my aunt's death?

Without looking up from her paperwork, she offered a crisp "No."

I stood, but before leaving, I asked one last question. "Just curious. Where exactly did the accident happen?"

"Not far from her driveway, near that yellow warning sign where the road curves. I only know because law enforcement still had the area taped off when I drove by on Monday afternoon."

There had been no tape when I arrived at the cottage late Tuesday. It must have been removed by then. I took all the documents she'd given me and left.

On the street, I again questioned my aunt's so-called intuitive powers. If Walter's claims were valid, why didn't she foresee her death? Walter said Lydie likely didn't tell me everything. It pained me that any secrets she'd kept might be lost forever. I had one more stop to make where I hoped to find clarity. I tucked the legal papers in my jeans and retrieved the bike.

* * *

The police department occupied a former church a block from the library. I rolled the Schwinn into a designated bike stand. With the legal papers tucked under my arm, I entered the building to find pews lining the walls below stained-glass windows. The scarred wooden floors creaked as I approached a four-foot-high counter displaying a nameplate: Chet Greene, Chief of Police. A well-endowed woman in her early twenties with feathery fake eyelashes and long dark hair that matched her brown lipstick stood by a file cabinet. She ran a blood-red fingernail along the tabs that sounded like fluttering bat wings. With a set of vampire teeth, she'd be a shoo-in as the TV hostess of late-night horror films. I introduced myself and requested an update on my aunt's hit-and-run case.

She maintained a calm and uninterested demeanor. "You'll have to ask the chief about that."

"Is he in?"

She hesitated for a moment and then bellowed, "Chet!"

My ears were still ringing a moment later when a man in his early forties with a military haircut and a badge pinned to his blue uniform rounded the corner. His lusty smile faded as his gaze swept past the file clerk and landed on me.

He shifted his sturdy frame into a macho stance, legs spread, arms crossed, a position meant to intimidate. After years of dealing with cranky travel agents and frantic cruise passengers, I was immune to posturing.

"How can I help you, ma'am?"

I restated my mission. When I mentioned Lydie's name, his brow furrowed.

"Sorry about your aunt's accident."

My jaw clenched. "Hit-and-run is no accident. It's a serious crime."

"Not sure you know this, but there aren't any street lights on that stretch of road. People drive fast out there because they're in a hurry to get someplace else. That's why folks shouldn't walk out there after dark."

"I know that. Lydie knew that. The question is what forced her out to that dangerous place and why. It's almost like you're blaming my aunt for her death."

His eyes narrowed. "No, ma'am, I'm not saying that at all. But there were no witnesses. No physical evidence. It's a downer, but finding the driver won't be easy."

I wanted to tell him it wouldn't be easy to fill eighteen cabins for the Cabo Fiesta cruise, but I planned to give it my best effort because that was my job. Maybe I could loan him a few of my old Nancy Drew novels to stimulate his investigative juices.

"My aunt's death is more than just a downer to me."

He softened his tone. "I get that. But there's nothing to tell you at the moment. I'll let you know if anything changes." He turned and walked toward the back room.

"How will you let me know? You don't have my phone number."

He flipped his hand. "Give it to Pam. She'll put it in the file." He continued walking.

"I'd like a copy of the police report."

I couldn't see his expression, just the taut, twitchy muscles in his back as he stopped. "We charge thirty bucks to process and copy those reports. I don't have time to do that right now."

I couldn't understand his hostility toward me, but his attitude forced me to respond. "I assume you already wrote the report. Maybe Pam can take a break from fluttering her file tabs and make me a copy."

Over his shoulder, he shot me a hostile glare before turning to Pam and nodding. She disappeared into the back office. He followed, leaving me alone in the lobby to search for ancient gum under the church pews.

A couple of minutes later, Pam returned with a two-page report. *Two pages?* I thought. For thirty bucks, I expected a novella. I could probably have duplicated the case file at the library for ten cents a copy. Beyond my aunt's personal information and the accident location, the document contained nothing revealing. A responding officer named Kowalski found no property with the body, not even Lydie's cell phone.

"Thanks," I said, handing her a ten and a twenty. "Can I get a receipt?"

"We don't give receipts."

I didn't need a receipt and wouldn't have pressed for one, but Pam's sullen attitude only encouraged me. "Maybe just write the amount on a piece of paper and sign your name."

I left the station with the number three zero and an illegible signature on a sticky note, thinking *that went well.*

I hadn't eaten breakfast, so I again stuffed the bulky legal documents into the back waistband of my jeans and rode the Schwinn down the street to C'est Shells café in search of brunch. I propped the bike against a tree and checked out the menu posted by the door.

Through the window, I saw Walter Kestrel sitting with another man at a table in the center of the small dining room. Hungry though I was, I backed away, hoping to avoid detection should he hold any residual hostility from our discussion the night before. A moment later, Walter smiled and waved me inside. I figured whatever had set him off had dissipated.

Walter glanced at the documents stuffed into the back of my pants but didn't comment. He pointed to the man across the table. "Emmaline, say hi to my nephew Cooper Dane."

Cooper looked somewhere in his early-to-mid thirties with an athletic build and spikey hair the color of a weathered catcher's mitt. A dusting of light stubble had spared his cheeks from the sun, but his toasted bronze nose suffered from overexposure.

During my thirty-one years on the planet, I'd racked up an impressive list of failed relationships, including my latest with Brad. But if I weren't leaving town in two weeks, I'd have questions about Cooper: Is he funny? Is he smart? Does he look good in a suit?

Cooper's eyes were a shade of blue that reminded me of forget-me-nots, my father's favorite flower. He stood and offered me a firm handshake, a warm smile, and a pleasantly old-fashioned pleasure to meet you, Emmaline. That gesture, plus the fact that he'd pushed several boulder-sized croutons to the edge of his crab salad, made me like him instantly—points awarded for the non-traditional breakfast, plus extra credit for the crouton wisdom.

He borrowed a chair from another table and gestured for me to sit as I removed the legal documents from my waistband.

"Coop is on his way to Mexico," Walter said, chowing down on his scrambled eggs and catsup-smothered hash browns. "He just stopped by for a short visit, right, kid?" Walter winked. Cooper rolled his eyes and sat down. The exchange sounded like the continuation of a long-running private joke.

"That's a long drive," I said, wondering if I should mention Fortuna's Cabo Fiesta cruise as an alternative. I had it on good authority that there were some vacant cabins.

"He's not driving," Walter said. "He's sailing. You might have seen his boat anchored in the bay."

I'd spotted a boat in the fog the night before but hadn't paid much attention. I guessed the length to be around forty feet. Working for a cruise company, I'd learned the seas were unpredictable, and sailing that far alone on a boat

21

that size sounded dicey.

"You're going solo?" I asked.

Cooper glanced at his uncle and smiled. "At the moment. Subject to change."

"I told you," Walter said. "No way I'm crewing on that floating bathtub of yours." He turned to me. "Did you look at my rental?"

"I did. I love it."

"I suspected as much. So, when do you want to move in?"

"As soon as possible. I have to be back at work in two weeks."

"Why don't you drop by my place tonight around six? You can pick up the keys and sign the rental agreement. Stay for dinner. Coop's making his famous clam chowder."

I glanced at Cooper to judge his reaction to the invitation, but his expression remained neutral.

"Asking your nephew to make dinner for a guest seems above and beyond the call of duty," I said.

Walter waved away my concern. "Six o'clock. Tonight. I'll bring my truck over to your place tomorrow morning. The kid and I can help you move into the shop."

How could I refuse?

After leaving the café, I stopped by the bank and added my name to my aunt's accounts. The teller told me how to access the transaction history online and suggested I call Lydie's former employer to notify them of her death and, if indicated, cancel the monthly pension deposits. She also helped me set up a device on my cell to accept credit card purchases at the shop. I withdrew some cash in small bills in case I needed to make change.

Before heading home, I called Helen Marché to advise me if any laws prohibited me from selling collectibles from a storefront. She said if a private person sold used goods, there were usually no tax consequences. My situation might be more complicated. She'd check and let me know.

The invitation to dinner at Walter's should include wine. The bike didn't have a basket. I couldn't possibly stuff bottles into my waistband, so I rode back to the cottage to pick up my car.

Danny's General Mercantile was only a half-mile from the house. It's an old-fashioned country store with barn plank floors and an impressive beer selection. I bought a few supplies and a couple of bottles of Chardonnay. On the way home, I ticked off possible items I could sell and brainstormed a catchy name for the shop—Gently Used Mementos or Nostalgia with a Hint of Fame—when movement and something red caught my eye.

A moment later, a red ball rolled in front of the car. My head snapped to attention. An instant later, a young boy appeared, chasing after it. I slammed on the brakes. The car skidded to a stop moments before impact. My clammy hands gripped the wheel to quell the tremors in my body. I squeezed my eyes closed.

Nothing appeared on the road ahead when I opened them a moment later. No red ball. No small boy. I sat motionless, unsure of what had just happened. I glanced in the rearview mirror to check if traffic had backed up. Behind me, a triangular yellow sign with an arrow snaking up the center warned of curves ahead. According to Helen Marché, I'd stopped in the exact spot where a hit-and-run driver had killed my aunt.

Chapter Four

Five minutes later, I sat in the Audi in front of my aunt's garage, trembling from another vision—this time of my car bearing down on that phantom child. The experience had felt so real, but unlike what had happened to Lydie, nobody had died.

I couldn't move, so I waited until my head cleared and my breathing returned to normal. Once inside the house, I went to the place I'd always felt safe—the porch swing on the veranda where I'd spent many happy hours listening to my aunt's tales of faraway places.

Every summer, starting at eight years old, my parents sent me to Justice Bay to spend two magical weeks with my aunt. Lydie had several rules she strictly enforced. I didn't have to be practical. I didn't have to use my inside voice to discuss things that excited me. Caution was reasonable but only in moderation, and she only gave advice when asked.

All that ended the summer before my thirteenth birthday when my father's death shattered my world. My mother's relationship with Lydie had always been strained, so she stopped arranging trips to Justice Bay. My aunt and I talked on the telephone periodically and exchanged funny greeting cards. I loved Snoopy. Lydie loved puns; the cornier, the better. But it wasn't the same as seeing her in person.

I'd left the French doors ajar, and a moment later, Boo jumped onto the far end of the swing. I thought she might run away, but she remained crouched there, staring at me but making no attempt to come closer.

Out on the bay, Cooper's dinghy wasn't tied to the stern. He must still be in town or maybe at Walter's making chowder. Dinner wasn't for several hours. I wouldn't have time in the morning to pick out items to sell at the shop, so after fifteen minutes of staring into mid-space, I forced myself out of my fugue state and went inside. Boo followed.

My search began upstairs in the library/office, hoping I might discover some clue to explain why Lydie was on that road the night she died. Books filled the shelves on three walls. I'd already read many of those novels, so I stacked them in piles to take to the pop-up shop. Several were overdue library books that I had to return. I searched for collectibles that would appeal to buyers, excluding anything I wanted to keep—like the mate cup. My first find sat on a table by the window, a hand-carved decoy in mottled shades of beige and gray. It looked old, so it would likely appeal to somebody. I'd never seen the duck before, nor did I remember Lydie mentioning where she got it.

Writing a short paragraph on a display card describing each item might be an exciting marketing strategy. That way, I could share some of Lydie's stories with others. I'd have to create histories from scratch for things of unknown origin, like the duck. I began writing.

A merchant found the duck battered and bruised in the Marrakesh souk beside a pile of Berber carpets. There were rumors, but no one could confirm how he got from a Minnesota slough to a vendor's stall in a Moroccan back alley. If you look deep into his glassy yellow eyes, perhaps he'll reveal his secrets. But proceed with caution. Outside the well-lit tourist areas of this medieval red city where spies and wanderers dwell, they only whisper his name—Decoy.

That prose wouldn't win a Pulitzer, but writing it reached Lydie-level corny and made me smile. I researched vintage decoys online and found that prices varied from fifty to one thousand dollars. I decided to charge thirty, which I considered more than fair. I added that amount to the bottom of the display card.

Under Boo's supervision, by late afternoon, about thirty items and display cards were ready to load into Walter's truck, including a music box inlaid with silver fleur-de-lis. Someone had broken the internal mechanism, so no music played, and the tiny ballerina didn't twirl on her toe when you opened the box. Even broken, the silver made it valuable. I decided to sell it "as is."

Boo alternately observed, napped on the office couch, and threaded through the display cards without tipping over a single one—bonding progress.

A call from Reggie Press, Fortuna's Alabama district sales rep, interrupted my afternoon. Confirming he got my cruise cancellation message, Reg promised to look for another group to fill the space. I told him I'd do the same. After I ended the call, I wondered how I would juggle filling Cabo Fiesta cabins and settling my aunt's estate in two weeks. I channeled Scarlett O'Hara and decided to worry about that tomorrow.

Since Boo and I were becoming best friends, I ditched the other names I'd brainstormed for the shop and branded it with her given name, Cassandra's Collectibles. I hoped Lydie would be pleased.

I got lost in my work and was shocked when my watch read five-thirty—time to prepare for dinner at Walter's. I hadn't brought many clothes. I doubted Walter expected me to come in formal attire, but I didn't want to look grubby. Boo followed me upstairs to the guest room and lounged on the bed as I put on my good jeans and one of my better T-shirts. When she walked with me toward the stairway landing, I began to feel like a cat whisperer. But as I reached down to pet her, she squirmed away from my touch and raced into Lydie's bedroom.

I hadn't gone in there since I'd arrived at the cottage. I considered it an invasion of my aunt's privacy. As I stood in the doorway, my gaze traveled from Lydie's bookcases to the window seat overlooking the bay to her king-sized bed, so expansive for a petite woman like my aunt. Again, I remembered Walter's warning that there were things she hadn't told me and realized that Lydie may not have always slept there alone.

Boo jumped onto the bed next to a splash of cinnabar red. The memory of that phantom red ball rolling across the road jolted my senses. A silk blouse with ruffles cascading down the front hung from an expensive-looking wooden hanger as if Lydie had just removed it from the closet. A sales tag from Bay Threadz, the shop below Helen Marché's office, was attached to the label with a tiny safety pin. It looked out of place compared to the muted gray and green clothes in her closet. My aunt had never worn the blouse. I wondered if she'd meant it as a gift.

I heard a loud meow. Boo stood at my feet. "Hey, Sweet Baby Girl." She nuzzled my leg. I picked her up. This time, she didn't try to run away. I rested my head against hers. "I miss her, too."

Boo responded with a low murmur. I didn't want the cat purrs to stop or the memory of Lydie to fade. I carried her downstairs and grabbed a can of tuna from the cupboard, intending it as a treat. While opening the can, I spilled oil on my T-shirt. The tuna seemed like a bad omen, so I put it in the refrigerator and gave Boo kibble instead.

The smelly fish oil soaked into my good T-shirt. I didn't have anything else appropriate to wear to a dinner party. I checked my watch. Time had melted away, so I ran upstairs to Lydie's bedroom. I slipped the red blouse from the hanger and removed the tags. I held the silk to my nose. It smelled of cedar.

My aunt stood 5'4" to my 5'7," but I was thin, so the blouse fit, except the sleeves were too short. I rolled them up, hoping nobody would care. I looked at myself in the closet mirror. The blouse wasn't my style, and I never wore that shade of red, but even paired with jeans, I had to admit the blouse looked good.

* * *

Walter told me his place was only a couple of blocks up the road. I zipped my leather jacket up to my chin and, at the last minute, decided to walk. I'd forgotten to bring the two bottles of Chardonnay in from my car, but the nippy outside air had kept the wine chilled.

At precisely six, I arrived at Walter's two-story rustic log cabin with its charming stone chimney. An orange and cream vintage Ford F-150 pickup truck slumped in the driveway. The paint job reminded me of a Creamsicle.

On the door panel, a logo of a fish leaping from the water accompanied the faded but still readable lettering, Ed's Bait & Tackle.

The front door was ajar. Through the crack, I called, "Knock. Knock."

Walter answered from somewhere inside. "That you, Emmaline? Come in."

I pushed open the door. The aroma of bacon and clams welcomed me. The first floor consisted of one large room—what designers called open-concept. Living room to the left. Kitchen to the right. Next to the sliding glass doors at the far side of the room sat a table holding a partially finished jigsaw puzzle. Nearby, a telescope stood aimed at the bay. Walter knelt before the fireplace, lighting a stack of logs with a long match.

"Is that your truck out there?" I asked.

"Yup. Came with the house. She's a beauty, isn't she?"

"A sight to behold, all right."

Cooper stood over a burner on the kitchen island in a bibbed chef's apron over jeans and a teal flannel shirt, with sleeves rolled to his forearms. The overhead light accentuated the sun-bleached threads in his sandy brown hair. A few wet curls lay against his neck as if he had just stepped out of the shower.

I held up the wine bottles. "I come bearing gifts."

"Excellent," Cooper said, stirring the pot of chowder. "Can you put them in the fridge?"

The refrigerator stood against the wall behind him. The space between Cooper and the appliance left little room to navigate, but I opened the door without injuring anybody. When I leaned over to find room for the bottles, I accidentally bumped my rear end against his thigh. My embarrassment regressed to high school level.

"Sorry," I said.

He laughed, activating the smile lines at the corners of his eyes. "Don't worry. My uncle considers cooking a contact sport. He designed the kitchen with that in mind. Thanks to you, I finally understand the fringe benefits."

My cheeks warmed from embarrassment because I wasn't sure how to interpret his comment. Jokey? Flirty? He might just be making conversation, so I averted my gaze toward the dining room table near the window. There were four place settings. Walter didn't mention inviting another guest. I wondered who it might be.

"What can I do to help?" I asked.

"Nothing at the moment," Cooper said. "Why don't you just relax by the fireplace? Walter told me about your aunt. Must be tough."

"Did you know her?" I asked.

"I met her once," he said, "but Walter talked about her often. He thought she was pretty special."

Walter's hands were sooty from the fireplace logs. "What are you two gabbing about?"

Cooper set the spoon on the counter. "We're debating the merits of using canned clams instead of fresh."

"Canned?" Walter's tone sounded incredulous. "Who told you that was okay? My sister?"

"Nope," Cooper said. "Julia Child."

I'd asked myself several theoretical questions about Cooper at the café. He'd just answered one of them. He had a sense of humor.

Walter frowned. "Don't get me started."

He handed me a sheet from a yellow-lined legal pad and washed his hands at the sink. At the top of the page were the handwritten words—Rental Agreement. I should have asked what he charged for rent before now. Apprehensive, I continued reading. A short paragraph permitted me to use the property for a collectibles shop for one hundred dollars per week for two weeks, as long as I agreed to clean the bathroom and sweep the floor before I moved out. The last line read: Terms extended upon agreement of both parties. Walter said my aunt thought I'd stay in Justice Bay. Perhaps he was mirroring her magical thinking.

I looked up from the page. "That's generous."

"It's only two weeks, right? That covers utilities, so we're good."

"I don't know what to say…thank you."

"Cooper and I'll be at your place tomorrow morning at seven. It's early, but sleep deprivation is good practice for those long, lonely nights at sea, right, kid?" He glanced at my jacket. "You look like Nanook of the North. Give me your coat. I'll hang it up."

"Thanks," I said, removing the jacket and fluffing the ruffles on my aunt's red blouse.

I held the jacket out for Walter. He stared in shock at the blouse. His jaw went slack. The color drained from his face. The doorbell rang before I could determine what triggered his odd response. The mysterious fourth guest had arrived.

Chapter Five

Walter returned to the kitchen, absent any evidence of his strange reaction to my aunt's red blouse. A woman followed close behind him. She looked around my age, petite with an angular fringe hairdo—cut close on the sides and left longer on the top—highlighted with purple streaks. She wore a black pea coat, skinny jeans, and short black boots. A dainty diamond stud pierced her left nostril, twinkling like a tiny star in a distant galaxy—très avant-garde until she caught a cold.

The woman flashed a wide-eyed smile. "Em?"

She did look vaguely familiar, but I wasn't sure why.

"Maddie Balister," she continued in that polite way people have of jogging the memory of the clueless. "I haven't seen you since…forever."

Walter leaned his forearm on the kitchen island. "I heard you two were pals when you were kids. Thought you might need a friend in town, Emmaline, so I invited Maddie to join us."

The mental fog cleared. Maddie Balister and I had spent time together during my summer vacations in Justice Bay. She'd been a quiet, artistic girl and always eager to follow any harebrained idea I had back then.

After my father died, those Justice Bay summer vacations ended. Maddie and I kept in touch like thirteen-year-old girls do—for a while. Years ago, my aunt told me she'd moved to New York City to study art. I'd always wondered what happened to her, but never attempted to find out. Life moved on for both of us, it appeared.

We wrapped our arms around each other as questions tumbled out in commingled, overlapping word spurts. "How have you been? How are your

31

parents? How long are you staying?"

Maddie pulled away with a resigned sigh. "I'm not sure how long I'll be here. My dad had a heart attack. I came back to help my mom run the store. He's getting stronger, but…" Her sentence faded into a shrug.

Maddie's parents owned one of those small-town hybrid businesses— a hardware store that sold boxes, shipped packages, and made copies. Her parents reminded me of actors in one of those 1950s sitcoms my grandparents used to watch—lovely people with negligible faults and conflicts they resolved in thirty minutes minus commercials. Maddie's mother loved to bake, filling their house with the yeasty smell of homemade bread. As I recall, Mrs. Balister gave Lydie her cinnamon roll recipe.

"I'm so sorry about your dad," I said.

She nodded, her eyes tearing up. "And Lydie, too. She came into the store the Saturday before she died. I didn't know that would be our last hug. I hope the police find the monster who killed her."

Walter interrupted. "Maddie, you remember Cooper?" I wondered if he changed the subject to avoid dwelling on my aunt's death or because he enjoyed controlling the conversation.

"How could I forget Cooper?" she said. "We met a few years ago. I breezed into town to visit my parents, and you stopped by the store to buy fishing flies."

Cooper must have visited his uncle's place occasionally, but our paths had never crossed. I glanced at him hovering over the chowder, but his expression remained neutral. If they'd met before, he didn't seem to remember. Still, he did what most of us do under similar circumstances. He punted. "Good to see you, Maddie."

"Come with me," Walter said to her, pointing to the bar on the other side of the room. "You look like you need a glass of wine."

Maddie removed her coat and tossed it on the couch. When they were out of earshot, Cooper walked over to me and whispered. "Em? Is that what I should call you?"

I had no reason to whisper back, but I did because it provided the chaste intimacy I craved.

"I answer to anything—Em, Emma, Emmaline, Hey-You. Call me whatever feels right."

He smiled. "That may take a while to figure out."

This time, it did seem like he was flirting with me.

Walter and Maddie returned from the bar with their wine. Walter set the bottle on the coffee table as we settled onto the overstuffed furniture.

"Cheers," I said, clinking glasses with Maddie. "Tell me everything about your life."

She laughed. "You mean everything I've done in the eighteen years since we last hung out together?"

"Okay, maybe just the highlights."

"After high school, I ditched Justice Bay to study photography and illustration at the School of Visual Arts in Manhattan. I worked as a graphic designer for a small newspaper—crappy pay, good people. Now I'm a packaging designer for a software start-up—good pay, crappy people. And I've had more bad boyfriends than I care to remember, so I've sworn off men forever. What about you?"

I collected my thoughts before answering. Since Maddie had brought up the subject of boyfriends, it provided the perfect opportunity to mention that I didn't have one. That sounded too pathetic, so I stifled the urge.

"Lydie inspired my love of travel and reading—especially spy novels—so after graduating from UCLA, I landed a dream job with Fortuna Cruise Lines instead of joining the CIA. One of the job's perks is visiting exotic places worldwide."

"Sounds perfect," Maddie said. "What about you, Walter? You look too young to be retired. What's your story?"

He chuckled. "It's boring. If you're looking for a cheap thrill, ask Coop to teach you how to flush a holding tank."

I turned to Cooper. "I'll pass on the holding tank info. I'd rather hear about your boat and your story."

He hesitated. "Not much to tell."

Maddie winked. "We'll be the judge of that."

Cooper reached for the wine bottle and refilled each of our glasses. "Don't believe my uncle. He's the one with an interesting history. Twist his arm."

Walter stoked the fire with a poker. "I'm not telling you people anything." He meant his tone to amuse, but the meaning was clear. His personal life would remain off-limits. "Come on, kid. Play nice. Regale us."

Cooper stared at his wine glass, his mood quiet and reflective. "Born in Seattle. University of Washington undergrad. Harvard Law. Passed the bar. I worked in a big corporate law firm in San Francisco. Made a lot of money. Lost my way. Now I'm taking a break." He looked up from his glass and smiled. "I should have gone with the holding tank lecture, right?"

Maddie and Walter chuckled, but Cooper's response unsettled me. There was a great deal to unpack in those few words that might explain the complexity of this man and perhaps his inner turmoil. My inane comments about school and work were trivial in comparison. I didn't know the details of Cooper's background, but I'd learned about lawyer stress from my dad. I often wondered if the profession had contributed to his early death.

"My nephew's being modest," Walter said. "He graduated law school magna cum laude with honors. Made the law review. Passed the California bar on his first try. Top firms all over the country were bidding against each other to hire him. And wherever he hangs his hat at night, once a month, he flies home to take his mom to dinner. I know because my sister gives me a blow-by-blow account of everything they ate."

"Whoa," Maddie said, grabbing Cooper's left hand to check for a wedding ring. "You sound like a catch. Come on, confess. You must have faults." She flashed a come-hither look. "I'll tell you mine if you tell me yours."

Cooper took a sip of wine, eyeing Maddie over the rim of the glass. "I have plenty of faults," he said, smiling, "but it's more fun if people uncover them without my help. Trust me. It doesn't take long."

Walter stood. "I'm hungry. Let's move to the dining room." It was noteworthy that he continued his unbroken pattern of truncating conversations.

Moments later, we reassembled at the table. Everybody heaped praise on Cooper's culinary skills. His chowder and the fresh bread from Tarts & Bars, the new artisanal bakery in town, were divine. I listened while the others shared local gossip.

The sliding glass doors were open a crack, ushering in the fragrance of fir needles, carried into the room by a gentle breeze. I closed my eyes to enjoy the moment. My ears began to ring. The voices at the table faded into white noise.

I saw my aunt running in the dark, breathing hard. Tree branches, bent by the wind, scraped her face and whispered a warning—run faster. A second set of footsteps echoed hers. She stopped and turned toward me with terror etched on her face. Then, her image merged into mine, which pitched me into a nightmare I often had as a child. Someone chased me, but as hard as I ran, it seemed like jogging on a treadmill. I didn't go anywhere.

"Emma?" Cooper's voice brought me back to reality. "Are you okay?"

My breath became rapid and shallow as my eyelids shot open. I glanced around the table. Everyone gaped at me.

Maddie reached over and touched my arm, keeping her tone light. "Hello, Em. Was it something we said?"

I forced that unsettling scene of my terrified aunt into a dark compartment of my brain, but I couldn't shake the belief that it mirrored her last conscious moments before the car hit her. Sweat formed on my chest under the red ruffles of my aunt's blouse. I sensed Cooper's focus on me, but didn't want to look at him because I had no clue what had just happened or what it looked like to others.

That vision added the second unexplained out-of-body experience since this morning. It frightened me to think this might be the new normal and that my life had changed forever. I didn't know what to do, so I decided not to tell anyone because I feared the creepiness would repel them. The three were my only friends in Justice Bay, and I didn't want to jeopardize that.

"Sorry," I said. "I guess I've had too much wine."

Walter's gaze darted from me to Maddie. "Emmaline says she's fine, people. Let's move on."

Maddie frowned. "Right. As I said, seeing how upscale Justice Bay has gotten is surprising. Buyers turn charming old summer places into multi-story vacation homes for the rich and famous."

"That's good for selling Lydie's house, right?" My voice cracked, but at least I sounded lucid.

"I guess," Maddie said. "Waterfront property is always valuable, but whoever buys the cottage will likely tear it down and build some huge view-blocking monstrosity."

That had been the trend for years in Los Angeles—developers buying one-thousand-square-foot houses and replacing them with six-thousand-square-foot boxes with no yards. It changed the character of neighborhoods forever and rarely for good. However, the thought of a gigantic excavator claw destroying Lydie's home horrified me.

After dinner, Walter feigned exhaustion and went upstairs to bed. Still unsettled, I nonetheless offered to help with the dishes.

"Sorry to leave you with the mess," Maddie said, "but I have to get home. My dad likes me to read to him before he goes to sleep. He's into Dostoyevsky at the moment, The Brothers Karamazov. Snore. Literary Valium."

"No problem," Cooper said, "We've got it covered."

"I hope we can get together for lunch while I'm in town," I said. "I'm opening a pop-up store to sell some of Lydie's antiques. I'm naming it after her cat, Cassandra's Collectibles."

"Cassandra?" Maddie asked. "How fun. Like that Greek mythology lady that told true prophecies nobody believed."

"I forgot about poor cursed Cassandra," Cooper said.

So had I, but now I wondered if Lydie's choice of a cat name was a nod to the skepticism from people who doubted her intuitive abilities.

"Here's my prophecy," Maddie went on. "Your shop will be a hit. Believe it. It's just what Justice Bay needs. I'll stop by tomorrow and check it out." She grabbed her coat from the couch and turned toward the door. "See you soon." She waved. "Bye, Cooper."

Cooper waved back, and then the two of us loaded the dishwasher and cleaned the kitchen as we chatted about the logistics of moving Lydie's collectibles into the store. Several times, I thought he wanted to tell me something, but he held back.

My attention fragmented. My thoughts drifted back to Lydie's belief that I shared her intuitive gifts. I hadn't thought that possible, but I couldn't ignore the unsettling visions I'd experienced since arriving in Justice Bay.

After Cooper and I finished cleaning the kitchen, he walked me to the door. Under the glow of the porchlight, I looked up at him and said, "Thanks for dinner. Everything was wonderful. See you in the morning?"

He gently placed his hand on my arm as I turned to leave. "Wait. There's something you need to know."

Chapter Six

Cooper released my arm, but instead of inviting me back inside Walter's house to continue the conversation, he remained on the porch, closing the door behind him. The temperature had dropped during the evening. A brisk breeze pinched my face as I zipped my jacket and pulled up the collar to cover my cheeks. Cooper rolled down the sleeves of his flannel shirt, his only accommodation to the chill.

"If this is about that weird thing at the table," I said, "please don't tell me I drooled and hooted like a loon, even if it's true."

He flashed a puzzled frown, followed by a smile. "Nothing like that. You zoned out for a minute. We got worried when Maddie asked you a question, and you didn't answer immediately."

Relief washed over me. "I'm not sure what happened. A bad dream, maybe, except I wasn't asleep."

He nodded toward the beach. "Can I walk you home?"

Most women might consider a man suggesting a moonlit stroll along the water's edge romantic. But I'd just met Cooper, so I labeled it exercise.

As we walked along the rocky shoreline toward the cottage, he said, "What happened tonight, if you don't mind me asking?"

I swallowed hard before speaking. "I saw Lydie running through the woods. Someone chased her. She looked terrified. It felt like I was reliving her experiences the night she died."

He stopped, caught my gaze, and held it. "You should know that Walter cared a great deal about your aunt. Her death has been hard on him."

"Cared about her like a neighbor or something more personal?"

He resumed walking. "That's not for me to say." His tone sounded soft, almost reverent.

"Sure it is. Your uncle. My aunt. We're practically related."

He rubbed the back of his neck. "As you already know, Walter can be… abrupt."

"What does that have to do with my question? And don't feel obligated to apologize for your uncle. I've dealt with my share of grumpy cruise passengers and overbearing travel agents. I can handle Walter."

"Touché." He stopped to pick up a smooth, flat rock on the path, wiping away the dirt with his finger. "Okay, I think they were more than just friends."

"Like in a relationship?"

He skipped the stone across the water and continued walking. "It's complicated."

"Don't be coy," I said, frustrated. "I wore Lydie's blouse tonight. Walter looked at me like I had my finger looped through the pin of a hand grenade. There has to be a reason. If you know what it is, just tell me, okay?"

He turned toward me. "Walter knew that blouse belonged to your aunt."

"How? The tags were still on it when I found it on her bed. I doubt she ever wore it."

"She didn't. That's the point."

"What's the point? Did he give the blouse to her as a gift?"

Cooper struggled to find the right words. "No, but he was with her when she bought it. Walter told me Lydie sensed danger shortly before she went to Tibet."

I felt a jolt as I remembered my blackout at the table and Lydie's terror. "Did she say why?"

He headed toward my aunt's overturned rowboat tethered to a tree near the house. "Not to my knowledge, but your aunt's premonitions didn't always come with details."

"Why do you have more information about her psychic abilities than I do?"

"All I know is what Walter told me." He wiped the moisture from the wood with his shirt sleeve so we could sit down. "Walter said they were at lunch when she told him about her fears. After they left the café, they walked by a dress shop. Lydie spotted that blouse in the window and bought it, specifically because the color and the ruffles weren't her thing. She joked that if she ever wore it, Walter should send help. He didn't make anything of it at the time. Then, Lydie died three days ago, and tonight, you came to the house in red ruffles."

Walter may have dismissed Lydie's prediction, but it had been accurate. The appearance of the red blouse felt shocking and creepy. I thought about my aunt's official name for her cat, Cassandra, after a woman in Greek mythology whose prophecies nobody believed. If people had dismissed Lydie's foreshadowing abilities before, she might have considered Cassandra a kindred spirit.

Something forced my aunt out of her house the night she died. A phone call? A knock on the door? Maybe it frightened her enough to run onto the road. Chief Greene hadn't made any progress in identifying the car's driver. He didn't seem to consider it a priority. I had to keep pressuring him to find out what happened that night.

My feet were frosty, and a chill seeped through my jacket. I moved close enough to draft the warmth radiating from Cooper's body, but not close enough to give him the idea it was a come-on.

"So, when Walter saw me wearing Lydie's red blouse, he thought it was a message from the grave?"

"I'm not sure what he thought. You'll have to ask him yourself."

I looked out at the ripples of water shimmering in the moonlight. "I gather your uncle isn't psychic?"

"No," he said, "but he has unique insights about risk and threat."

"Let me guess. Walter used to sell life insurance."

Cooper slowly turned toward me, almost like he wanted to judge my reaction. "He's a former Special Agent for the FBI in the counterintelligence division."

In my wildest fantasies, I never expected to find that on my Justice Bay bingo card.

***

The following day, I awoke to the sound of my cell phone alarm, still thinking about Cooper's bombshell news that Walter had been an FBI Special Agent. He'd told me his uncle investigated foreign intelligence operations and espionage, especially economic espionage—theft of military weapons systems, among other crimes. The Bureau had trained him to keep a secret. That explained why Lydie trusted him.

I reached over to turn off the alarm and touched a warm spot next to me where Boo must have camped out during the night. I forced myself out of bed, showered, and then searched the kitchen, hoping to locate a stash of leftover cinnamon rolls. I found only crumbs. Maybe I'd look for Lydie's recipe and make a batch myself.

Boo gazed out the French doors. I picked up the cat and hugged her. She tolerated it for a moment and then squirmed to get down. I sat outside on the porch swing, admiring the view as I called the office. Reservation agents had sold three of the Cabo Fiesta cruise cabins to individual travelers. That left fifteen more to peddle.

Before Walter and Cooper arrived, I called Lydie's former employer, the defense industry consulting company Spellman Polk & Kimble. I didn't expect anybody to be there this early, so I planned to leave a message. To my surprise, a woman named Kelly Hinson from employee benefits answered the call. She'd already been notified about Lydie's death and confirmed she would suspend the monthly pension payments and send paperwork for me to fill out to receive the life insurance payout.

"Losing her was a huge blow to all of us," she said. "Such a bright and vibrant woman." She hesitated for a moment. "I don't want to intrude, but would you mind if we posted an obituary in the *San Francisco Chronicle*? Just to let her friends and colleagues in the Bay Area know about her passing."

"That would be lovely."

"The last time I interacted with your aunt was at her retirement party. She was excited to leave the following day for Tibet."

I sensed a pang of guilt. I'd planned to attend that event, but an emergency at work forced me to cancel. Thinking back, I couldn't even remember the crisis, only that I'd chosen career over family.

"I'm sorry I couldn't be there."

"I took a bunch of photos. I can send you copies."

"Perfect." I rattled off my email address.

If there's anything else I can do to help," she said in parting, "please let me know."

I wondered if Kelly had any insights about Lydie's death. It was a long shot, but worth a try.

"Just curious," I said. "Did my aunt ever mention anything that was troubling her?"

She hesitated. "We didn't talk about our personal lives if that's what you're asking. The company frowned on that sort of sharing."

"Got it. Thanks."

After ending the call, I moved the first batch of Lydie's antiques and the display cards from the upstairs hallway to the door, where they'd be more accessible to load into the truck. I also found a drawer full of old plastic bags for customer purchases.

Walter and Cooper arrived at the house fifteen minutes early with some empty boxes, take-out coffee, and croissants from the Tarts & Bars bakery. I'd never known an FBI agent before. I tried to figure out if he wore a Kevlar vest under his bulky jacket, but I couldn't tell. I probably wouldn't look at him again without wondering.

The three of us had coffee and croissants at the breakfast nook. Cooper's sailboat swung on its bow anchor in the bay. The wind and current had shifted the vessel's position from the previous night.

"What's the name of your boat?" I asked.

He looked up from his coffee, and I admired his blue eyes again. "Brief Encounter."

"Is that a lawyer pun or a more complicated story?"

A subtle smile appeared on his lips. "A little of both, but definitely complicated."

That sounded intriguing. I wanted to know more. "How long have you been sailing?"

Walter leaned into the conversation. "My sister is descended from mermaids. She started taking him out on the family's sailboat before he could walk."

Walter's expression became a mixture of admiration for his sister and amusement at a memory he hadn't yet shared. I tried to imagine him in Lydie's big bed, but wasn't ready to go there yet.

I glanced at Cooper. "Interesting genealogy."

He grinned. "You have no idea."

After eating, we loaded Lydie's books and treasures onto the bed of the Creamsicle. Walter and Cooper rode to town together. I followed them in my car. I slipped the key into the lock of the shop's front door, but the door wouldn't open until Cooper lent his shoulder. When we unloaded the boxes and stacked them inside the shop, Walter went to the bakery on another coffee run while Cooper helped unpack enough items to fill the shelves. He chuckled a couple of times as he read the display cards, which made me inclined to forgive him for his cryptic answers to my questions the night before. Walter returned from the bakery with coffee and a box of chocolate-dipped macarons for the customers.

A few minutes later, Maddie arrived, carrying a large poster board.

"Tah-dah! Look what I made for you."

The poster featured a mustard yellow background with a giant cartoon cat resembling Boo. Under a pair of black paws, on the right side were three lines—Cassandra's Collectibles and below that, Browsers Welcome and Emmaline McCoy, owner.

"Impressive," Cooper said.

"Spectacular," I added.

Maddie propped the poster in the window. "I almost added a line that read, 'Gifts that inspire your mews,' but at the last minute, I decided that was a pun too far."

Walter chuckled. "I like it."

"Lydie loved puns," I said, overwhelmed with gratitude. "The cornier, the better. The sign is beautiful. Thank you, Maddie."

She beamed. "It's just temporary, but you need something in the window to tell people what you do. I have to sell hardware now. If there's anything I can do to help, you know where to find me." She headed toward the door. Over her shoulder, she added, "Enjoy."

A moment later, a middle-aged woman wearing gray sweatpants and a matching hoodie entered the shop. Dark circles rimmed her eyes. She looked unwell or maybe just sad.

"Are you open?" she asked.

Walter looked at me and shrugged. "Sure. Why not?"

I held my breath as she picked up various items and read the display cards. The woman smiled a couple of times, which lifted her spirits. She left with a Depression-era glass candy dish and a couple of macarons. Most depression glass wasn't valuable, but that first sale made me happy.

"Time to go," Walter said. That jigsaw puzzle isn't going to put itself together. Move it, Cooper, if you want a ride."

Cooper followed him toward the door but waited until his uncle left before handing me a phone number on a slip of paper. "Call me later. I'll try to arrange a get-together with my uncle. Just the three of us. But there's no guarantee he'll answer your questions."

"Should I bring anything?"

He raised his eyebrows. "Maybe a heat shield. He doesn't like to be interrogated."

For the next half hour, I worked alone in the shop. I used the time to make a few cold calls to travel agents and one to Brad to discuss events at work. He seemed anxious that reservations agents had only rebooked three of the eighteen cabins.

"It's crazy busy here," he said. "When are you coming back?"

"Not sure, but I'll need the full two weeks. There's a lot to do. Justice Bay is adorable. I've met some interesting people."

I told him about the shop and Maddie's poster, but he sounded distracted.

"It must be costing a fortune to rent a retail space," he said, in a tone I labeled cranky. "Why don't you hire someone who runs estate sales and be done with it? They'll invite looky-loos to the house, take a cut of the profits, and there are no out-of-pocket expenses for you."

I could easily cover Walter's low-cost rent. I just wished Brad would be more sympathetic. "It might come to that, but I'm committed to Cassandra's Collectibles for now." I almost expressed my commitment to stay until law enforcement found the driver who killed my aunt, but I sensed he wasn't interested in hearing that, either.

A well-groomed man in his early fifties with aquiline features and tortoise-shell glasses peeked through the glass window. "Sorry," I said to Brad. "Got to go. I have a customer."

I ended the call just as the man stepped inside. He wore expensive-looking gray slacks, a charcoal sweater, and an air of privilege. He didn't acknowledge me or speak. He just browsed around, inspecting items and returning them to the shelf with maximum force.

"Can I help you find something?" I asked.

"Just checking out the kitschy trinkets," he said. "I'm John Orson Osgood. I own the antique store at the end of the block. But don't worry. I'm not your competition. My inventory appeals to a different class of clientele."

"How lovely," I said, feeling defensive. "I have great admiration for people like you. So many fakes in your business. Must be hard to figure out what's genuine and what's not."

He smirked. "Not difficult when you're an expert." He reached for the decoy. "This might work as a display item on a Chippendale desk I have for sale." He pointed to my display card about finding the duck in a Marrakesh back alley. "I love a good spy story. I'll give you ten dollars for it."

His arrogance and the lowball offer irritated me. I had only asked thirty dollars, far less than the range of prices I'd found online, and I'd marked the amount on the card. "I'm sorry. Double Agent Decoy is on hold for another customer."

He frowned. "How's that possible? It looks like you just opened."

"I know," I said, feigning surprise. "I guess it's true—word travels."

He squinted as though my lie had just dawned on him. "Nice little shop you have here." I expected him to finish the sentence like a mafia capo. It would be a shame if something happened to it. Instead, he turned and stomped out.

For a moment, I questioned the wisdom of alienating customers, especially a neighbor shopkeeper like John Orson Osgood, but I dismissed the thought. He'd been rude and the opposite of neighborly. Besides, I only planned to be in town for two weeks. What difference could it possibly make? Then grimmer thoughts intruded. I imagined Osgood driving down a dark rural road so focused on plotting ways to screw over his competition that he didn't see a petite blonde woman walking along the shoulder. If he'd killed my aunt, maybe he just dropped by to see what I'd learned about the investigation.

I shook off a shill as I removed the decoy from the shelf and slipped it into an empty box in the bathroom. Maybe I'd give the duck to Walter. If anybody loved a good spy story, I guessed it was a former FBI counterintelligence agent.

Chapter Seven

B y noon, a mix of Justice Bay locals and people driving through town had drifted in and out of Cassandra's Collectibles. Many of them bought at least one of Lydie's treasures before leaving.

There were still a few boxes I hadn't unpacked. With everything I had to accomplish before returning to L.A., I needed somebody to help me run the shop for a few days while I made arrangements to sell the house and find someplace to store Lydie's furniture and other personal effects. Maddie ran her parents' hardware store. Walter? Not an option. His grumpy demeanor wasn't compatible with retail sales. Cooper might agree, but pitching the idea abused our budding friendship. I didn't know anyone else in town well enough to ask them for help. Even if I did, it would be an imposition.

Fortuna Cruise Lines used temporary employees, especially during the busy season. I wondered if Justice Bay had a similar service. I searched my cell browser and found a listing for ABB Office Consultants, which provided data entry, bookkeeping, and receptionist personnel. I called the number.

A woman answered the phone with a low, husky voice. I told her I needed a salesperson, a self-starter who could collect money and process credit card payments for the next couple of weeks. I agreed to the fee.

"As it turns out," she said, shuffling papers, "Mr. Bromley can be at your shop in about an hour."

"Perfect," I said, thinking Mr. Bromley might be an older gentleman seeking a reprieve from bingo at the senior center.

Fifteen minutes later, a young man wearing a camel-colored cardigan approached the shop on a black and fluorescent lime-green road bike. He dismounted, repositioned the cross-body strap of his distressed leather messenger bag, and leaned the bike against the building. He adjusted a red paisley bowtie around the neck of his blue oxford shirt, opened the door, and stepped inside the shop, looking like a young Mister Rogers.

His willowy physique, light brown curly hair, and long, bony fingers made him seem no more than fourteen. Close up, I estimated his age at nineteen or twenty. Bold black-framed glasses accentuated his hazel eyes. When he closed the door, I half expected the air turbulence to blow him over.

"Hi, I'm Emma," I said in a neutral tone in case he was here to deliver a telegram.

He put his hand over his heart and sighed. "I know. I admired the sign when I passed the shop this morning on my way to the bakery for a mocha frappé. I love what you've done with the place." He walked over to a shelf and straightened a display card that had tipped over. He stepped back, pleased with his work.

With a straight spine and a smile that spread across his pale oval face, he said: "Arthur Baxter Bromley reporting for duty." I half expected him to salute.

I realized Arthur Baxter Bromley had to be the ABB in ABB Office Consultants. Aside from the woman who answered the phone, he might be the only employee.

"I didn't expect you so soon," I said. "Your assistant estimated you'd be here in about an hour."

"That was my mom. She thinks it's a good business strategy to pretend I'm busier than I am."

"Good to know," I said. "Let me show you how to take credit card payments." That's when I realized I'd been using my phone to process sales.

Arthur dipped his hand into the messenger bag and pulled out a wad of old-fashioned two-part credit card slips separated by carbon paper. "I guessed you'd be processing credit cards and assumed you used your cell. My mom's best friend works for the bank. She tells me they still accept these bad boys."

The door opened, and Cooper walked in with a leather tool bag over his shoulder and a six-foot, carpeted cat tree in his arms. His hair stood up in random spikes. A small coil of rope peeked out of a pocket in his polar fleece vest.

Arthur hustled over to Cooper and extended his hand. "Arthur Baxter Bromley. Welcome to Cassandra's."

Cooper propped the cat tree against the back wall.

"Nice to meet you," he said, shaking Arthur's hand.

"Where did you get the cat tree?" I asked.

Cooper slid the tool bag off his shoulder. "I stopped by the hardware store this morning to pick up tools to repair your sticky door. The tree was collecting dust in a back corner. I guessed Boo might get a kick out of it."

"That's so thoughtful," I said. "Boo will love it."

"Oh," Arthur said to Cooper, "I didn't know you two were friends. I'm the new temporary employee. The tree would also be a great place to display your aunt's antiques."

"I love the idea." Arthur and I were definitely off to a great start.

Cooper unzipped the bag, revealing a jumble of tools, including a wood plane, an array of screwdrivers, and a small can of lubricant.

"How did a *Hahvid* attorney learn how to unstick doors?" I said in my best Boston accent.

"When he bought a boat," Cooper said. "If you're single-handing, you have to know how to fix things."

We didn't have time for further discussion because Cooper stepped away from the entrance a moment later as a woman in her sixties swept through the door. A tailored coat opened to reveal a sleek wool dress draped elegantly over her thin frame. Her angular features and blade-thin nose made her look severe. Diamond stud earrings sparkled in the overhead light. At least three carats per ear, I guessed. Whoever said, "You can never be too rich or too thin," had this woman in mind.

"You must be Emmaline McCoy," she said in a saccharine tone. "I simply had to see what you've done with the place. I'm so sorry about poor Lydie. Terrible accident. Just terrible."

I didn't know how she'd learned about the shop or why she thought my aunt's death was an accident and not homicide. Somebody mowed Lydie down with their car and left her to die on the side of the road. That's illegal. Still, I decided to accept her condolences with grace.

"The shop just opened this morning, but feel free to look around. If you have any questions, please ask."

Cooper tightened the top door hinge while the woman strolled along the built-in shelves, oohing and ahhing over every item on display. Arthur watched her movements with suspicion.

"The writing on these display cards is so intriguing and seductive. It makes me want to buy everything." She gazed at me and sighed. "What a clever young woman you are. This shop is exactly the new business we need in Justice Bay."

The woman extended a leather-gloved hand. "I'm Sylvia Medwin. I'm on the city council. What you've done here is simply dazzling. Perhaps you'd like to speak about entrepreneurship at our next meeting."

I had no idea why this woman gushed over a stranger, especially me. I flashed Cooper a side-eye to judge his reaction to the excessive flattery. He seemed amused but continued to adjust the hinges. Arthur looked troubled.

"Cassandra's Collectibles is what you call a pop-up store," I said. "It's temporary. It'll only be here for a couple of weeks."

Her eyes widened. "How titillating. At least come to my home for lunch so I can give you a proper, even though temporary, welcome to Justice Bay." She handed me a card with her name and home address printed in fancy calligraphy. "Let's say Sunday at noon." She didn't wait for my response. Instead, she sashayed past Cooper as he held the door open for her. She stepped onto the sidewalk with a final wave and a "Tout à l'heure."

I could have declined her lunch offer and told her I couldn't take time away from the shop, but Sylvia Medwin intrigued me. After all the rave bombs she'd dropped, she hadn't bought a single "seductive" thing. I questioned her true motive for inviting me to her home.

"That performance was Oscar-worthy," Arthur said as he rearranged the unsold collectibles, moving items that still shared space to a separate shelf.

"Since I'm going to her house for lunch on Sunday," I said, "who is she?"

Cooper opened and closed the door a couple of times. It didn't stick anymore. "Arthur is a local. Maybe he should answer that question."

"Sylvia is the grand pooh-bah of Justice Bay society," he said. "She and her husband Franklin live in that mini-castle in the hills above town."

"I've seen the place from a distance," I said. "It's on a private road, so nobody can get close, right?"

Arthur nodded. "I've never been inside, but if you believe the rumors, plan to arrive wearing a string of garlic around your neck."

Arthur moved a matryoshka doll Lydie bought in St. Petersburg, Russia, to an empty shelf. "It's a scaled-down replica of a European castle. Lumber baron Bartholomew Halyard built the place in the early 1900s for his fiancée, a member of Romania's royal family. The engagement imploded, and poor Mr. Halyard lived alone the rest of his life in that drafty old place."

"That's sad," I said, "and also a little dark and gloomy for the Medwins."

"I wouldn't worry about them," Arthur said. "They have plenty of money to hire interior designers to lighten the mood."

"Where did the Medwins' money come from?" I asked.

Cooper glanced at me. "Franklin Medwin made his fortune processing and packaging frozen seafood."

"You mean like fish sticks?"

He smiled. "Exactly like fish sticks."

Lydie's leather Buckingham Palace notebook sat alone on one of the shelves, which reminded me of my limited wardrobe. "I have nothing to wear to a castle owned by fish-stick gazillionaires. Jeans and a T-shirt don't seem appropriate."

Cooper knelt on the floor to return his tools to the bag. "Maybe you can borrow something from your aunt's closet."

"You mean like the red blouse?"

His lips pressed together in a grimace. "You're right. Not a good idea."

"Nothing would fit. I'm three inches taller than my aunt. Maybe I'll stop by Bay Threadz and see what they have on sale."

"When are you closing the shop?" Cooper asked.

I scanned the room, noting that Arthur had nearly completed his rearranging handiwork—no bunches or bald spots. "There's not much left to do. Arthur, do you mind locking up?"

"I'd be honored. What time shall I be here in the morning?"

I gave him the key. "Whenever it's convenient. Nine? Ten?"

Cooper zipped the bag closed and stood. "I'll walk with you to the dress shop."

No, no, no, I thought. Clothes shopping with a man you'd just met reeked of intimacy taboos. It wasn't as personal as if he'd volunteered to do my laundry, but it rated at least two notches above dinner at a romantic Italian restaurant. Did he plan to drop me off at the door or—God forbid—go inside and watch while I searched the racks? And what about trying on clothes? Did he expect me to twirl around, modeling frocks and matching mules like we were in a 1950s Doris Day rom-com?

Making such a big deal out of a bit of shopping was ridiculous. Cooper waited for me to put on my jacket. The music box hadn't sold. At the last minute, I dropped it into my backpack, hoping I could find a way to fix it at home. Cooper and I chatted until we arrived at our destination.

"I'm going to leave you here," he said. "I have to get back to the boat. That holding tank isn't going to flush itself."

I smiled. "Thanks again for helping me move into the shop, fixing the door, and especially buying Boo that cat tree."

He caught my gaze and held it. "I hope you find what you're looking for."

A lump formed in my throat. Cooper meant a fish-stick outfit, but I latched onto a deeper meaning. What was I looking for? A life in the L.A. suburbs with somebody like Brad, only better? A nine-to-five job with a 401K and a boss I had to coax and cajole to give me two weeks of bereavement leave?

Cooper must have sensed my change in mood. "You okay?"

"Yes," I said in the most upbeat tone I could muster. "Fine. I'm fine. Everything's fine."

He paused, tilting his head slightly to the side. "So...see you later?"

Small talk aside, I sensed he didn't want to leave as much as I didn't want him to go. After he disappeared around the corner, I stood alone on the sidewalk outside Bay Threadz, feeling more let down than expected.

Chapter Eight

Twenty minutes later, I left Bay Threadz with a perfect outfit for the Medwin-castle luncheon—a pair of form-fitting olive-green slacks and a coordinating floral shirt. On the way to my car, I remembered Cooper had promised to arrange a get-together with his uncle to discuss his relationship with Lydie. He hadn't mentioned it. I wondered if he'd forgotten to ask or if Walter had refused to meet me. I'd just have to be patient and wait for his next move.

Boo waited for me at the door. The cat blasted a loud meow to voice her displeasure at being left alone all day and then retreated to the kitchen window seat overlooking the bay to watch for birds. My L.A. apartment had a "no pets" policy. I needed to find Boo a new home, but my friends in Justice Bay were limited to Walter, Maddie, and Cooper. Of the three, only Walter lived in town. Arthur was more an employee than a friend. Besides, I didn't know him well enough to press him about pet adoption.

I called the office for an update on the Cabo Fiesta cruise. The reservations team had booked three more cabins from travel agents I'd contacted. I reached Brad on his cell, but he cut me off before I could tell him the good news.

"When are you coming back to work?" he said. "It's chaos here."

"I still have lots to do in Justice Bay. I'm guessing it will take the whole two—"

"Look, I'm heading into a meeting. I don't have time to talk. Just come back to L.A."

"Call me later?" I asked.

"Sure. Whatever." Brad ended the call.

I understood the pressure Brad felt, but somebody had killed my aunt, and I had to pick up the pieces. As a friend, he should have been more understanding.

After dinner, I went for a short run. When I returned home, I looked for more books and collectibles to sell at Cassandra's. I hadn't searched the closet in Lydie's office. When I opened the door, the unmistakable aroma of incense drifted from an oversized duffle bag on the floor. I pulled it out and set it on the desk.

Inside were items that appeared to be travel gear from Lydie's trip to Tibet. She'd returned home on the Friday before her death Sunday evening. She hadn't had time to unpack. Inside the bag were hiking boots, insect repellent, a device to sterilize water, and a treasure trove of souvenirs, including swatches of weathered cloth featuring horses surrounded by squiggly writing and a couple of small hand-made rugs. Several paper lanterns that, once unfolded, were the size of pumpkins. I picked up an oblong black stone with a smooth, waxy feel. Embedded in the surface were ivory geometric markings, including circles, zig-zags, diamond shapes, and a series of tiny cinnabar dots. I couldn't identify the stone, so I put it aside and kept digging.

Also in the bag was a boarding pass with "Seamus" written next to a telephone number, plus a small package wrapped in white tissue paper with my name written on top. When I picked it up, heat radiated up my arm. I didn't let go because the sensation felt strangely comforting. I removed the tissue and found a book about the size of a number-10 business envelope, the cover made of wood. What once had been three images carved into the surface were so degraded from age and use that I couldn't tell whether they were Buddhas, lotus flowers, or something else.

A strip of worn crimson fabric held the book together. I untied the cloth and found twenty unbound parchment pages charred around the edges. A beautiful script in a language I couldn't identify filled both sides of each page. Also inside lay a scrawled note written by my aunt.

My dearest Emma, this Tibetan Buddhist prayer book is a belated birthday gift. I hope its blessing brings you enlightenment. You have always been the most important person in my life. I will love you until the day I die and forever after. Remember always to trust your instincts and question everything. Om mani padme hum. Love, L

The text didn't sound like my aunt. It read more like a script from a hostage video. I examined each book page but found nothing that explained her cryptic message. According to the date on her note, Lydie wrote it on Sunday, the day she died. I collapsed on the desk chair, trying to interpret her words and feeling bereft that they were her last.

I searched online for the meaning of om mani padme hum. I learned that the ancient Buddhist mantra, loosely translated as "praise to the jewel in the lotus," and that saying the mantra only once had the power to release negative karma and achieve enlightenment. That sounded too easy.

I removed Lydie's boots and travel supplies from the duffle. In order to learn more about the items she'd brought home, I'd ask Arthur to search the internet when traffic stalled at the shop.

Before going to bed, I thought about calling Brad for an update at work, but rejected the idea. It was late, and he'd been unpleasant the last time we spoke. I read for a while, then lay in bed for hours, staring at the ceiling as random thoughts and images cascaded through my memory. Foremost among them—the phantom red ball, the red blouse, and the frayed crimson ribbon around the prayer book. A shrill voice in my head told me the repetition couldn't be coincidental, that the color was sending some kind of message. An unsettling shiver rattled my body, the same sensation I'd experienced when I unlocked Lydie's door two days ago. Finally, with Boo pressed against my leg, her purrs lulled me into a fitful sleep.

* * *

As soon as I woke up the following day, I dragged myself out of bed and contacted the travel agent who booked the three Cabo Fiesta cabins. She expressed gratitude for the personal thank-you call and promised to recommend the cruise to other clients. There was no need to notify Brad.

By now, somebody at work would have told him the good news. A boycott might be in order since he hadn't initiated even one supportive call to me since I'd left L.A.

I had to write the display cards and find more items to sell. That's when I remembered the broken music box in my backpack. Maybe it just needed a glob of grease. If I'd been thinking, I would have borrowed that lubricant Cooper had in his tool bag. Better yet, he might repair the box since he'd mastered the fine art of unsticking doors.

I pulled the music box from my backpack and attempted to twirl the ballerina with my finger. She wouldn't budge. I concentrated on avoiding damage to the tutu and lost focus. The box slipped out of my hand and crashed to the floor. I yelped, slapping my hands against my cheeks. Boo must have interpreted the sound as a call to action because she galloped into the room like Secretariat racing for the Triple Crown.

I inspected the damage. The side panel looked ajar. I picked up the box. Something small and black fell to the floor when I tried to slide the board back in place. I thought it might have come loose from inside the box, and that's why the music didn't play. Boo arched her back and batted the object across the room like a hockey puck. I hurried over and scooped it up before she damaged it.

It looked like a USB drive, but I didn't see a likely slot inside the box where it would fit. Plus, using a storage device to power a music box didn't make sense. I slid the panel back in place and set the box on the nightstand until I could find a professional to repair it.

Before I could close the lid, a tinny waltz by some long-dead composer began to play, and the ballerina started spinning. Hearing the sound, Boo let out a piercing meow. I picked her up. Her heart beat fast, or maybe it was my heart. I couldn't tell. She jumped from my arms onto the bed.

I closed the lid and looked at the black device again. It didn't belong in the music box, so why leave it there? I slipped it into my laptop port and opened a file labeled Tibet. Inside were about twenty photos.

One picture showed my aunt in her parka and hiking boots poised above a barren valley, and in another, she stood in front of an extraordinary building on a hill with snow-covered mountain peaks in the distance. Next to her was an older man with a wispy mustache and chin whiskers, wearing vivid carnelian robes, matching shoes, and elaborate headgear. Lydie hadn't identified the locations, but they had to be shots of her recent trip to Tibet.

One picture stood out from the others—a man in a parked car near a flowering bush. The driver had rolled down his window, exposing a ballcap that only partially concealed his oversized ears. He appeared to be jabbing his left finger while talking into his cell. The photo looked innocent enough, so why had Lydie hidden it inside a music box? As far-fetched as it sounded, I thought my aunt had summoned me to a scavenger hunt to search for clues to her death. Only, this scavenger hunt wasn't a game. It was deadly serious.

I had to know more about that photo, so I used my aunt's color printer to run off a copy. With Boo's food and water dishes filled, I loaded the new batch of collectibles, novels, and overdue library books into my car and headed for town. There was no need to hurry since Arthur would open the store at nine or ten, so I stopped by the library before heading to Cassandra's. If the man in the photo lived in the area, I hoped the librarian could identify him.

* * *

The library sat on prime waterfront property near the police station. Mature trees and stone benches dotted the lawn facing the bay.

Inside the lobby, fluorescent lights competed for relevance with a row of narrow rectangular windows near the ceiling. A young woman with short hair sat at the front desk wearing a T-shirt printed with, *I like to party, and by party, I mean read books.*

On the floor near her were several plastic grocery bags filled with hardback books, possibly donations for a fundraiser. I cleared a space on the front desk for Lydie's overdue books by pushing aside a lacy plastic basket filled with pens that looked like somebody had once filled it with farmers' market strawberries. I asked to speak to the librarian. Party girl told me to wait by a small desk a few feet away that displayed a name plaque that read: Pia

Bianchi, Librarian.

A moment later, squeaky wheels rolled over the tile floor. A curvaceous woman in her late fifties with curly gray hair, a kind face, and a genuine smile pushed a cart stacked with books. A pair of glasses hung by a leopard-print lanyard around her neck. As she got closer, I noticed the name on her badge read: Pia Loves Books.

The woman gazed at me with wonder. "Emmaline?" She opened her arms wide and enfolded me in a hug that would make an anaconda proud. "Lydie showed me so many pictures of you," she said enthusiastically. "I'm delighted to meet you, even under these tragic circumstances."

Given the decibel level of her greeting, Pia Bianchi didn't enforce a shooshing policy in her library. Good to know. As it turned out, Pia had known Lydie for years. They'd become close after my aunt hosted a Friends of the Library fundraiser at the cottage. We shared memories of my aunt as I followed her along the stacks, past a copy machine announcing ten cents per page for black-and-white and twenty cents for color, confirming that Chief Greene had conned me out of twenty-nine dollars and eighty cents. As she shelved books, I told her about the collectibles shop and Sylvia Medwin's invitation to lunch.

"The castle's history sounds sad and gloomy," I said.

She ruffled the pages of *Grapes of Wrath*, perhaps searching for contraband bookmarks before returning the book to the shelf. "If you're interested in tragic love stories," she said, "the romance section is on aisle three."

That seemed oddly dismissive of poor Mr. Halyard's broken engagement. There had to be more to the story.

"At the moment, I'm more interested in mysteries." I pulled out the photo I'd found in the music box of the man in the car by a bush. "What do you make of this?"

Pia parked her glasses on the bridge of her nose as she studied the snapshot. "At least I know where Lydie took this picture," she said, pointing to the bush. "It's the rest stop just outside of town. That Oleander bush is a local joke— the city overspent building those restrooms. That limited the landscaping budget to only one measly plant. Nobody watered it. Everybody thought it would die. But there it is, all alone and still thriving after all these years, a testament to the mismanagement of taxpayer dollars."

"Do you recognize the guy?"

"No, but lots of folks have second homes around here. Some of them rent out their places for short-term stays. The Chamber of Commerce has an online members-only database of local homeowners, including photos and a brief bio. Not everybody chooses to participate—privacy issues and all. It's password-protected, but I can get you in for a peek. See if he's in there."

I raised my eyebrows. "You're a wealth of knowledge."

Pia chuckled. "Librarians don't know everything, but we know where to find it. Follow me." She led me past various Dewey Decimal classifications to a small alcove with low bookcases, small squatty chairs, and a sign announcing a children's story hour.

She leaned over to rest her hand on my shoulder as she logged me on. "No popcorn available for the show, but have fun."

I scrolled through the entries, but the man with the big ears wasn't listed as a resident, confirming he didn't own property in Justice Bay or chose not to broadcast his presence.

As I logged off, cold air and the smell of incense surrounded me. My breathing grew labored, and my body appeared to lift off the chair. A soft gong sounded in the distance like low-pitched church bells. My eyes closed. My head emptied of cluttered thoughts.

Coins jingling and the copy machine coughing out pages brought me out of the vision and back to reality. My eyelids popped open. I glanced at my watch. I'd been at the library for over an hour. Arthur had proven trustworthy, but as a new hire, I couldn't leave him alone at Cassandra's Collectibles forever. At least I'd fulfilled my mission. Pia didn't know Big-ears.

I made my way toward the lobby, where Pia arranged a semi-circle of those sturdy squat chairs in the kids' area under the watchful eye of a half dozen five and six-year-old children.

She walked over, smoothing her nubby knit dress. "Find what you were looking for?"

"It was enlightening to see who lives in the area," I said, "but I didn't find my mystery man."

Pia raised her eyebrows. "You will. Sometimes answers become apparent when you rephrase the question."

I had no idea what Pia meant. The front door opened before I could ask for clarification, and a woman walked in with a young girl.

Pia winked at me. "It's our regular Friday morning story hour, and the last straggler just arrived. I have to go."

Chapter Nine

I'd planned to park in front of the shop to unload the new merchandise, but there were no open spots when I arrived. A half dozen people stood on the sidewalk out front. At first, I thought *great*. Word is spreading. Everybody loves the place. My concern grew when I realized they were all talking and gesturing toward a piece of paper on the door. I parked the car a block away and ran down the street to join them.

As I made my way to the front of the crowd, Arthur had his arms spread across the door like the last man standing at the Alamo. Behind him hung an official-looking poster attached to the glass with green masking tape. My cheeks burned as I nudged him aside and read that Cassandra's Collectibles would be closed due to its failure to obtain a city business license. Helen Marché had promised to check on tax consequences but hadn't mentioned needing a permit. I kept my composure as I peeled the paper off the glass.

"Sorry," I said, glancing at the crowd. "There must be some mistake."

The group shouted a chorus of questions. What's going on? How soon will you reopen? Can I just sneak inside and buy that wood vase on the cat tree?

Nobody had barred the entrance with an overriding lock, so I took the key from Arthur and opened the door. The crowd flooded inside and went directly to the shelves to look at the inventory. I brushed off their questions because I didn't know who had posted the notice or why. I'd call Helen Marché for advice when I had a moment.

In the chaos, my phone beeped with an incoming email. Kelly Hinson from SP&K had attached a file with photos from Lydie's retirement party.

Looking at pictures would have to wait until I dealt with this crisis.

Arthur and I kept busy with customers for fifteen minutes until the bell over the door trilled. I looked up to see Maddie walking into the shop. Her black shredded leggings and gray tunic were a smidge goth for sedate Justice Bay, but I liked the look.

"What are you doing here?" I asked.

"I took a break from selling crescent wrenches to see if you needed anything."

Arthur mediated an argument between two customers who claimed first dibs on a Bohemian crystal pelican Lydie brought home from the Czech Republic.

"Maybe some advice?" I handed her the closure notification. "I just found this on the front door."

Maddie studied the paper while Arthur sold a framed black-and-white photograph of a sign in front of a Turkish prison Lydie had taken by stealth during a trip to Istanbul. The sign read: *No Photographs!*

"This document is a total fake." Maddie pointed to the page. "Look, the edges of the city seal are fuzzy, and the first paragraph of the text has a different typeface than the last paragraph. And this green painter's tape? We sell it at the store, and it's not even the expensive stuff. Trust me. This notice is a cut-and-paste job done by an amateur."

I glanced at the customers to look for culprits who might have returned to the crime scene but failed to see any guilty expressions or suspicious sidelong glances. "Why would anybody do that?"

Maddie pointed to her Cassandra's Collectibles cat poster in the window. "Maybe they didn't like my sign." She grinned. "Just kidding. Who wouldn't love that edgy masterpiece?" She took my hands in hers. "Who will gain if your shop closes?"

I told her about my run-in with John Orson Osgood, the antique dealer down the street.

"Nice try, but no," she said. "Osgood is well-schooled in the fine art of Photoshop. He designs his newspaper ads. They're good. This so-called official document is the work of a prankster."

Prankster or not, I felt unsettled that somebody in town disliked me enough to scare away my customers. "What if Osgood intentionally made it look unprofessional as a red herring?"

"He knows you'll only be here for two weeks. It makes more sense for him to grit his teeth and wait for the shop to disappear organically."

I clenched and released my fists to curb my unease. "So, you think I should just ignore this?"

Maddie passed the document back to me. "Keep it in a safe place in case something else happens."

I cringed at the thought. "Something else? That sounds ominous."

"Look, don't worry. Pranksters want a reaction. Don't give them one. Meanwhile, I have fifteen minutes before returning to the garden tools aisle. Put me to work."

Her assurances weren't exactly reassuring. "Thanks, Maddie. Arthur and I have to unload boxes from my car, but that's about it." At hearing his name, he turned toward us.

"Artie?" Maddie said.

Arthur winced at the adulteration of his name.

I glanced at Maddie. "You two know each other?"

"Artie's mom was my sixth-grade teacher. Is she still shaping the character of future generations?"

"Retired," he said, "but she'll substitute in a pinch."

"Looks like Artie's busy with customers," she said. "I'll help you unload."

I moved the car to a newly opened space in front of the shop. With Maddie's help, we set the boxes of books and collectibles inside by the front door, including the duffle bag containing Lydie's Tibetan souvenirs.

"Sorry, I can't stay longer," she said. "Hardware must be sold." She waved to Arthur. "Say hi to your mom."

Moments after she left, my phone beeped with an incoming text. The mortuary called, advising me that they'd transferred Lydie's ashes to her columbarium niche at the cemetery.

"Arthur, I have to take care of a few things. Will you be okay alone?"

"Don't worry," he said. "I've got it covered. What should I do with the items not marked with a price?"

"Your guess is as good as mine. Check online. If you can't find anything comparable, just make the number reasonable. By the way, there are some items in the duffle bag from my aunt's Tibet trip. While you're on the internet, could you maybe find out what they are? I'll be back in thirty minutes or so. Call if you need anything." I rattled off my cell number and headed to the car.

The directions on my cell app led me to the Kinsdale Memorial Gardens, a few miles from downtown Justice Bay. A narrow, paved road led me onto the property, past headstones that ran the gamut from flat bronze rectangles embedded in granite to seven-foot statues with ornate angels and crosses, and one marble carving that looked suspiciously like an Old English Sheepdog. The pavement ended. I continued on a dirt road that opened onto a cul-de-sac surrounded by thick woods. Stone benches dotted the perimeter, but the strong wind and cold discouraged sitting in stillness and reflection.

It was a relief that Lydie had made arrangements in advance. I remembered my father's death and the overwhelming responsibility of helping my mom in the aftermath. Much of the planning had fallen onto my thirteen-year-old shoulders because my mother had been overcome with grief and incapable of action. Lydie offered to help, but my mother's relationship with her had always been complicated, so my aunt came to the funeral but stayed in the background.

A neighbor told me how proud my father would have been that I planned the wake and organized the potluck. She said, knowing that should bring me closure. Back then, I couldn't see how asking friends and neighbors to bring tuna casseroles and deviled eggs would make anything better because there would never be closure. The pain was permanent.

A flagstone path led to the columbarium niches, which looked less like a wall of post office mailboxes than I'd feared. The oblong-shaped structure spanned about ten feet long and six feet high. Smooth river rocks were embedded in the rounded corners. The ends and sides had marble-faced doors containing the ashes. A bouquet of wilted white roses lay on the ground.

There hadn't been time to install a permanent marker on Lydie's niche, but I would have found it even if the mortuary hadn't told me the location. As I swept my hand over the area, I sensed an unexpected jolt of energy. I rested my head on the smooth marble and closed my eyes.

"What happened, Lydie?" I whispered. "Who was driving that car?"

Something cracked. My eyelids snapped open. It could have been a dead tree branch broken off by the wind. But it sounded more like footsteps in the underbrush. Something or someone lurked in the woods. My neck tingled with fear as I slowly turned around to look.

"Who's there?" I shouted.

Silence.

My legs trembled as I remembered my vision of Lydie running through the woods, chased by an unknown assailant. I wondered if somebody had followed me from the store. I crouched down to lower my profile and said, "Hello." Still nothing, no sounds of a human or animal running away, no sounds at all except for the wind whistling through the trees.

I stood slowly, cautiously, and did a three-sixty swivel. Maybe I'd imagined the sound, but I sensed someone had been concealed among the trees, watching me. I crept toward the edge of the woods, scanning the area. That's when I spotted a red object on the ground. My mind flashed back to the phantom child chasing a red ball and the red blouse foretelling danger. As bizarre as it sounded, I still wondered if the color was associated with my aunt's death. As I drew near the object, I noticed an asthma inhaler with a red plastic holder lying in the debris.

I decided against collecting it as evidence. My stalker might be imaginary. If not, there was no way to tell how long it had been there. Inhalers were medicine. If the owner came looking for it and found it missing, it could jeopardize an innocent person's life.

I didn't stick around to weigh the pros and cons. I snapped a photo of the inhaler with my cell and jogged back to my car. Once inside, with the doors locked, I gulped enough air to calm my rapid heartbeat and to puzzle over what had just happened. All my senses told me that somebody intentionally murdered my aunt. I couldn't shake the feeling that I should be doing more to ease Lydie's path into the afterlife. I could think of only one way—to find out who drove the car that killed her.

Chapter Ten

I glanced at the car's clock and realized I'd been at the cemetery for over
an hour. I couldn't face returning to the shop, so I called Arthur to ask
if he'd mind closing up. He hesitated as if he had something to tell me,
but we agreed to meet at ten the following day.

I remained unsettled after I got home. I found it impossible to concentrate
on anything except tidying the house for my meeting with the real estate
agent the following day. I became overwhelmed as I glanced around the
living room for a place to begin. L.A. homeowners often staged their houses
to appeal to potential buyers. One of my coworkers at Fortuna had hired a
film company to move her lumpy couch and thrift-store lamps into storage
and bring in rental furniture and art. The transformation made the place
look like a photo spread for *Architectural Digest*. Even the clothes in her
closet were arranged by type and color and placed on identical hangers
precisely two inches apart. Looking back, I'm not even sure they were her
clothes. They may have been costumes from the wardrobe department.

I doubted I'd find any film company employees in Justice Bay, but I
welcomed the staging challenge. I stored books and collectibles in the garage
to create open space. Then I dusted and spritzed lavender air freshener
throughout the house. The scent wouldn't last, but what did? When I fired
up the vacuum cleaner, Boo skulked into a hiding place known only to her,
emerging later that night after I went to bed.

* * *

Saturday morning, I awoke feeling anxious. I'd already been in Justice Bay for five days and still had much work to do before returning to L.A. It looked increasingly like two weeks wasn't enough time to settle Lydie's estate. My boss wouldn't be happy if I asked for additional bereavement leave, but if it came to that, he'd have to deal with it.

Arthur could run the place alone, but I still planned to work a few hours before my noon meeting with the real estate agent. I made a few more adjustments to the décor and then drove to the shop, arriving just before ten.

As I approached Cassandra's, my concern spiked. People packed the shop, and an overflow crowd waited on the sidewalk. After the legal notice debacle yesterday morning, I thought, *what now?* My imagination ignited a flurry of scenarios, all bad. I ran the last few steps and swung open the door. A dozen people mingled inside, drinking tea, laughing, and talking.

I glanced around the room. Arthur had unpacked the books and knickknacks and placed them on the shelves next to their display cards. He'd used string and clothespins to join the cloth swatches from Lydie's Tibet trip and hung them around the ceiling like festive crown molding. Plates of pastries and paper cups covered the surface of a card table that had magically materialized, creating the ambiance of a cozy home library.

Arthur bounced toward me, glowing like a lighthouse beacon. "Attention, everybody," he said, clapping his hands. "This is Emma. Emma, meet the Justice Bay Literary Society."

Everybody waved and called, "Hi, Emma."

He swept his arms to highlight his handiwork. "By the way, those cloth squares are Tibetan prayer flags. Festive, don't you think?"

"Amazing."

He acknowledged my approval with a grin. "After you left yesterday, I unpacked everything. All those boxes of beautiful hardbacks left me no choice. I had to invite my book club to browse this morning. Did you know your aunt had a signed first edition of *Postmortem*, Patricia Cornwell's debut novel? I checked. It's worth a pretty penny. I've sold all the other mysteries, thrillers, and literary novels. People also snapped up a bunch of other collectibles for our club's annual Secret Santa gift exchange."

I stared at him in disbelief, convinced I'd just won the lottery. "That's fantastic, Arthur. Who brought the tea and pastries?"

"Angie from Tarts & Bars donated them. I'm in love with her lemon squares. She's also working with Pia on our new Authors on Tour series, so I told her to bring some business cards to hype her shop to our customers."

"Perfect."

"The only problem," he said, "is once everybody takes the novels home, we're low on inventory. Do you have more? If not, the chair of our bimonthly non-fiction selection committee has a few biographies and self-help books she can offer on consignment."

I didn't have the heart to remind him that Cassandra's Collectibles would soon be gone and forgotten.

I offered a strained smile. "I have more books. I'll bring them tomorrow."

He pulled me over to a quiet corner of the shop. From his pocket, he pulled out a key. "Since we come and go at different times, I duplicated the front door key. I hope you don't mind."

"Brilliant idea, Arthur. You think of everything." I loved his fun-loving attitude, but feared he'd get so invested in Cassandra's that it would jeopardize his temp business.

He grinned at the praise. "Oh, one more thing. After you left for the cemetery, a man came into the shop and asked for you. I forgot to ask his name."

"Describe him."

"Sort of hippie-like. I told the guy you were at the cemetery and didn't know when you'd return. He got so worked up that he started to wheeze. I almost called 911, but he took a couple of hits on his inhaler, and his breathing improved."

The hair on my arms rose. "What color was the cover?"

Arthur looked puzzled. "You mean the cover of the inhaler? Orangey-red, I think."

I squeezed my eyes closed. I sensed somebody was watching me in the woods near Lydie's niche. A red inhaler lay in the underbrush when I investigated. My imagination hadn't gone wild. Someone had been there. Maybe the same man who'd come into the shop. Arthur pointed him toward the cemetery, so he drove there and dropped the inhaler while spying on me. Most people in town knew my aunt had died and that I now lived in her house. If the man had found me at the cemetery, locating me at the cottage wouldn't be challenging.

A sound buzzed in my head like a hive of agitated bees. The noise blocked out the voices in the room, leaving me without a logical explanation for all these troubling events. I had to learn the identity of this man because I had a strong feeling that my life depended on it.

Chapter Eleven

I presented a happy face as I mingled with Arthur's book club members, but under the surface, I couldn't stop worrying about the man in the woods. I wondered what he wanted with me and if he'd come back.

Around eleven forty-five, I told Arthur I had an appointment with Pearl Potts about selling the house. I didn't want to leave him alone again, but he appeared happy chatting with his book group and agreed to close the shop later that afternoon. At the last minute, I moved the decoy from the empty box into my backpack. The duck would have to remain out of sight since I'd told John Orson Osgood that I'd sold it.

On my way home, I stopped by Danny's Market to buy a bouquet of fresh hydrangeas for the living room coffee table, arriving home a few minutes before my appointment. Meeting with a real estate agent made losing the house seem too real. Undoubtedly, I would miss this place and all the memories, but I couldn't afford a vacation house. Plus, my life centered around L.A.

At exactly noon, I answered a knock at the door. A petite woman in her mid-seventies with a blonde bouffant hairdo stood on the porch. In L.A., real estate agents tended to be young and glamorous, nipped and tucked, Botoxed and body-licious. But aside from Pearl Potts's heavy-handed makeup, she appeared to be rocking her wrinkles.

She sashayed into the living room like she owned the place, wearing a fuchsia bouclé knit dress with a matching Chanel-inspired jacket, every edge fringed in loopy yarn.

"What did you do in here?" she asked in a nasal tone. "Looks nice. Not that it didn't look nice before, mind you. It just looks tidier. That's good. Buyers don't want to see your clutter in the house. They want to imagine their clutter."

"I didn't ask when we spoke on the phone," I said. "How are you advertising the house? Newspapers? Internet ads?"

She batted away the question with a flip of her hand. "Let's just say I have a boutique agency with an exclusive list of clients—people who know people."

"Are any of those people interested in buying the house?"

She bent over to sniff the bouquet of hydrangeas on the coffee table. Her hairline drifted to her eyebrows when she returned to an upright position. Wig. She pushed it back in place with her index finger. Walter told me Pearl was Justice Bay's only real estate agent. But I couldn't help thinking— *seriously?*

"I showed pictures of the place to a young couple. They might be interested." Pearl opened the French doors. "Husband wants the place. Wife isn't so sure." She continued onto the veranda to gaze at the bay. "They have two little ones, so the waterfront is a negative for her. I told her kids don't stay little forever, but she wants to keep looking. Too bad. That view!"

I read somewhere that women made most house-buying decisions, so the wife's reluctance didn't sound hopeful. "Any other prospects?"

"Chill, okay?" Pearl returned to the living room. Her gaze traveled from the adjacent turret's ceiling beams and leaded glass windows and landed on Lydie's favorite reading chair. "In the meantime, eighty-six the ratty wingback over there. Fill the space with some potted ferns. Three is good."

My jaw dropped open from her cheeky comment. She walked to the couch, raised her hand over a pillow, and landed a swift karate chop in the middle, leaving the two ends pointing upward like a horned owl. She continued down the row of pillows until I had enough owls for a Hogwarts messenger service. I'd watched many design shows on TV and understood that karate-chopped pillows had peaked in the 1980s. The new style trended toward letting pillows be pillows, fluff only.

"Okay," she said, "that's about it. And don't worry about unloading the place. I have a track record. Top-selling agent in Justice Bay."

"Um, Pearl, you're the only agent in Justice Bay."

She raised her chin and glared at me. "What's your point?"

"No point, just an observation."

Pearl didn't have to install the standard communal lockbox with a key inside since she remained the sole Justice Bay real estate community member. However, she would need to get inside to show the house to prospective buyers.

"I'll make an extra key for you," I said.

"Why would you do that?"

My answer glided out, slow and measured. "So, you can get in to show the house when I'm not here."

"Don't bother." She reached inside her purse and brought out a key. "I already have one."

"You have a key to my aunt's cottage?"

Pearl turned and headed toward the door. "I sold her this place back in the day. She never asked for it back. What's the big deal?"

The big deal? Somebody other than me had a key to Lydie's house. I wondered who else occupied a spot on that not-so-exclusive list.

"I'll give you a ring when I'm ready to show the place," she said. "And by the way, stop calling it a cottage. It's a two-story, three-bedroom house."

Pearl was right. That description sounded better on a sales flyer, but I'd always considered Lydie's house a cottage because of its fairytale magic. That was unlikely to change.

I lingered on the porch, watching Pearl enter her late-model black Lincoln Continental and drive toward the main road. I made a mental note to warn the new owners to change the locks.

Since there might be a buyer soon, I had to find the title to the house. Lydie had paid off the mortgage long ago. Helen Marché hadn't included that paperwork in the documents she'd given me. My aunt didn't have a safety deposit box, so the deed had to be in the house.

Boo had made herself scarce while Pearl prowled around, but she sauntered out as soon as the door closed. She shadowed me as I began searching Lydie's office. The desk drawers were jammed with labeled and alphabetized files, the mundane records of daily living—credit card receipts, earthquake preparedness instructions, and insurance contracts. I located a file labeled house, but it only contained old statements from various contractors, including a locksmith, roof repair, and termite inspection.

I sat back in the chair and wondered where my aunt kept her important papers. They would be well hidden and protected from fire and earthquakes. A wall safe? That sounded like hammy theatre, but possible.

I moved throughout the house, peeking behind every painting and wall hanging, but found no safe. I drifted into Lydie's bedroom, which I hadn't entered since the red blouse episode. Boo disappeared into the closet, probably for a nap. After looking behind the only painting on the wall, a seascape by a gifted local artist, I sat on the window seat, eyes closed, hoping for another premonition to reveal the perfect hiding spot for a house deed.

After a few minutes, I realized that deed channeling wouldn't solve the mystery. As I passed the closet, I noted Boo using a sweater on the floor as a bed. When I picked up the garment, I noticed a slit on the carpet. I grabbed an edge and pulled, exposing a foot-long flap. Embedded in concrete on the floor was a safe.

I needed the combination. Then I remembered the locksmith receipt I'd found in the House file. Pearl claimed Lydie had never changed the locks, so why did she need a locksmith? I decided to call the company and ask if they'd installed the floor safe and if they could help me open it.

I ran downstairs, removed the statement from the file, and entered the phone number into my cell contacts. As I crammed the paperwork back into the file, a credit card receipt stapled to the back ripped free. Handwritten on the bottom were four double-digit numbers—10-18-3-26. Those numbers could represent anything, but I suspected it meant the combination of the safe.

I ran back upstairs to the bedroom closet. There were no instructions on how to turn the dial or how many times. I was right-handed, so I started by turning four times to the right, stopped, then three times to the left, continuing until I hit every number in the grouping. I continued experimenting until ten frustrating minutes later, a click. The handle turned. The lid opened.

Inside, I found a velvet bag full of gold earrings, a diamond tennis bracelet, a jar of silver dollars, Lydie's passport, and the ownership papers to her VW Beetle. The deed was there next to an envelope addressed to my aunt from the San Francisco headquarters of the California Coastal Commission. It contained a one-page letter dated three months before.

My jaw clenched as I read. Some unnamed person had reported that the cottage had been built too close to the water in violation of the Commission's regulations and claimed the courts could impose civil penalties of up to thirty thousand dollars if their investigation confirmed the allegations. They might also require Lydie to demolish the veranda.

The air around me took on an unnatural stillness. My limbs were heavy as I considered the consequences of these threats. The prior owner added the veranda years before Lydie bought the house. The Coastal Commission should have grandfathered in the porch. I couldn't bear the thought of somebody tearing it down.

The letter didn't mention who'd objected to the veranda. I doubted it was Walter, especially since Cooper hinted that he and my aunt were in a romantic relationship. An unoccupied vacation cabin to the north had been there for as long as I could remember. Lydie once told me the owners were a wealthy Nevada couple with multiple properties who never used the place. After all these years, I doubted they knew the porch existed. But somebody did, and that somebody might want Lydie's house, maybe enough to kill for it.

I had to find out if my aunt settled the issue or if it might threaten the house sale. I closed the safe, leaving everything inside except for the letter. I sat on my beloved porch swing, staring at the bay. So much had happened since I'd arrived in Justice Bay. Lydie's photo of the big-eared man in the car at the rest stop still puzzled me, not to mention the prank document on the shop's door and that bizarre incident at the cemetery. Now I had this threatening letter.

I considered myself an independent person and a problem solver. I could handle this alone, but liked to bounce ideas off Brad. In the early days of our friendship, we'd go out after work for a glass of wine and talk about everything from why honeybees were dying off to whether cookies were better soft or crunchy. We were still friends, or at least I thought so, but I decided against calling him since our last few telephone conversations had been brief and prickly. For the next few minutes, I debated the wisdom of my next move. I picked up the phone. My finger hovered over the keypad briefly before I made the call.

Chapter Twelve

Ten minutes after Walter Kestrel answered my call, the Schwinn leaned against the bench in front of his cabin, and I sat on a chair across from him at his kitchen island. I pulled the decoy out of my backpack and set it next to a charcoal gray Glock that lay disassembled on a white terry-cloth towel on the counter.

I nodded toward the duck. "I brought you a gift."

Walter read the story card about the Moroccan back alley where spies and wanderers dwell and offered a deadpan, "Funny."

"Cooper told me you used to be with the FBI," I said. "Do they still make you shoot things after you retire?"

"Targets mostly," he said with a wink, "but I've got to keep up my skills because you never know. And by the way, if this conversation is classified, you should know my nephew is in the house, doing his laundry."

The thought of Cooper in the next room washing his underwear qualified as too much information. "We're good."

Walter began pushing a brush back and forth through the gun barrel. "Regale me."

"Sooooo," I said, stretching out the word. "I met Pearl Potts. She's a character."

Walter chuckled. "I sense you didn't appreciate Pearl's quirky vibe."

"She's the only real estate agent in Justice Bay? Really?"

He squirted cleaner fluid onto a cotton square and attached it to the end of the brush. "I won't lie to you. Some people hire agents from out of town, but Pearl knows the area. She'll do right by you and, more importantly, by

Lydie."

"I hope so." I pulled out the photo of the man talking on his cell by the oleander bush. "You recognize this person?"

He stared at the image. "Nope. Why?"

"The librarian told me Lydie took it at the rest stop outside town. Just wondering what this guy had to do with my aunt."

Walter set the brush on the towel. "No idea. Where did you find it?"

"On a flash drive hidden in a music box."

His eyes narrowed. "I assume you'll tell me more, so I'll be patient…for now."

I ignored the pressure. "I found the photo with Lydie's Tibet pictures. It didn't belong with the others. Is there any secret FBI technology that can identify this person from a profile view?"

Walter grabbed the photo. "I'm retired. Remember? That said, you can tell by his hand that Mystery Man is a white male. His baseball cap covers his hair, so we can't see the color. But no fringe shows at the edges, so it's likely either short, shaved, or the guy is bald." Walter squinted and moved the photo closer. "The coat he has on is too big for him and looks cheap. Maybe the guy lost weight or has no sense of style. He's wearing a watch. The picture's grainy. It's hard to tell the brand. Gold face. Lots of dials and doodads. Black band. It could be a Patek Philippe. It could also be a knock-off. But if it's real, the guy is either a crappy dresser with disposable income or a thief. That might not help now, but it could be important later."

Walter's words seemed like an FBI Academy course on what to look for when you think there's nothing to see. "Impressive," I said.

"Check out his body language," he continued. "He's jabbing his left finger in the air like he's angry. Whoever he's talking to is telling him something he doesn't want to hear."

My gaze locked onto the photo. Walter's observations confirmed my suspicions that I had no intuitive instincts. I wasn't even particularly perceptive.

Walter's generic description of the driver meant it could be anybody, even the neohippy guy who came to the shop looking for me. Maybe he had his hair stuffed under the ballcap. I told him about my trip to the cemetery and my suspicion that somebody lurked in the woods.

"When I went to look, he'd gone but left an inhaler on the ground."

"Did you pick it up?"

"No. It was medicine. I thought the owner might come back looking for it."

I showed him the pictures I'd taken and told him every detail I remembered about the incident. "Do you suppose this man had something to do with Lydie's death?"

"I'll pass it by Chief Greene," he said, his expression unreadable. "Anything else?"

I laid the Coastal Commission letter from my backpack on the counter beside him. "Do you know anything about this? I found it in Lydie's safe."

He raised his eyebrows as he read. "You're turning into a regular Miss Marple."

I snatched the letter from his hand. "Glad to see you recognize my many talents."

Walter picked up the brush with the cotton square attached. "About four months ago, Lydie told me some suit from a venture capital firm in San Francisco sent her a letter offering to buy her house. She turned him down, but he kept upping the ante. She finally told him to bug off. He did, but a few weeks later, that notice arrived."

"Did he want the house for himself or a client?"

"Not sure."

"Is the Coastal Commission investigation still open?"

"That setback allegation was a load of crap, but somebody with leverage had to know a big shot at the commission for this letter to happen. Lydie sent them a copy of all the former owner's building permits. After that, they dropped the whole thing."

"Sounds like a pressure campaign to force her to sell."

"That's what she thought, too." He ran the cotton square through the barrel a few times. It came out black and sooty, making me think he'd fired the gun recently. "But it didn't work," he went on. "Just made her mad."

"Do you remember the man's name or the firm he worked for?"

Walter continued cleaning the Glock with cotton swabs. "Don't recall if she mentioned the man's name. The firm sounded heroic, like an America's Cup yacht—Intrepid or Indefatigable. Lydie must have kept the paperwork."

"I haven't found it yet."

He squinted as if trying to read imaginary tea leaves. "Keep looking."

"Hey, Emma." I turned to see Cooper standing in the doorway in a plaid flannel bathrobe. He held a wicker basket full of clothes. He glanced at the decoy and smiled.

"Jeez, Cooper," Walter said. "We have company. I hope you're wearing something under that robe."

Cooper set the basket on the couch. "Sorry, my clothes are still in the dryer."

Walter beckoned him over. "Have a seat. Just watch yourself."

Cooper pulled up a chair next to me, ushering in the aroma of peppermint soap. "I'm glad you're here. You saved me a call. Tonight, I'm throwing together my version of bistro chicken pasta. I thought you might want to join us for dinner."

I glanced at Walter. He frowned, which gave me the impression that he vetoed the idea. If so, I wondered why. Perhaps he suffered from Emma overload.

"Maybe another time," I said. "I have my lunch with Sylvia Medwin tomorrow. I need to brush up on my castle etiquette so I don't embarrass myself."

"How about Monday after work?" Cooper asked. "You can tell us if you passed muster with the Queen."

Walter finished cleaning the Glock and began reassembling the pieces. "Leave the woman alone. She's going to think you're a stalker."

Cooper leaned toward me. The robe parted, revealing one bare, muscular thigh. "Is that what you think, Emma? That I'm stalking you?"

My cheeks were warm. How should I answer that? No, but there may have been an actual stalker watching me at the cemetery. I'd told Walter about the incident, but didn't feel like burdening Cooper with the details. I preferred to dwell on the positive, that being pursued by Cooper Dane was not a horrible thought.

"A stalker? Uh, no. That's not how I think of you."

Walter redirected the conversation as he often did. "Coop told me about your lunch with Sylvia. I can't figure out why the Medwins live in that moldy old relic. They could turn it into a museum and ditch Justice Bay for one of those sterile high-rise penthouses in San Francisco."

"Maybe they enjoy looking down on the peasants from their hillside castle," I said, standing. "Thanks for all your help, Walter. Look, you've had me over for dinner. I'd like to reciprocate. How about both of you come to the cottage on Monday? I'll invite Maddie. If you survive my cooking, our friendship might have a real chance. Is six okay?"

"Perfect," Cooper said. "I'll bring wine."

Walter mumbled something unintelligible that sounded like humph.

The sun slipped toward the horizon as I swung my leg over the Schwinn and pedaled toward home. The air had turned crisp and cool. Traffic was light. I thought about Monday's dinner menu and already regretted extending the invitation. Everyone who'd suffered through one of my dinner parties agreed I couldn't cook. Nobody would speak to me again if they survived dinner at all. I might have to ply them with a few bottles of wine to dull the memory.

The turnoff to Lydie's driveway was in sight when I glanced toward the woods on my left. Something glinted in the afternoon sun. Intrigued, I stopped and wheeled the bike across the road and onto the shoulder. I leaned the Schwinn against a fallen log and walked through the dense underbrush, following the light source.

About fifty feet from the road, I spotted a familiar cell phone cover in a pile of fir needles. I'd had it custom-made for my aunt's last birthday using one of my favorite photos of Lydie in Machu Picchu, Peru. It was encrusted with multi-colored rhinestones and crystals depicting clouds surrounding the mountain. In the foreground, Lydie stood smiling, wearing hiking gear, including a bucket hat and a heavy sweater.

I felt dizzy and disoriented. A million unanswered questions circulated through my head. Had she dropped the cover while out on a walk? Had it been knocked off her phone when the car hit her? If so, why hadn't the police found it? Had they investigated at all? According to the police report, first responders found no phone among her possessions. Where was her cell? I'd been so busy with the shop that I hadn't looked.

Since the cover might be evidence, I photographed it and the surrounding area before picking it up with a tissue from my backpack. I dropped it in a paper lunch bag when I returned home. Then I thoroughly searched the house and Lydie's car, but her cell wasn't there.

It had now been six days since my aunt died. Without her password, I couldn't use the find-my-phone option. Her cell battery had probably lost its juice by now, but I had to do everything possible to find it.

I walked from room to room, punching in her number and listening for a response. I had just redialed from inside her office when the ringing suddenly stopped. I heard heavy breathing, followed by a cough. There was only one conceivable explanation. Somebody had just answered Lydie's phone.

Chapter Thirteen

S econds later, the cell connection ended. My hands felt clammy as I resisted the urge to hide under the bed or return to Walter's kitchen. I couldn't deny the possibility that some Joe Blow had found the phone at the side of the road and stolen it before the police searched the area. But more likely, the driver who killed my aunt got out of the car, took her phone, and discarded the cover before leaving. It was unclear why anybody would do that unless they thought it contained something incriminating—like texts or photos.

I considered contacting Walter, but the cell cover and the call were related to an open police investigation, so I decided to share the information with my biggest skeptic, Justice Bay Police Chief Chet Greene. I called his direct line but got a recorded message. I could have dialed 911, but my information didn't qualify as an emergency, except to me, so I left a voice mail telling him I'd found the cover. I also said there were several other matters to discuss, without mentioning the mouth breather who answered Lydie's phone.

At ten p.m., I still couldn't sleep. I didn't want to burden Maddie with my problems at this late hour because she was likely reading Dostoyevsky to her dad before he fell asleep.

My boss had scheduled me to deliver a marketing pitch at a travel convention in Dallas in two weeks, so I began inputting a list of talking points. After a few crappy paragraphs, I lost focus. I'd written dozens of similar presentations. I could write another one. I just didn't want to.

I roamed the house for the next hour, looking for that venture capital offer on Lydie's house. Walter thought she kept the paperwork. I already confirmed it wasn't in her office file cabinet. I searched other places where my aunt might keep her essential papers, but found nothing. Chief Greene didn't call back. I read until about eleven before falling asleep.

* * *

It irritated me that Greene still hadn't returned my call by the following morning. Before my lunch with Sylvia Medwin, I took the cell cover, still in the paper lunch bag, grabbed the photo of the man in the parked car by the oleander bush, and drove to the police station, hoping to find Greene. Somebody had locked the front door but left a light on in the back office. I knocked. Chet Greene peeked around the corner and frowned.

I noticed his wrinkled uniform shirt and undone top two buttons as he unlocked the door. "What can I do for you?"

"Did you get my message?"

"You're on my things-to-do list for tomorrow," he said without inviting me in.

"Why wait until tomorrow? I'm here now."

He glanced toward the back office. "I'm working on something. Can it wait?"

I pushed open the door. "No. It's important."

As I walked toward the front desk, I saw a woman's handbag on the clerk's chair. I wondered what Chet Greene was doing and with whom.

I handed him the paper bag with Lydie's cell phone cover inside. "As I mentioned in my message, I found this in the woods near the scene of my aunt's murder."

His eyebrows darted up. "Lydie Halstad's death isn't classified as a murder."

"I hope you'll change that after reviewing the new evidence."

He opened the bag and looked inside. "You should have left this where you found it. You broke the chain of custody. Even if I reclassified your aunt's death as a homicide, the district attorney wouldn't admit the phone cover as evidence in court."

I shook my head, unsure if he was telling me the truth. "That doesn't sound right. I didn't leave my fingerprints and documented where I found it." I reached for my cell phone to show him the pictures I'd taken in the woods, but he brushed me off.

"Forget the cover. It's no good to me. What else you got?"

I expelled a blast of air, frustrated by his skepticism. "Somebody is using my aunt's phone."

I told him about the mouth breather who'd answered my call. "If you get records from Lydie's cell carrier, they might pinpoint where the phone is now and what other calls the person has made since my aunt died."

From the back office, the sound of a creaky chair interrupted our conversation. I craned my neck to have a peek, but couldn't see inside. Greene raked his hand through his bristly hair as he eyed the doorway. "Give me your aunt's number."

I found the wine receipt from Danny's market in my backpack, jotted down the number, and handed it to him. Then I placed the photo of the man near the oleander bush on his desk.

"My aunt took this picture shortly before she died. Do you have any idea who this person is?"

"Nope."

"Maybe you could ask around. If the guy is local, somebody might recognize him."

"What if they do? It's not illegal to make a phone call at a public rest area."

"My aunt hid the photo. Don't you find that interesting? That's not normal unless something frightened her."

"A lot of things your aunt did weren't normal," he said with thinly concealed contempt. "And you're starting to sound like her—a kooky conspiracy theorist."

His rudeness shocked me. I wondered why he dissed me since we'd just met. He'd also dismissed potential evidence I'd uncovered, making me feel like a Cassandra.

"I thought cops took some kind of protect-and-serve oath when they took the job," I said. "All I'm asking is for you to find out who killed my aunt."

Angry red blotches appeared on his cheeks as he handed me the paper bag with the cell cover inside. "I'll let you know if I find the phone."

He led me to the front door, locking it once I stepped outside. His attitude annoyed me, but I couldn't do anything about that now. Since he'd rejected the cell cover as evidence, I slipped it onto my phone like a talisman—a perfect fit.

A few hours before my lunch with Sylvia Medwin, I returned to the house and forced myself to work on the travel show presentation. It included a typical pep talk. I sang the praises of Fortuna Cruises and peppered my remarks with a few travel jokes, including this crowd-pleaser: What's the definition of an international bathroom? When you enter, you're Russian, inside European, and when you leave, you're Finnish. On second thought, I deleted it for being too indelicate.

In preparation for my lunch with Sylvia Medwin, I put on the new outfit I'd bought at Bay Threadz. The body-hugging green pants and coordinating floral top made me feel like a model on my way to a photo shoot at a creepy castle.

My car navigated the S-curves leading up the hill to Medwin's Romanian-inspired castle at eleven-forty-five. I wondered why an upper-crust doyenne of Justice Bay Society and city council member had invited me for lunch. Despite her praise for my sales know-how, I wasn't under consideration for any Entrepreneur of the Year award just because I'd opened a temporary pop-up store. There must be an ulterior motive. Still, getting into the good graces of a town luminary might be essential. Plus, I looked forward to seeing the castle and learning more about its history.

As I cleared the final switchback, the view expanded to showcase a gray stone edifice with multiple cone-shaped spires that reminded me of a theme park fantasyland. A man answered my call on the intercom and buzzed me through the gates. I parked in a circular courtyard and approached the massive front door.

A young woman named Celia, dressed in a gray cotton uniform with a white collar, gestured me into a chilly foyer that smelled of floor wax. She led me through a labyrinth of dark and gloomy wood-paneled hallways past rooms with arched doorways, heavy ceiling beams, and maroon velvet curtains covering the windows.

I arrived at the dining room, relieved that the Medwins had softened their Vlad-the-Impaler décor with white walls. A crystal chandelier hung above the table, twinkling with reflected noon sunlight. A lovely vase of peonies sat on the table, but on closer inspection, they were the type that needed dusting, not watering.

Celia pulled two placemats and napkins from an ornately carved wood bureau and set them on the table. Then she left me alone with an appetite-suppressing dead animal rug in front of the fireplace. A wolf? I resisted the urge to lean over and smell the thing, preferring to believe it was a faux-fur reproduction.

Moments later, Sylvia made a grand entrance in another gorgeous dress made of clingy blue silk draped perfectly over her thin frame. She smiled and gestured for me to sit at the table.

"So glad you could come, Emmaline. I'm sorry my husband couldn't be here to meet you. He's out of town on business."

"Maybe another time." My gaze swept the room. "What a great place. Such an interesting backstory."

"What exactly do you know?" Her tone sounded clipped and suspicious.

I repeated what I'd learned about Halyard's broken engagement with a Romanian princess and the grief-stricken, lonely life that followed him to his grave.

Celia entered from the kitchen and placed a basket on the table that looked like a tiny coffin. Thankfully, it was filled with bread.

After Celia left the room, Sylvia continued. "Bartholomew Halyard was brokenhearted when his engagement fell through, and he did die a single man. But he didn't die alone."

I smelled gossip. "That sounds intriguing."

"He had a years-long affair with his housekeeper."

A noise interrupted the conversation. I glanced toward the kitchen door. Celia stood in the opening, holding two salad plates and glaring at Sylvia.

"It exploded into scandal in the late 1920s," Sylvia said, oblivious to Celia's eye daggers. "Halyard never married the girl, but he left her everything when he died."

I placed my hand on my heart. "What a great love story."

Celia set the plates in front of us—crab salads. I wondered if they came from Medwin's frozen fish-stick factory.

Sylvia shook out the folds of the napkin with her long, bony fingers and laid it across her lap. "Love story? The girl was a gold-digger who took advantage of a lonely, much older man."

What's the problem if they were happy? I thought, but I said, "What happened to her?"

"She's dead now, of course. Good riddance, if you ask me."

I wanted to know more, but Sylvia's disapproving tone cued me to drop the subject. After that, we avoided any talk of Bartholomew Halyard and his housekeeper. Instead, we chatted about the minutiae of Justice Bay life and nibbled on romaine leaves, which were crisp and fresh. The crab may have once been frozen, but it tasted delicious nonetheless.

During a lull in the conversation, Sylvia said, "Emmaline dear, I hear you're selling your aunt's house. Any offers yet?"

"No, but it's only a matter of time," I said, parroting Pearl's optimism.

"I might know an interested party." Her tone was matter-of-fact on the surface but sly at its core.

"Great. Tell the buyer to contact my real estate agent, Pearl Potts."

Her mood soured. "Pearl? Are you serious?"

I managed to keep the defensiveness from my tone. "Yes. Pearl. She came highly recommended."

Sylvia pushed her salad aside. "The buyer would prefer to negotiate directly with you." Her shrewd tone made me suspicious.

"Who's the interested party?"

She hesitated. "My husband and I would like to purchase the place."

"Why would you want it? You live in a castle."

"The house isn't for us. It's for our son. He lives in the city, but having a pied-à-terre in Justice Bay makes visiting more convenient."

The castle must have a gazillion rooms, including a guest room or two. The son could probably have a whole wing if he wanted it.

My shoulders tensed. "I can't cut Pearl out of her commission. It wouldn't be fair. She's already put effort into pitching the place."

From her sour expression, I gathered Sylvia must be unaccustomed to hearing the word no. She touched one mega-watt diamond earring, maybe to remind me she had enough money and power to crush me like a bug.

"Did you sign a contract?"

"Uh…not yet," I said. "We have a verbal agreement."

"Then it's not binding. You're free to change your mind."

My jaw muscles tensed. All that flattery Sylvia dished out when we met at the shop now looked like manipulation and deception. "Except I won't. Because I promised."

"I know you're eager to sell," she said. "To help you out, we're prepared to be generous."

She threw out a number that exceeded even L.A. standards. I paused to consider the offer, but I'd given quirky Pearl the listing, and I wouldn't go back on my word.

"As I told you," I said, "I'd love to sell the place to you, but only if you go through Pearl."

"There are obstacles to unloading a house in Justice Bay," she said with an unpleasant edge in her tone. "It can sometimes take a very long time."

Call me crazy, but her words sounded like a threat.

"You can speed things up by contacting Pearl. I have her number if that helps."

Sylvia tilted her head back, leaving her thin blade nose pointing at me like a switchblade. "If you change your mind, you know where to find me." Her chair scraped against the hardwood floor as she pushed it back from the table. "Celia will see you out."

After she left the room, I waited around for at least five minutes, but Celia never materialized, so I made my way back toward the front door through the maze of hallways.

I must have taken a wrong turn because the territory looked unfamiliar. I glanced into one of the rooms to get my bearings. There was a window, but curtains covered the view. I stepped inside to look around. A rusty suit of armor stood at attention near the door. I'd never seen one up close before. I wondered if Sylvia might be interested in selling it on consignment at Cassandra's Collectibles. Probably not.

I opened the face flap to see if a dead knight lurked inside when footsteps echoed in the hallway. A man spoke in a one-sided conversation on his cell phone.

"Is she gone?" He paused. "Her car is still parked in the courtyard." Another pause. "Are you telling me she's wandering around the house unescorted?" His tone became angry. "Find her!"

My mouth dried as I speculated about the guy's identity. Security guard? Igor? Renfield? I could have stepped into the hallway and asked for directions, but something stopped me—fear. Sylvia's response after I refused to cut Pearl out of the house deal landed like a threat. With the woman's wealth and influence, I could imagine the multiple levers of power she could press to cause me trouble.

As the sound of Renfield's footsteps came closer, my leg muscles tightened, ready for flight. My head jerked from side to side as I looked for a place to hide. Everywhere seemed too obvious. I glanced toward those maroon velvet curtains on the windows as a vein in my temple pulsed. My mind again flashed back to shades of red. Everywhere red. I forced myself to shake off the memories like a dog repelling water and took cover behind the curtains, sitting on the windowsill to hide my feet like a tortured heroine in a B movie. Outside, I saw my car parked in the courtyard. So near and yet so far away.

My heart pounded as the footsteps approached and paused near the open doorway. I didn't want to peek to see who was there for fear of being discovered. I held my breath so the sound wouldn't give away my position. As soon as the footsteps continued down the hall, I opened the window and lowered myself to the ground. Then I ran.

Chapter Fourteen

On the drive home from the castle, I wondered what explained the recent interest in my aunt's house. Justice Bay hardly qualified as the hub of commerce or a well-known vacation destination. It offered a picturesque view for buyers looking for a second home, but it was hours from a major airport. There were minimal tourist attractions and no hotels to accommodate visiting guests.

The cottage sat near the water, which hiked the asking price. But with all its charm, the Justice Bay area featured more desirable homes. For one thing, nobody had remodeled Lydie's kitchen since the 1990s, and the roof over the garage leaked. And yet, four months ago, a mysterious buyer had offered multiple escalating bids to acquire the place. They may have even filed a bogus complaint with the Coastal Commission, thinking that would pressure Lydie to sell.

And then, a short time ago, Sylvia Medwin had proposed paying me big bucks for the place. She'd suggested a sneaky end-run around my real estate agent to avoid paying commission. I wondered why Sylvia had insisted on cutting Pearl out of the transaction. Maybe she assumed I'd never sold a house before and wanted to isolate me from any professional who had. That allowed her to manipulate me into accepting unfavorable terms.

I had to learn details about any prior house offer, so I contacted Pearl Potts when I got home. She confirmed there were no recent attempts to purchase the place. I didn't tell her about Sylvia Medwin's sleazy plan to cut her out of the deal because Pearl had to coexist with the Medwins in this small-town environment.

After ending the call, I went online with the one clue Walter Kestrel had provided—the mystery buyer worked for a venture capital firm in San Francisco with a heroic-sounding name. My search for VC firms produced multiple links. I checked the websites for projects that were related to real estate but found nothing that triggered any suspicions. I paused when I came to one called Endeavor, Inc. Walter might view that name as heroic, but I considered it a tad needy. We Try!

Scrolling through the site's content, I came across a list of principals. My shoulders rippled with tension when I glimpsed a familiar name—Medwin—not Franklin or Sylvia, but Kevin.

Endeavor's website didn't include detailed personal information on Kevin, so I typed his name into my computer's search engine and found his profile on several social media accounts. Kevin appeared to be a single guy in his early thirties, with short blond hair and an engaging smile. He lived in San Francisco but had attended a private high school in Palo Alto and earned an undergraduate degree and an MBA at Stanford. He'd claimed no hometown, but Sylvia said her son lived in the "city." San Francisco was the largest city near Justice Bay. It sounded like Kevin might be Sylvia and Franklin's son.

I wondered if Kevin or somebody representing him had made the mystery bid to buy my aunt's house. Maybe he asked his mother to approach me with her shady offer when that failed. It was convenient that my aunt had died in the interim, leaving the house available.

Lydie must not have mentioned the buyer to Walter because he would have recognized the Medwin name. On a whim, I zoomed in on Kevin's photo to see if he might be the man in the picture by the oleander bush, but I found zero evidence of a Patek Philippe watch. Rich people probably had drawers full of expensive watches, but the man in Lydie's photo looked at least fifteen years older than Kevin and had much larger ears. It appeared that the Medwins had lived in the castle for a while, so Kevin must have spent his early life here. I'd ask Maddie tomorrow at dinner if she knew him and if they still kept in touch.

I sat on the veranda porch swing to think about my next step. Sylvia had made a generous offer for the house. If I accepted her proposal, I could always write a check to Pearl to compensate her for the lost commission. A quick house sale will allow me to finish my work in Justice Bay and return to Los Angeles. I could move the unsold collectibles into storage until I found them new homes. That would at least make my boss happy, but I doubted returning to L.A. would make me happy.

A series of loud meows echoed from inside the house. Boo stood in the kitchen over a hairy object with a tail. It appeared to be some kind of rodent. Rat? My feline-owning friends had told stories about cats bearing gifts. I wondered if the beast still lived or had died a noble death. I was already planning the funeral when I went inside to investigate.

My relief was profound when I discovered only a stuffed toy that Boo had hauled out of one of the many hiding places that housed her collection of bottle caps and paperclips. Its long, thin snout reminded me of Sylvia's nose. I took that as a sign that I'd done the right thing by turning down her cheesy offer.

I called Maddie to invite her to dinner the following night, telling her that Walter and Cooper would also be there. She couldn't talk, so I ended the call after she agreed to join us.

My terrible cooking history left me clueless about menu options. To avoid embarrassing myself, I did the unthinkable. I ordered take-out from C'est Shells for pick up tomorrow afternoon—fresh salmon tartare, crab cakes with avocado salsa, Tuna Mornay (whatever that was), and a green salad. The hostess talked me into a Chiriboga Blue cheese and a French Brillat-Savarin. I planned to stop by Tarts & Bars for after-dinner lemon squares.

After that, I sat on the porch swing to collect my thoughts. I had to notify my mother of my aunt's death. Lydie was her sister-in-law and my father's only sibling. Even though they'd never been close, she needed to know.

My mother and I loved each other, but her reserved nature made her seem emotionally contained. While the mothers of my friends acted like giggly guests at a slumber party, mine was the adult in the room, telling you to tone it down and not leave cookie crumbs on the bed.

She remarried during my senior year in college and moved to Paris. On my first visit to her new Montmartre apartment, I told her I'd resumed my regular visits to Justice Bay. She apologized for keeping me away from Lydie all those years and confessed she felt threatened by how much closer I was to my aunt than her. I thanked her for letting me know, but ended the visit feeling sad about all the time I'd lost with my aunt.

After thoroughly depressing myself with that tortured history, I couldn't muster the courage to call her. I used the time change between Justice Bay and Paris as an excuse. Instead, I sent a short email with the essential information, hoping that would suffice.

The rest of the day became a blur. At around seven p.m., I stood in the kitchen when a beam of light appeared at the end of the driveway. I went to the front of the house and stared out the window. Somebody loitered in the woods near the road, sweeping the area with a flashlight near where I'd found Lydie's cell cover. Maybe Chief Greene finally decided to search for evidence that would lead to a suspect in my aunt's death, but I feared something more sinister prowled those woods.

Chapter Fifteen

I didn't file a police report about the light in the woods to avoid insulting Chief Greene if he'd been investigating. He would only take it as confirmation of my so-called kooky conspiracy theories. The person hadn't come near the house. I couldn't confirm their identity. Regardless, I planned to pull Walter aside at dinner the following evening and ask his advice about what to do next, if anything.

My boss expected me back at work on Monday, a week from tomorrow. That would be difficult. I'd made progress thinning out some of Lydie's collectibles, but Pearl hadn't sold the house, and I hadn't explored any options to dispose of my aunt's furniture and other household items. I could lock the cottage and return to L.A., but driving back on weekends to finish the job sounded exhausting. More than that, I wasn't ready to leave Justice Bay and return to work. I needed more time to stay in the cottage surrounded by my aunt's cherished memories.

I played dangle-the-string with Boo, her all-time favorite game. After that, I relocated my laptop and Lydie's small printer from the upstairs bedroom to the kitchen island so I could keep an eye on the driveway.

I searched online for nearby moving companies with storage facilities that could accommodate the contents of the house. There weren't many, so I did a similar search for businesses in L.A. Storing the household goods closer to home would make it easier to sort through everything whenever I had a few minutes to spare. I also left a message for Pearl Potts, asking for an update on any prospective house buyers.

Chief Greene had given me no updates about Lydie's hit-and-run investigation. He should be checking every mechanic in the area for a damaged car. Maybe I'd help him since I already had my laptop open. I searched for auto body shops within a twenty-mile radius of Justice Bay. I copied and pasted the information into a table with name, address, and phone number columns. There was no way to know where the driver lived, so I expanded the search to within fifty miles.

I printed my list and weighed the possibility of anonymously slipping it under the door of the police station, but decided against it. Greene would suspect me and discount the information. I'd find a trusted ally to deliver it for me.

At around nine p.m., as I shut down my computer, I heard a knock on the door. I flinched. Between the creepy stalker at the cemetery and the unknown person searching the woods, my concern escalated about who was outside my house at this late hour.

An imaginary scary movie trailer full of assassins and monsters under the bed began running on a loop through my brain. I grabbed a cast-iron skillet from the kitchen and crept to the door with my back against the wall. A shadowy figure stood on the landing. Every nerve ending fired as I raised the skillet over my head.

"Who's there?" I shouted.

"It's just me," Walter said.

My legs trembled as I lowered the skillet and opened the door. "You scared me half to death."

"Sorry," he said as he stepped inside, holding a bag of cat litter. "I know it's late, but I found this at my place. Thought you might need it."

"Thanks, Walter." I ushered him inside with a sweep of my arm. He set the litter on the island countertop and draped his black down jacket on the back of one of the stools.

"Has Chief Greene shared any information about Lydie's death investigation?" I asked.

Walter sat on the stool next to his jacket. "Look, Greene has faults, but he's not a doofus. Besides, he's not the only one looking into Lydie's death."

I leaned toward him. "Who? I thought Greene worked alone."

"All I can say is the investigation is moving forward."

"How do you know? You're not on the Justice Bay police force. You're not even an FBI agent anymore. You're retired."

"For all the crime novels you claim to read, I'm surprised you don't know that law enforcement doesn't talk about ongoing investigations with citizens like you. Me included."

"I thought you were a counterintelligence specialist. How does catching spies help solve a hit-and-run?"

He leaned toward me with his forearms on the island's granite top. "All investigations boil down to who and why."

"It wouldn't kill you to give me a detail or two," I said. "You can trust me." That argument didn't seem to move him. "I bet you told Cooper."

"Sometimes I need a legal opinion, but whatever we discuss is privileged."

"And in exchange for that legal advice, you give him free rein over your laundry room."

His lips twitched in a smile. "As I said, Cooper never betrays a trust. Even if your interrogation ended with him under a light bulb and handcuffed to a chair, you couldn't break him."

I laughed. "I'll get Maddie right on it."

Walter looked puzzled. "Maddie Balister?"

"I get the impression she's interested in him."

He raised his eyebrows, surprised. "He never mentioned that."

"Does he always share details of his love life?"

"Sometimes," he said with a wink. "What would you like to know?"

"That qualifies as too much information." I grabbed the body shop list and slid it across the countertop.

He glanced down at the page. "What am I supposed to do with this?"

"Give it to Chief Greene?"

"I'm guessing he's already made a list."

"Have you seen it?"

Walter sighed. "Fine. I'll stop by the station tomorrow." He put on his jacket and slipped the papers into a pocket. "And Emmaline, you're not going to contact any of these body shops, right?"

Walter didn't know me well. I didn't want to lie out of respect. But I had no confidence in Greene's investigation. If I didn't see some progress soon, I'd have no choice but to do the chief's work for him. Otherwise, he might never find my aunt's killer.

"Don't tell Greene where you got that list, okay?"

Walter nodded and headed toward the door. He glanced over his shoulder as he reached for the knob. "Just to clarify, you can talk to Cooper about anything. He's a good kid who knows how to keep a secret. You could do worse." A moment later, he disappeared into the darkness.

I wondered what he meant by that last comment. Did Walter believe I had a closer relationship with his nephew than I did? I worried that my attraction to Cooper had been too obvious. He flirted with me, but some guys were like that. It didn't mean anything. Walter denied Cooper had designs on Maddie, but I sensed she had a few of her own. I brushed those complications aside and read until I drifted off to sleep.

After rolling out of bed the following morning, I called Mike Woods, intending to ask for another week of leave. His assistant put me through immediately.

"Emma, I'm so glad you called." His voice vibrated with stress. "It's chaos around here. I've scheduled an emergency meeting for the entire management team next Monday, a week from today. We have big decisions to make. I need you here."

A lump formed in my stomach. "What's going on?"

"One of our ships collided with a fishing boat in Mexican waters. Repairs are underway in Puerto Vallarta, but the ship can't leave port for a few days. We've offered all passengers free shore excursions while waiting, but some people want to go home. I've sent a couple of reservations agents to PV to smooth things over and handle travel arrangements."

"Mike, I'm so sorry. What a mess." I paused to gather my courage. "But here's the thing. It'll be challenging to leave Justice Bay in time to attend that meeting. That's why I'm calling. I underestimated how long it would take to sell my aunt's house and settle the estate. I need another week." I wanted to add or two but decided not to risk it.

After a long, chilly silence, he said, "No. That's not possible. I wanted you back earlier, but didn't ask because I promised you two weeks. There's no way I can authorize any more time off."

"I'll keep working from here—"

"What part of no don't you understand?" he shouted. "Either show up for work on Monday, or I'll find somebody who will."

My ears still rang as I stammered my reply. "Okay then. See you Monday."

Without so much as an attagirl, he hung up on me.

They say your life passes before you when you die. They don't tell you the same happens when your boss almost fires you from the only job you ever had, a job you love. Fortuna hired me before the ink dried on my college diploma. I'd devoted all my energy to building a career there. I'd worked overtime hours for no compensation, organized birthday cakes and funeral flowers for my co-workers, and given the company my undying loyalty. I'd worked my way up the ranks to almost—fingers crossed—vice president. I understood the ship's collision had torpedoed Mike's calm demeanor, but accepting that my usually mild-mannered boss refused to support me after my aunt's death hurt.

I pressed my hand on my heart and counted the rhythmic beats until I stuffed my feelings of helplessness into a compartment of my brain labeled things to worry about later. Somehow, I muscled Lydie's wingback chair into my car along with a handful of books and drove into town. I passed the waterfront library, the dolphin fountain, and all the charming shops I'd come to love.

Before going inside Cassandra's, I stopped on the sidewalk to feel the cool air against my cheeks and inhale the scent of brine and fir needles. I glanced at the poster Maddie had made, shelves filled with Lydie's treasures, and the Tibetan wind-horse prayer flags Arthur hung around the ceiling. Pain clenched my body. I had less than a week to move everything out, close the cottage, and drive back to L.A. In a day or two, Cassandra's Collectibles would be history. I'd miss it. I'd also miss Walter and Cooper, not to mention Maddie and Arthur.

"Love the reading chair," Arthur said as we struggled to extricate Lydie's wingback from the back seat of my car. Once the boxes of books were inside, he added, "I see you survived your lunch at the castle."

"You were right, though. I should have worn a garlic necklace."

"Did you find out why Sylvia invited you?"

"After plying me with crab salad and some castle history, she asked to buy my aunt's house."

"Why didn't she call Pearl?"

"I'm guessing Sylvia didn't want to pay Pearl's commission on the sale."

He scrunched up his face. "What an awful person."

Several customers milled around the shop as Arthur rearranged merchandise on the shelves to accommodate the new books. "There were some real doozies in the latest batch of novels you brought in. I've never seen a boxed set of Lawrence Durrell's Alexandria Quartet. And *The Shell Seekers* is my all-time favorite Rosamunde Pilcher title. After reading that book, I wanted an Aga stove and a cottage in Cornwall."

"Have you ever been?" I asked.

"To Cornwall? No, but someday I'll go. For now, I'm having a blast researching the cost of Tibetan prayer flags, which brings me to that odd rock you found in your aunt's duffle bag." Arthur returned from the back room with the stone in his palm. "I searched online and discovered it's a natural agate called a 'zee' stone, spelled D-Z-I. If it's authentic, it can be worth a lot of money."

"Whoa," I said, shocked at the news.

"My advice? Keep it. Some say it's a spiritual amulet with protective powers, and from what I've seen, you could use the help right now. If you decide to sell it, you should have it appraised by the antique dealer down the street. If Mr. Osgood doesn't know the value, he might suggest somebody who does."

I flashed a skeptical stare. "The man doesn't like me."

"I can ask him if you like."

"Yes, please."

All the customers had left the shop by four o'clock, so we closed for the day. Arthur planned to meet with John Osgood on his way home. I headed to C'est Shells to pick up my take-out order, Tarts & Bars for dessert, and to Danny's store for wine. I got home, discarded the take-out containers, transferred the food into serving dishes, and then into the warming drawer, which I considered only a minor deception.

I vowed to conceal my alarm over my boss's demoralizing ultimatum. This evening would not include despair or everyday dishes, so I set the table with Lydie's Spode and her ornate Gorham silverware that matched the elegance of the white linen tablecloth.

To distract my guests once they learned about my cooking inadequacies, I searched online for how to fold napkins into everything from a bird of paradise to a courtesan's fan, eventually settling on four bishop's hats. I also found a site touting the fine art of garnishing. The carrot curls looked easy, but I didn't want to push my luck tonight. I bookmarked the instructions for scallion flowers pinned to an eggplant for future reference. That might make a quirky centerpiece someday.

I turned my phone to silent mode and stored it in the bread drawer. Moments later, Maddie swept into the house with her usual dramatic exuberance, dressed in black skinny jeans and a purple sweater that matched her hair.

"Mwah, mwah." She threw two air kisses as she brushed past me, carrying a bottle of wine.

"Something smells divine," she said, setting the wine on the kitchen island. "And familiar."

My cheeks flushed. "What do you mean?"

She chuckled. "I had a short but steamy affair with Gabriel Blanchet, the chef at C'est Shells, a man of many talents, I might add. I'd recognize the aroma of his Tuna Mornay anywhere—that hint of mustard, the Cheddar cheese he special-orders from Wisconsin, and his homemade bread crumbs. But don't worry. Your secret is safe with me."

I scoffed. "Come on, Maddie. I'm not going to lie about take-out."

"Of course you're not, sweet Em." She winked. "How can I help?"

"You can open the wine."

"I thought you'd never ask." She pulled out the cork and poured a glass for both of us.

I took the salmon tartare from the refrigerator and set the platter on the kitchen island alongside some crackers. "Maddie, do you know Kevin Medwin?"

She hesitated. "Why?"

Her evasive tone gave me the impression he may have been one of her romantic conquests. "He's Sylvia and Franklin's son, right?"

"Yesss," she said, drawing out the word.

I told her about the luncheon and Sylvia wanting to buy the house for Kevin. I noted the puzzled look on her face as if she were processing incongruous information.

"It's interesting," I continued, "because somebody else tried to buy the property four months ago. My aunt turned them down. You think that buyer might have been Kevin?"

She snickered. "As darling as this place is, I doubt any level of adorableness could persuade Kevin Medwin to buy your aunt's house."

I straightened my spine, feeling offended. "Why do you say that?"

"Kevin left Justice Bay years ago to escape his awful parents. You met Sylvia. Her husband is even worse. Kevin rarely visits anymore. The last thing he'd want is a house near those two."

"Then why did Sylvia make the offer?"

"Who knows? Maybe Franklin wants to build another fish processing plant on the land." She scooped some tartare onto a cracker. "Kevin and I are still in touch. If you'd like, I can ask if he knows anything."

"That would be great."

We were interrupted by a knock on the door. Walter walked in first, said hello, and retreated to the breakfast nook. The first thing I spotted when Cooper entered a room was his startling blue eyes. Most eye colors were like the vegetables in minestrone soup—a tad of this, a smidge of that. Dedicated colorists could find Cooper's eye shade in a box of twenty-four Crayolas labeled simply blue.

Maddie threw her arms around Cooper before he could hand me the vase of flowers he carried—pink roses, ferns, and a delicate white bloom I couldn't identify.

"Thanks for stopping by the house to help with my dad," she said.

Cooper's eyes widened. So did mine. His free arm floated in the air without purpose until it finally landed on Maddie's back. He patted it a couple of times until she released her grip. Her enthusiastic embrace made me wonder if the gesture implied gratitude or something deeper. Maddie liked to hug people, but it also lent credence to my theory that she had a thing for Cooper.

"My pleasure," he said.

"Thanks for taking that cat tree off my hands," she added. "It's been in the store forever. Where did it end up?"

Cooper glanced at me. "Not sure, but I think it's still at Emma's shop."

"The perfect place for it, right, Em?" Maddie poured a glass of wine for both men.

"Time will tell," I said.

Walter watched our interactions but remained distant, both physically and emotionally. Maybe being in Lydie's house churned up painful memories.

After I centered Cooper's bouquet on the dining room table, everyone moved into the living room with our wine, where we chatted and nibbled on salmon tartare.

Maddie sat on the couch next to Cooper. After about fifteen minutes, she bumped his shoulder with hers. "Let's go look at your boat."

"Not much to see in the dark."

Maddie pulled him off the couch and led him outside to the veranda, leaving me alone with Walter. A moment later, the porch swing chain creaked.

My gaze drifted to Walter. "Are you okay? You seem unusually subdued."

"I'm fine," he said. "How's it going with you? Does Pearl have any prospects for the house?"

I processed his words, but my attention darted back to Maddie and Cooper on the porch swing. "Nothing definite."

He nodded. "Be patient. It'll happen." He glanced at me with an unflinching FBI stare. "Anything else on your mind?"

Walter had a gruff and guarded exterior, but I was also confident that anybody who loved my aunt had a kind heart and a generous spirit. Walter cared about me. I viewed his last question as an invitation. I told him everything—finding the cell cover, Sylvia's house offer, the flashlight in the woods, my boss's ultimatum, and Chief Greene's inexplicable rudeness.

"It makes me angry that Greene doesn't seem interested in discovering what happened to Lydie."

I became so wrapped up in cataloging my grievances that when I finally glanced at Walter, he stared at me with an expression as chiseled and stony as a president on Mount Rushmore. That alarmed me.

"Sorry," I said. "I didn't mean to rant."

He leaned toward me with his forearms on his thighs. "Look, Emmaline, here's my advice. I hope you take it. Stop investigating Lydie's death, including conjuring up any more theories about Chet Greene. Let it go. I said I'd look into it for you. You have to trust that I will. Focus on your job situation. And talk to my nephew."

"Cooper? Why?"

"Because he's dealt with the same work-related decisions you're facing now. He may not have all the answers, but he can walk you through some options for handling your boss."

I glanced out the French doors. Maddie's head rested on Cooper's shoulder. In a petty moment, I felt left out or, more accurately—envious. Schoolgirl crush or not, I'd begun to have feelings for Cooper.

When we'd first reconnected, Maddie told me she had given up on men. Maybe Cooper had restored her faith in relationships. If so, I wished them both happiness. I had to abandon Justice Bay in less than a week, returning to L.A. and my job at Fortuna Cruise Lines. Until then, I would stay in the background. I didn't trust myself to speak with Cooper about my decisions. In nautical speak, that ship had sailed.

Chapter Sixteen

My dinner guests left at around 11:00 p.m. Walter's warning to back off investigating Lydie's death still bounced around in my brain as I dropped the table linens into the laundry basket and loaded the dishwasher.

I poured myself a glass of wine and headed to the living room. A light rain began to fall. Boo sprawled paws up on the couch, recuperating from her last nap. I gazed at the bay, watching Cooper's boat sway with the current as I organized my thoughts.

I didn't doubt that Walter would look into my aunt's death as promised. He had skills, FBI skills. But I had skills, too. I'd worked ten years in the cruise industry. I understood what happened to people when their plans went sideways.

Even if Lydie's death was an accident, as Chief Greene wanted me to believe, I doubted the driver went sightseeing that night. He had plans. Interruptions in a person's schedule produce emotional reactions from mild irritation to total meltdown. Killing somebody with your car veered into disaster territory. If that happened, any responsible person would have called for help. But if Lydie's death had been the goal, as I sensed, the driver had already calculated his path forward. In my mind, I created bullet points for those next steps and ran them by Boo.

"For sure, the driver would explain any damage to the car by claiming he hit a deer, right? And once he fled the scene, he'd scrub DNA from the car's exterior." Boo's eyes were at half-mast. At least she listened, so I continued. "Except we both know from watching true-crime TV that it's hard to get rid of trace evidence."

Boo opened her eyes wide and stared at me.

"What would the driver do next? Set fire to the car to destroy anything incriminating or hide it in a private garage until the police investigation cooled down."

Boo yawned and, with a silent meow, rolled over with her back toward me, indicating I'd have to continue mapping out the plot without her help.

I opened the French doors to get some fresh air and paced the living room because it helped me think. My aunt was petite, but the impact must have caused damage to the car. The person left the scene, so the vehicle remained drivable. Assuming minimal damage, such as a broken headlight, they could buy parts from an auto supply store or a junkyard and repair it themselves. If not, they had to find a body shop outside Justice Bay that could discreetly fix the car. But the shop might have to order a replacement part. That could take time.

My pacing abruptly stopped, causing the wine to slosh onto the floor. My muscles grew rigid as I remembered the person with the flashlight searching the woods last night. I'd assumed they were looking for my aunt's cell cover, but what if they came back to find a piece of the car that had fallen off during impact, something that might lead back to the owner?

All my senses were on high alert as I returned to the kitchen and removed my cell from the bread drawer. I set the wine glass on the counter and switched the cell's silent mode off.

Brad had called a half dozen times earlier in the evening. He'd left only one message—call me. My watch read just past midnight. He'd been working long hours, so I hesitated to contact him this late in case he was asleep. But all those calls so close together were unusual.

A woman answered his phone. Brad never let anyone use his cell. Something was wrong.

"Who is this?" I asked.

"Just a minute." I didn't recognize the woman's voice, but she sounded nervous, which only heightened my concern.

Brad must have seen my name on his cell display. "Why didn't you call back earlier?" He sounded on edge.

I released the breath I'd been holding. "Sorry, I had people over for dinner and turned off my phone. What's up?"

"What the hell did you say to Mike? I met with him this afternoon about Cabo Fiesta, and he nearly bit my head off."

I grabbed a towel from the counter and returned to the living room to clean up the wine spill. "Don't worry. I handled it, but I asked Mike for another week off. He said no. So, I'll be back next Monday as planned."

"What were you thinking?" His voice sounded edgy and frantic.

I cleared my throat to keep from overreacting to his panicky tone. "I'm in Justice Bay alone, dealing with my aunt's death, plus trying to continue working from here. It's hard. I needed more time."

"I'm sorry for what you're going through, Em, but Mike is dealing with a crisis of his own, and he's freaking out. He even told me he might replace you."

Mike had said that to me, too, but his sharing it with Brad troubled me. I dropped the towel on the wet floor and moved it around with my foot. Then I walked onto the veranda and breathed in the brittle night air. I convinced myself that firing me during a crisis made no sense, especially given those promotion rumors floating around the office.

"He didn't mean it," I said. "He's just blowing off steam."

"Mike already thinks you're not working hard enough to fill those cabins. Then you strong-arm him to get more time off. Now he's convinced you're gaming the system to get extra vacation time."

My lips parted, but for a moment, no words came out. "My aunt just died. That's hardly yoga on the beach at Club Med. Did you tell him it's not my fault that the library ladies decided on a Canadian Rockies bus tour over our Mexican cruise?"

"It's more than that. Mike got a complaint from your Alabama sales rep. The guy claims you're putting too much pressure on him to fill the space."

I again focused on Cooper's sailboat peacefully swinging on its anchor in the bay to maintain my composure. "This is an all-hands-on-deck situation, Brad. The library group is in Reggie's sales territory. I merely asked if he could persuade the group to reconsider. And in case you forgot, I'm responsible for all the cabins rebooked so far."

"I get it. Reggie's a whiner. I know you're doing your best, but it's not enough. Forget Monday. You should come back as soon as possible, like tomorrow. Otherwise, you may not have a job to come back to."

The lights beamed from inside the cabin of Cooper's sailboat. He must still be awake. I sat on the porch swing and soaked up the warm glow. "I can't just lock the door and walk away from my responsibilities."

"I'm worried, Em. Everybody at work knows we used to be a couple. I'm afraid any wrong decision you make will damage my career, too."

My frustration bubbled to the surface. "We had a short fling, Brad, and people learned about it because you told them, even though I warned you not to."

"Okay, I made a mistake. But you need to find some way to appease Mike."

In the background, a woman's voice called Brad's name.

"What's going on?" I asked. "Where are you? Who answered your phone?"

Brad hesitated. "She's just a friend. Look, it's late. Let's talk when you get back."

He avoided my questions. I wondered why. Boo sensed my agitation because she bolted off the couch and joined me on the swing. I patted her back as her purrs vibrated up my arm.

I squeezed my eyes closed. "If you're involved with somebody, just say so. We're both free agents."

"For your information, I'm at work. Mindy from accounting answered my phone. She's helping me with spreadsheets due first thing in the morning because she's an accountant. There. Satisfied?"

More likely, she helped Brad on the sheets. Mindy was a flirty young redhead. I'd always meant to ask her what products she used to make her hair so shiny, but it was too late for that now. Brad had always been a ladies' man. More than once, I'd observed him having intimate conversations with Mindy. I should have connected the dots.

"Were you involved with her while we were together?"

"Look," he mumbled. "I have to go."

He ended the call without answering my question, which answered my question. I held the phone to my ear long after the call ended. I didn't care who Brad dated now, but if he'd been two-timing me with Mindy during our short relationship, I couldn't help but feel betrayed.

Boo grew tired of my company and abandoned me for the couch. Even my cat thought I was a loser. I missed my father's unconditional love in times like these. I thought about calling Walter for emotional support, but forcing an acquaintance to play substitute dad would make me feel even more pathetic.

I wondered how much loss I could endure. My dad and Lydie were both gone. My mother lived in Paris with her new husband. I'd met most of my friends at work. If I lost my job, I'd lose them, too. They would promise to stay in touch, but they wouldn't, just like my early friendship with Maddie had faded over time.

Brad and I had ruined a solid friendship with a short-lived romance. For the sake of our careers, we agreed to go back to being friends. Even that arrangement teetered on the brink because I didn't trust him anymore. I'd go back to L.A., and we'd continue to work together, but his lack of support had permanently altered our relationship. It felt like a sumo wrestler had slammed down on my chest. Nothing stayed the same, but why did this change feel so crushing? I sat on the porch swing, staring at the bay until Cooper's cabin lights went out.

Chapter Seventeen

I woke up the following Tuesday, the sixth official workday of my bereavement leave, to find thick fog shrouding Justice Bay. Brad's plea that I return early to appease Mike Woods and save my job had merit. Except returning now wasn't possible. Before leaving town, I had to tackle a substantial things-to-do list. I didn't have the time or emotional wherewithal to dispose of Lydie's things, so I'd rent facilities to store furniture and household goods. I would take every day that Mike had authorized, regardless of the consequences.

Helen Marché hadn't returned my call about that fake closure demand posted on the shop's door, but her feedback didn't matter. Cassandra's Collectibles would disappear in a few days. I needed to tell Walter I would vacate the shop on schedule instead of extending the rental agreement.

Meanwhile, Pearl Potts hadn't even posted a for-sale sign at the end of the driveway. I wondered if I'd made a mistake not selling the place to Sylvia Medwin. I decided to call Pearl to discuss the offer with her at least.

I went for a run to clear my head. When I got home, the fog still ghosted around the house and surrounding woods. The damp earth from last night's rain lingered, filling the air with the smell of decaying leaves and saltwater from the bay. I changed clothes and found waterproof garden gloves in the garage, and orange rubber boots with frog faces painted on the toes. They were too small, but I put them on anyway because they'd keep my feet dry.

The air outside remained nippy and damp as I walked down the driveway toward the main road. I hoped to test my theory that the person in the woods with a flashlight searched for a part that had broken off the murder car. My aunt had been headed toward Justice Bay when the driver hit her, so I started exploring the side of the road near the yellow warning sign where the hit-and-run occurred. It still gave me chills to be in the place where Lydie had died.

Faint tire tracks appeared in the soil just off the shoulder, now muddy from the rain. There were no skid marks, but they may have worn away in the week-plus since my aunt's death. My mystery-solving bona fides from watching true-crime TV shows were finally paying off. I snapped a couple of close-up shots with my cell camera. Given Chief Greene's blasé attitude toward the investigation, I couldn't assume he'd taken impressions.

I continued walking for about a quarter-mile, scanning the area from the shoulder to approximately six feet into the woods. Nothing looked out of place except for a few paper cups and cigarette butts that some irresponsible jerk had thrown into the fire-prone underbrush.

Nothing likely flew off the car and landed on the other side of the road, but I turned back and looked anyway. About four car lengths from Walter's driveway in a ditch adjacent to the shoulder, I noticed another set of tire tracks. From the direction of the imprints, it appeared that a vehicle had used the trench to make a U-turn. The tread looked similar to the tracks near the crash site.

My gaze slowly swept the terrain. Something protruded from a mud puddle. My rubber boots sank into the gooey earth as I ventured closer. My gloved hand plunged into the cold, opaque water and herded the object toward me.

My neck tingled with tension when I spotted a side mirror with attached wires. I had no idea how long the mirror had been submerged, but it wasn't rusty. Etched into the chrome was the unmistakable three-point-star emblem of a Mercedes-Benz.

I stood and backed away, leaving the mirror where I found it. I wouldn't make the same "chain of custody" mistake again. The mirror may not have anything to do with the car that hit my aunt, but all my senses told me otherwise. The mirror may have come loose on impact. The driver left the scene and made a U-turn a short distance away. As he drove into the ditch, the jolt caused the cables to give way, and the mirror dropped to the ground.

Reporting this potential evidence to Chief Greene would be as useful as hawking globes at a flat earth convention. Walter Kestrel was the only person I trusted with the information.

A roaring sound emerged through the darkness as he answered my call.

"What's all that racket?" he asked.

I shouted over the noise. "Not sure. Look, there's something you need to see."

A motorcycle emerged from the fog, traveling at a high rate of speed. The driver's shoulder leaned perilously close to the pavement as he rounded the curve.

"Where are you?" Walter asked.

"Not far from your driveway—"

As the motorcyclist attempted to maneuver the bike upright, he lost control and swerved toward me. I clutched my phone in a death grip and stepped back just in time to avoid a collision. But I miscalculated the depth of the trench. My arms flailed as I struggled to regain my balance. I smelled engine exhaust. Heard a hollow thump as my head hit the ground. Every nerve ending pulsed as I envisioned dying on the same road where Lydie had lost her life.

My eyelids fluttered. Above me, gray fog spread across the sky. I hadn't lost consciousness because I heard a squawking sound. I pivoted my head and experienced a jolt of pain in my neck. My phone lay in a heap of fir branches. I reached for it when I recognized Walter's voice on the line.

"Emmaline! Emmaline, can you hear me?"

I wiped away dirt and debris from the screen before answering. "Walter?"

He exhaled audibly. "You scared the hell out of me. You said you were close to the driveway, so I sent my nephew to look for you."

My vision cleared enough to see Cooper running toward me at full speed, the front panels of his gray hoodie flapping like the wings of a giant pterodactyl.

"He's almost here. I see his wings."

"Wings?"

Cooper's breathing had escalated by the time he knelt next to me. "You okay?"

"I think so."

He took my phone and put it to his ear. "I found her. I'll take her home. Meet me there in a few, okay?" Then he ended the call.

His earnest expression and apparent concern triggered fantasies of me drawing hearts and doodles around his name with a pink Sharpie.

"What happened?" he asked.

I touched the back of my head and discovered a small knot. "A motorcycle almost hit me. I fell. Hit my head."

Cooper appeared alarmed at the news. He held up three fingers. "How many do you see?"

My eyes widened in disbelief. "You're joking, right?"

His rigid jaw confirmed he wasn't. "Just answer the question."

I shrugged. "Three."

"Do you feel dizzy? Nauseated? Any blurred vision?"

"No." I lied because I had Lydie's murder to solve. I didn't have time to play invalid.

"What's your all-time best Scrabble word?"

I paused for a moment to think. "Quixotic."

"Who was your first prom date?"

"Jason..." I realized he was playing with me now. "None of your business."

He tilted his head and smiled. "I have other questions. Shall I ask them later?"

"As long as they're not about Scrabble and prom dates. Look, I found a Mercedes side mirror. It's over there. In the water. I have to tell Walter." I ignored the pain in my neck as I crawled over to the puddle and pointed to it. "It might have come off the car that killed my aunt."

"Emma, you could have a concussion," he said in a soft voice. "I think you should see a doctor."

I punched each word like a standalone sentence. "I. Don't. Need. A. Doctor." I shivered from my wet, mud-caked clothes. I planted my hands onto a nearby log for leverage, but stumbled when I tried to stand.

Cooper grabbed me around the waist, making me feel ridiculous and unexpectedly giddy.

"Why don't you sit for a minute?" he said. "I'll go get Walter's truck and take you home."

I shook my head. "I can walk. I just need to talk to Walter."

"He'll be at your place in a few minutes."

He threaded his arm through mine and gently pulled me upright. With his help, I hobbled to Lydie's cottage. When we got there, my toes were so swollen that the froggie eyes on the boots bulged. Boo met us at the door with several loud meows, which weren't therapeutic for my raging headache.

Try as I might, I couldn't get my swollen feet out of the frog boots. Instead of cutting them off, Cooper coaxed them off my feet, using a couple of positions that reminded me of poses from the Kama Sutra that a classmate smuggled into our high school gym class on her cell phone.

I used the downstairs bathroom to wash up and swap my wet clothes for my aunt's hoodie and sweatpants, which hit me mid-calf like a pair of vintage pedal-pushers. I surveyed the damage before wandering into the living room. Cooper propped me up on the couch under Lydie's wool afghan and Pearl's karate-chopped pillows.

He made me a cup of tea. Walter arrived a few minutes later. He inspected the knot on the back of my head.

"That's an impressive bump. You should get a medical once-over. Make sure you didn't scramble your brain."

"I'm fine."

"Emmaline, you saw wings."

"Think of it as a prehistoric bird metaphor." My tone sounded more defensive than I'd intended.

He rolled his eyes. "I can't force you to see a doc, or I would, but you can't stay here alone. Cooper can crash on your couch tonight in case you need anything."

I didn't think Cooper needed to spend the night, but it wasn't worth arguing over. "Please stop talking about doctors and concussions. I found a Mercedes side mirror. I think it dropped off the car that killed Lydie. You have to call Chief Greene. Ask him to come out immediately and pick it up before it goes missing. He'll listen to you. Then we should list everybody in Justice Bay who owns a Benz. Next, if Chief Greene hasn't already done it, we should use my list to call body shops in the area to see if the owner brought it in for repairs."

I babbled on. Walter and Cooper stared at me with sympathetic, there-there-dear expressions as if I were suffering from some exotic mental disorder.

But that didn't stop me. "And that motorcyclist? At first, I thought he'd just lost control of the bike. I jumped out of the way before he hit me. He must have seen me fall, but he didn't stop to make sure I was okay. What if it wasn't an accident? What if he meant to run me down?"

Walter leaned in, forearms on his thighs. "What motorcycle?"

In my eagerness to tell Walter about the mirror, I'd forgotten to mention the guy on the bike. I filled him in on the details.

"Do you think he targeted me?"

"I doubt it," Walter said. "I've seen him speeding down that road before. I gave Greene his license plate number a while back and told him to look out for the guy before somebody ends up as a splat on the road."

"Let me guess," I said. "Greene hasn't done anything."

"It's karma's problem now." Walter stood and walked toward the door. Over his shoulder, he said to Cooper, "Don't let her out of your sight until I get back."

Chapter Eighteen

After Walter left, I cajoled Cooper into taking me to Cassandra's Collectibles. As long as I remained in Justice Bay, there was no downside to moving merchandise. Besides, working among my aunt's treasures with Arthur brought me joy. Cooper insisted on driving my car, a small concession since I still felt dizzy from the blow to my head.

Before leaving, we went into the garage where I'd stored an array of collectibles in preparation for Pearl's inspection visit. I glanced at Lydie's lime green VW convertible. She'd wanted a Beetle since her early twenties, but never bought one until two years ago. She loved that car. I'd have to sell it, too, which made me sad.

"What are the plans for that?" Cooper pointed to a small round wicker table with a glass top and two matching chairs.

I smiled, reminiscing. "In the summer, Lydie set them on the beach. She'd pour herself a glass of wine and watch the sunset."

"We should take them to the shop. People could relax and admire the merchandise, like in a museum."

I had to admit the idea had merit. "The wicker is good outside on the sidewalk, too. But who's going to serve the wine and sunsets?"

He laughed. "That sounds like a job for Walter."

Cooper lowered my car's backseat to accommodate the table and chairs, leaving just enough room for the collectibles, including an old Janis Joplin poster and a second one from that era: Today is the first day of the rest of your life.

When we arrived at Cassandra's, several shoppers waited by the door.

Word about the shop had spread, a good sign, at least for the next few days. Arthur had the day off, so Cooper arranged the table and chairs on the sidewalk while I moved the other items inside.

Sales were brisk for the first hour. Cooper offered to pick up lunch during a break in customer traffic. He headed toward the door as Maddie wandered in. Her flurried blinking indicated she was surprised to see him there.

I blurted out, "Poor Cooper. Walter ordered him to babysit me for the day." If she wondered why, she didn't ask.

Cooper smiled. "Hey, Maddie. I'm doing a lunch run. Can I get you anything?"

"I can't stay," she said. "I just dropped by to tell Em I spoke to Kevin Medwin." She turned toward me. "Sorry, but he knows nothing about his mother's offer to buy Lydie's house."

I appreciated Maddie's help in getting the information. Still, I'd conducted dozens of interviews in my travel career and learned that the key to successful snooping required guiding the conversation to suit your agenda.

"I thought of a few follow-up questions," I said. "Do you think Kevin would mind if I called him directly?"

"I don't think he'd mind at all."

Cooper opened the door to leave.

"I'll walk with you," Maddie said.

The fog had lifted, leaving behind a sunny autumn afternoon. I sat outside at the wicker table, watching the street for a Mercedes-Benz with a missing side mirror and enjoying the charm of village life.

A toddler sat on the rim of the dolphin fountain, giggling as his mother watched him bury his face in an ice cream cone. A young couple stole a kiss while waiting for a table at C'est Shells. Even the Sturm and Drang of seagulls competing over a spilled bag of French fries entertained me. All of it reminded me how much I loved Justice Bay.

Maddie hadn't given me Kevin Medwin's phone number, so I took advantage of the lull in activity to look up the one listed for Endeavor's central San Francisco switchboard. It astonished me how quickly he took my call.

"First," he said, "let me tell you how sorry I am about your aunt's passing. I hadn't seen Lydie in a while, but always liked her."

"Thank you. That means a lot to me."

"Maddie mentioned you had lunch with my mother. I hope she was pleasant, but that's probably too optimistic."

"We had a lovely crab salad," I said, aiming for noncommittal. "Your father couldn't join us. Traveling in Europe, I guess."

"He's not in Europe." His tone became suspicious. "He answered the phone when I called the house Sunday morning."

"Sorry," I said. "Maybe I misunderstood." Except I hadn't. I had lunch with Sylvia on Sunday. What a curious lie. At the time, I'd speculated that the angry guy in the hallway might be a security guard, but now I wondered if Kevin's dad barked orders on the phone as I hid behind the castle's velvet curtains.

From across the street, a woman waved to me. I recognized her as the sad-eyed customer who bought Lydie's candy dish on opening day. I waved back, pleased to know a few more people in town.

A customer approached and mouthed, "Okay to go inside?" I gave her a thumbs up.

"When did your parents buy the castle?" I asked.

I could hear his uneven breathing through the phone. "I don't remember the exact date."

Curious memory loss, I thought. Kevin's dismissal of my question made me confident there was more to the story.

"As I told Maddie," Kevin continued, "I have no idea why my mother offered to buy your aunt's place. I would never have lived there, and she knows that."

The customer waved goodbye as she left the store empty-handed.

"Another person offered to buy Lydie's property about four months before she died," I said. "I have reason to believe somebody from your firm made the offer."

"We have hundreds of employees. I have no idea if one of them wanted to buy a vacation house." Kevin's tone had shifted into detached business-speak.

"I sense something bigger than that. Is there any way to determine if somebody targeted Lydie's property as part of a real estate development deal?"

"I generally only keep track of the projects and acquisitions handled by my team," he said. "But I'll check. If I learn anything, I'll give you a call."

I didn't see the person talking on the phone in the castle hallway, but I wondered if Franklin Medwin might be the person in a photo my aunt took near the oleander bush.

"By the way, I may have seen your father at the castle, wearing a ball cap and a Patek Philippe watch."

Kevin scoffed. "I'm not sure who you're talking about, but my father wouldn't be caught dead in a ballcap. He owns a lot of watches, but he's been exclusively a Rolex guy for the past few years."

I'd never considered Kevin to be the unidentified man. But now I knew it hadn't been Franklin Medwin, either. For now, the big-eared guy remained a mystery.

After the call ended, the seagulls gave up on the French fries and moved on to greasier pastures. I stood to go inside when Cooper returned with a couple of salads and a pot of blue flowers. They were forget-me-nots, my father's favorite flower, which pleased me. It was uncommon to find them potted because they grew tall and spindly over time.

"Where did you find those?" I asked.

He centered the flowers on the wicker table. "At the garden store across the street from the bakery. The table needed a plant. This one seemed perfect."

I ran my fingers over the delicate petals. "Yes. Perfect."

Customers frequently used the wicker table ensemble as they stopped to rest on their way in or out of the shop. It added to the store's charm, just as Cooper had said. As it turned out, the guy was a natural salesperson. There was no canned pitch, just somebody genuinely interested in people. He charmed every customer.

I'd had a hectic day and a lingering headache. By three o'clock, we'd sold nearly everything on the shelves, so we decided to close for the day. As the car neared Walter's driveway, I told Cooper to stop.

"You've been with me all day," I said. "As you can see, I'm fine, so feel free to abandon ship."

He turned toward me, putting his hand on my seat's headrest, so close he could have run his fingers through my hair if he'd wanted to. "Let me at least drive you home. I can walk back to Walter's."

I didn't mind spending more time with Cooper. I just didn't want him to know I didn't mind. Life is so complicated.

I shrugged. "Whatever."

When we arrived at the cottage, Cooper didn't leave, and I didn't encourage him to do so, either. We spent the following few hours tagging items to sell at Cassandra's. He picked out the pieces, and I wrote the display cards. When we'd stockpiled enough for a carload, we went outside to sit on the porch swing.

After a few blissful moments of silence, he said, "Walter told me you're having issues with your boss."

My privacy antenna vibrated with tension. "Walter pressured you to ask me that, right?"

"Not exactly—"

I held up my hand to stop him. "Don't worry. It's nothing I can't handle."

He nodded. "Sorry. I didn't mean to pry."

I experienced a sudden and abnormal heaviness in my limbs. Seconds later, I almost told Cooper everything. After pouring my heart and soul into my job for ten long years, my boss threatened to fire me as I mourned the death of a woman who'd been a second mother to me. Furthermore, I suspected Brad had been cheating on me during our brief affair with Mindy-from-accounting, an ambitious young woman with little going for her except a lustrous head of red hair and impressive math skills. But I held back.

The chains on the swing creaked as I mulled over the wisdom of my dismissive response to Cooper's offer of advice. He had quit his job as a lawyer at a prestigious law firm in San Francisco to live alone on a sailboat. Earlier, Walter hinted that the reasons for Cooper's departure might be similar to my situation. Far-fetched, perhaps, but he might have helpful advice. I almost said—I'll tell you if you tell me. But before the words slipped out of my mouth, Cooper stood.

"I'm crashing at Walter's place tonight. Call me if you need anything."

After the door shut, I regretted not asking him to stay.

Chapter Nineteen

The following day, I wanted to go for a run or read a book. I didn't have time to do either, so I focused on my third favorite R—roaming around a charming gift shop—mine. When I arrived at Cassandra's, I found Arthur alone. He sat in Lydie's reading chair, his head bowed, staring at Lawrence Durrell's *Justine* on his lap.

I hurried over to him. "Are you okay?"

His gaze slowly lifted to meet mine. "I got a job offer."

"A temp job?"

"Permanent."

I glanced at Lydie's Janis Joplin poster on the wall, hoping it would provide an inspired response. But "Take another little piece of my heart" seemed too much on the nose.

I forced a smile. "That's great, right?"

He set the books on the floor and stood. "Shuffling papers at the County Assessor's office isn't exactly my dream job, but it comes with a steady paycheck and benefits."

"When do you start?"

"Monday." He threw his arms around me. "I wish you weren't leaving, Emma. I wish you'd stay, and we could work together to build Cassandra's into something special. We could redecorate. Go to trade shows together, like next year's antiquarian book fair. Those signed first editions of Lydie's would sell like hotcakes." Before I could return his embrace, his hands dropped to his sides. "It makes me sad to give up this gig."

I couldn't respond. I'd grown fond of Arthur. I understood from day one that we'd both be moving on, but I felt hollowed out by the loss of his presence in my life. He'd become the little brother I'd never had—intelligent, charming, always there with a bright idea and a helping hand. An old saying my mother often used to banish the gloom floated around my head: eat something, you'll feel better. It seldom helped, but it was worth a try in this instance.

"You know what we need?" I asked. "Pastries and tea. I'm going to Tarts & Bars for takeout."

His faint smile transformed into a grin. "You know I love their lemon squares."

I returned his smile. "You hold down the fort. I'll be back in a few minutes."

The bakery sat on a quiet side street off the main drag. It reminded me of a quaint Parisienne café with its cream-colored awning and the aqua paint on its wooden doors and window frames. Two metal tables on the sidewalk offered a peek-a-boo view of the bay.

I spotted Cooper at the cash register as I opened the front door. Before I could weigh the pros and cons of returning later, he swiveled toward me, holding two paper cups. Either he was undercaffeinated, or he was meeting somebody.

He nodded to acknowledge me. "Emma."

I nodded back. "Cooper."

"How's your head?"

"Fine."

He pushed the door open with his shoulder. "Good to see you."

My rejection of his offer of advice about my work problems likely caused his frosty reception. I should have handled it better. I was still reeling from Arthur's job news when I realized how much I wanted to speak with Cooper.

I struggled to say something appropriately neutral. Instead, I blurted out, "Arthur got a permanent job."

His expression softened as he held up the two cups. "Walter's coffeemaker died. I'll sacrifice my refill if you want to talk."

I let out a massive sigh of relief. "Thank you."

We sat at a table outside under the awning. Cooper added two creams to his coffee and grabbed a stir stick from a container on the table. As usual, I left my Java unadulterated.

"What's going on?" he asked.

I wrapped my hands around the warm cup, inhaling the aroma of dark roast beans and a whiff of chocolate floating from the bakery. "I'm not sure I want to return to Los Angeles."

He raised his eyebrows. "Then don't."

I mentally organized my arguments. "It's not that easy. My life is there. I love my job, at least I used to. But after all those years of loyalty to the company, my boss threatened to fire me because I asked for a few more days to settle Lydie's estate. And if Brad and Mindy-from-accounting are still an item, working there could be uncomfortable."

Cooper tilted his head and frowned. "Brad and Mindy?"

I flapped my hand dismissively, mentally kicking myself for bringing up their names. I'd have to find a better time. "Sorry. It's a long story meant for another day. My aunt left me some money, but it won't last forever, not with an aging house to maintain. Running Cassandras has been fun, but I'm not sure I can make it into a real business."

"How does Arthur feel?"

"Arthur starts his new job on Monday. You and Maddie are leaving soon. I only know a few other people in town; some don't like me very much, possibly including Walter." I rambled on until I ran out of steam.

Cooper took a sip of his coffee. "I assure you, my uncle likes you. And plans change. Maddie could decide to stay in Justice Bay and turn the hardware store into a design studio. Arthur might be willing to work the occasional weekend."

"What about you?" I asked. "When are you pulling up anchor and sailing away?"

He leaned back and laced his hands on the back of his head. "Not sure. Depends on the weather. I'm enjoying the freedom to do nothing except irritate my uncle."

I glanced at the tranquil water in the bay, wishing to mirror that serenity. "I feel overwhelmed with responsibility. There are so many decisions to make. I'm not sure what to do."

He rested his forearms on the table. "You'll figure it out."

I waited for him to say more, but he didn't, probably because I'd already said I didn't want him interfering in my life. But as Cooper had just said, plans change.

"What would you do if you were me? Stay or go?"

"I can only tell you what I did. When the culture at my firm became intolerable, I left."

"I can't believe you said goodbye to a career at a big-deal law firm."

"I still love the law. I'll probably practice again, but my new firm will have a moral compass."

"You could hang out a shingle in Justice Bay."

He gave me a tight-lipped smile but didn't comment. He seemed to search for a way to change the subject to something mundane, like the weather. I closed my eyes and waited. Except for the distant screech of a gull, Justice Bay remained quiet. The ever-present Los Angeles sounds of freeway traffic and jets roaring toward LAX were missing. A moment later, Cooper's voice broke my trance.

"Something went down at work," he said, crumbling the empty coffee cup in his fist, "and I couldn't look away."

His expression seemed tortured. I grasped for any words of comfort that weren't platitudes but came up empty. "Sounds serious."

"Friday night after work. One of our lawyers left the office. He went to his car and put a gun to his head. I had no idea he'd taken his life until I got to work on Monday and found a form letter from the managing partner on my desk. By that time, one of the paralegals had stripped the guy's office of all personal effects, and another attorney already sat in his chair. Not even death interferes with billable hours. That's when I decided I couldn't work for a firm that didn't mourn its dead."

My chest ached. "I'm so sorry, Cooper. How horrible for everyone."

"He left behind a wife and two young kids. That gutted me. I didn't even know he suffered from depression. The collective 'we' didn't talk about such things."

My situation wasn't as tragic as his, but I acknowledged that my boss had threatened to fire me during my bereavement leave because he stressed out about a few canceled cabins and a minor mishap with one of our ships.

"Leaving took guts," I said. "I wish I had that kind of courage."

He reached out and put his hand on mine. "You do."

I wanted to put my free hand on top of his, but that would be too much like a hand sandwich.

"I know it's a cliché," he continued, "but trust your instincts and question everything."

For a second, I stopped breathing. Cooper couldn't have known, but those were the exact words of advice my aunt had written on a note inside a Tibetan Buddhist prayer book.

Chapter Twenty

Cooper checked his watch. "Look, I have to go. How about we continue our gratuitous exchange of advice over dinner tonight?" My lips parted in a smile. "That could work."

We agreed to meet at C'est Shells at six. I walked inside the bakery and bought a half dozen lemon squares for Arthur and two cups of tea. When I returned to Cassandra's, I found him chatting with a woman in her late twenties. Her translucent makeup-free face and her shiny fawn-colored hair made her seem unintentionally beautiful. She reminded me of a movie version of the girl next door who cheers on the heroine but never gets the guy. Not valid in her case since she looked to be about six months pregnant.

Arthur pointed his finger at me. "Here's Emma now."

The woman's expression brightened. She walked over and offered her hand. "Great to finally meet you. All my friends are talking about your shop. Love the stories you've written about each collectible."

I set the tea and lemon squares on the cat tree and shook her hand. "Thanks for stopping by."

"I'm Abby Greene, by the way."

That familiar name ignited a bright red warning light. "Greene? Any relation to Chet Greene?"

Her smile looked sheepish. "Oh dear, I hope you didn't get caught in one of my husband's speed traps."

"Nothing like that. Chief Greene is investigating my aunt's death."

She pressed her hand to her heart. "Of course. I'm so sorry for your loss. Chet rarely discusses work, but I should have put two and two together.

Please forgive me."

"Nothing to forgive." *Not on my part, at least*, I thought.

I flashed back to the first encounter I'd had with her husband, his lusty smile aimed at the young file clerk, she with the chocolate brown lipstick and blood-red fingernails. I'd come to the station after hours the second time I ran into him. When he unlocked the door, Greene looked disheveled, and a woman's handbag sat on the clerk's chair. Chet Greene was a rude and lazy investigator, but I hoped my infidelity theory wasn't true. Abby deserved better.

I handed Arthur one of the cups of tea and offered Abby the other, but she declined.

"I'm planning another book club event at the shop on Friday," Arthur said. "You're welcome to come."

"I'm not sure I can make it. I have a three-year-old son at home. Sometimes, it's hard to find a sitter."

Arthur waved away her concern. "Bring him. Our group is full of substitute moms."

Abby headed toward the door. "I'll try."

After she left, Arthur turned to me. "She's sweet, isn't she?"

I didn't want to tell him that I suspected sweet Abby's husband might be cheating on her, so I punted. "Yes, she's lovely."

I sat on Lydie's reading chair and opened my laptop. I worked with complicated profit and loss reports as head of the marketing department at Fortuna. A simple spreadsheet would keep track of Cassandra's income and expenses. Thanks to Walter's generous rental agreement, those expenses were low enough to pay Arthur's temp fees, but the numbers indicated revenue was high enough to give him a bonus when the shop closed for good at the end of the week. I was about to break the good news to him when Kevin Medwin called. I retreated to the wicker table outside, which had become my ersatz office.

"I looked through all of our firm's projects but found no real estate deals that involved Justice Bay or your aunt's house."

"Are you sure? Lydie's friend thought he saw an offer on your firm's letterhead."

"He did." Kevin's tone sounded less confident than on our previous call. "When I spoke to my mother this morning, she admitted cutting and pasting our corporate logo onto her offer letter. She tried to get your aunt to sell several times but got nowhere. A fake letter appeared more persuasive to her. I warned her she'd likely committed a crime."

I wondered if Sylvia Medwin had cut and pasted that fake closure poster I found taped to the door of Cassandra's. It was odd that she would stoop that low unless she thought the unwelcome gesture would pressure me to dump the house in a quick sale and go home where I belonged.

"Why did she want to buy the place?" I asked.

He blew out a blast of air. "Boredom? I think she just wanted a project to occupy her time. She attended a Friends of the Library fundraiser at Lydie's about a year ago. The place had a stunning night view from the veranda along the shoreline to the downtown lights. Lydie told her the water got deep, around a hundred feet from the shoreline. My mother thought it would be a perfect place to build a bed and breakfast with a dock."

"Why tell me she wanted to buy the house for you?"

He cleared his throat and lowered his voice. "My mother may have hoped I'd stay there when I came to town, but I made it clear to her that after her cut-and-paste shenanigans, she needed to drop the idea of buying Lydie's house before she got into legal trouble. She agreed."

"Even if your mother owned the house, wouldn't the Coastal Commission object to a dock?"

"My mother is on the local board, but who knows? I told her since there are no guest accommodations in downtown Justice Bay, she should convince my father to let her turn the old sawmill into a boutique hotel if she wants to dabble in real estate development. I offered to pitch the idea to a project manager at my firm. She seemed enthusiastic."

"One more question," I said. "Your mother tried to remove my real estate agent from the deal and her commission. Any idea why?"

He sighed. "Trust me. Pearl Potts can take care of herself. As for my parents, they built a successful seafood processing business from scratch.

They didn't get where they are by being generous with their competitors."

I'd been in business long enough to know that, too, but I made a mental note that he didn't answer my question about the history between Pearl and his mother. I planned to find out eventually.

"Thanks, Kevin. I hope to meet you someday."

"I'm coming to town to see Maddie in two weeks. Maybe we can get together then."

He and Maddie had known each other since childhood and had kept in touch over the years. I wondered if he'd roll into town for a friendly visit with an old friend or if Maddie was plotting a new romance.

A heavy weight settled on my chest. "I'll probably be back in L.A. by then."

"Another time," he said.

After we ended the call, I considered the new information. It made no sense that Sylvia would kill my aunt if she aimed to strengthen the bonds with her son. After all, she'd abandoned the idea after Kevin offered to work with her on the hotel project. His plan cured both issues. She'd reconnect with her son and acquire a new project. None of that information eliminated her as a suspect, but the time had come to expand my list.

When I returned to Cassandra's, I told Arthur about the bonus I planned to give him. He thanked me for the extra cash but appeared sad that the shop would soon close.

Arthur helped unload the collectibles and books I picked out the day before. He opened one of the boxes and held up a hardback.

"Holy cow! A signed first edition of Sue Grafton's *A Is For Alibi*. Are you sure you want to sell this? It must be worth a bundle."

"I can't keep everything."

"Let me check my sources. I might be able to find a buyer."

I shrugged. "Okay."

I turned to see Pearl Potts hurrying past the shop, wearing a long white puffy coat that made her look like the Pillsbury doughboy. She had a Louis Vuitton purse slung over her shoulder. That pricy handbag meant she must be selling houses. Not mine, but somebody's.

"I'll be right back," I said to Arthur and ran out the door.

I called to her, but she hurried away. It didn't take long for me to catch up to her.

"Pearl, are you avoiding me?"

"What?" she said in her hyper-nasal voice.

I repeated the question only louder.

She put her hands over her ears. "Stop shouting. I'm not deaf."

"Did you get my message yesterday?"

"Yes, but I've got errands to run this morning, so let's cut to the chase. Nobody's made an offer on the house yet. I already told you about the young parents who nixed the place due to its proximity to the water. A middle-aged couple were looking for a retirement home but decided on Sausalito instead. A televangelist from one of those cable channels wanted to turn the place into a religious retreat. He lost interest after I told him your aunt died on the property."

True, at least technically. The driver had hit Lydie a short distance from her driveway. She'd landed in the woods within her property line.

I threw up my hands in frustration. "Why did you tell a potential buyer that?"

"Had to," she said. "People are superstitious. They get mad if you hide things like that. I got into a legal jam once because I didn't tell a buyer that the former owner had hung himself in the bedroom closet. Some people don't understand irony. Don't worry. Other prospects are coming down the pipeline. It's just a matter of time."

I'd never seen any evidence that Pearl had been inside the house with clients. Aside from that, I had no reason to disbelieve her claim. Still, I remained fixated on her inability to close a sale for a prime waterfront property with charm galore. I wondered if she sabotaged every potential deal for reasons I didn't understand.

Even though Kevin had warned his mother not to buy Lydie's property, I needed to sell the house. Since there were no other viable buyers, I told Pearl about Sylvia Medwin's offer, minus her plan to cut Pearl out of the agent's commission. Pearl's reaction was swift and emphatic.

"I'd sooner roller skate down Main Street in my birthday suit than let Mrs.

Caligula buy your aunt's house." She patted the curls on her wig and smiled. "But of course, dear, the decision is yours."

I vaguely remembered reading about Caligula in school, an inept and sadistic emperor who laid waste to the Roman Empire during his four-year tenure. Maddie, for one, shared Pearl's negative opinion of Sylvia. I wondered what else Kevin's mom had done to ignite that animosity.

As much as I wanted to explore Sylvia Medwin's history of bad behavior, I didn't have the time. It was Wednesday, and only four days remained until I had to pack up and return to L.A. The pressure mounted, and I still had a million boxes left unchecked on my things-to-do list, so I went back inside the shop.

We kept busy with customers until around five, when I went home to prepare for dinner with Cooper.

Chapter Twenty-One

I arrived at C'est Shells a little after six. Cooper sat at a table in a far corner of the restaurant. Like a consummate gentleman, he stood and pulled the chair out for me. He'd already ordered a bottle of white wine, the same label I'd brought to his chowder party—thoughtful—check. Attention to detail—check. He'd claimed to have faults early on, but I'd have to look closer to find them. Good thing I loved a challenge.

He poured wine into my glass. "Thought any more about your work situation?"

"It's hard to decide. I have a great job and an apartment back in L.A. My whole life is there."

He appeared let down by my answer. "You have a house here, too. And I thought you wanted to stick around and press Greene to find out who killed your aunt."

"True," I said. "Chief Greene is dismissive whenever I ask for a progress report. If I leave town, I'm afraid he'll rule Lydie's death an accident and close the case." I focused on my folded hands to avoid his scrutiny.

Cooper leaned forward, assessing me with his signature blue eyes. "I doubt Walter will let that happen."

"What's he going to do? He's not in law enforcement anymore."

"I've learned that you pay a price when you underestimate my uncle."

I hoped that was true. The waiter interrupted our conversation to jot down our orders and then disappeared into the kitchen.

"I met Chief Greene's wife today," I said. "Abby. Nice lady."

"At least the guy made one good decision."

I didn't share my suspicions about Chet Greene's possible infidelities. I had no proof he had an affair with his records clerk and worried Cooper would dismiss my theory as gossip.

Diners filled the tables. The noise level rose a decibel or two as the soup and salad arrived. I'd polished off my first glass of wine and started my second. My lowered inhibitions made everything Cooper said seem hilarious, profound, or provocative. At one point, I bent over laughing so hard at a story about Walter and a mishap with a chocolate éclair that a lock of my hair fell into the lobster bisque. Cooper reached out and handed me his napkin in a tender gesture.

He looked at me with an intense gaze. "Who's Brad?"

His question threw me. My cheeks burned with embarrassment as I wiped soup off my hair. "Just somebody at work."

I wasn't sure why I couldn't bring myself to tell Cooper the truth. Maybe I just wanted him to see me as unencumbered by failed relationships.

"Not that it's any of my business," he said, "but I sense you're not telling me everything. I'm not sure why."

We stared at each other while I gathered my courage. "Brad and I are coworkers who had a short fling. I realized we'd made a horrible mistake and ended the relationship a month before I came here."

He tilted his head. "Sounds complicated."

"Sort of like your boat name, I suspect. Brief Encounter, right?"

He winced. The gesture told me I'd probed something painful. "I had a relationship with an attorney in my office. I thought it would last. It didn't."

"Still, you named your boat with her in mind."

That sparked his tight-lipped smile. "Sometimes we need to remember our mistakes, so we don't make them again."

I glanced away so he wouldn't see what must have been a pained expression. "I called Brad late a couple of nights ago. A coworker named Mindy answered his phone. That's when I realized he'd been seeing her the entire time we were together."

He nodded. "I hate that."

"It's the worst."

"I'm sorry about Brad," he said. "It's hard to let go of our secrets, but it generally works better if we tell each other the truth."

My mouth was dry. "You're right." After a long silence, I redirected the conversation to cut the tension. "Since we're confessing past indiscretions, tell me something about you that your mother doesn't know."

He rolled his eyes. "We'd be here all night. What about you? Any other secrets I should know?"

I paused for a moment to think. "I once had serious spy cred."

He looked up from his salad. "Do tell."

"Lydie loved spy novels. When I was eight, she introduced me to a book called *Harriet the Spy*."

My mind snapped back to that exhilarating summer in Justice Bay. The book captivated me enough that Lydie started calling me Harriet, and I called her Ole Golly, the nickname for Harriet's nanny.

"My aunt bought me a notebook," I continued, "just like Harriet's. Every day, I wandered along the shore, noting the number of boats in the bay and shells in the sand. By the end of my two-week vacation, I'd collected information about everything from the food preferences of field mice to the type of shoes people wore to the beach."

The waiter collected my soup bowl and hurried off.

"Sounds like a life-altering experience. Did you catch any spies?"

"No, but when I got back to Los Angeles, I found Mr. Hayes guilty as charged for letting his dog out every morning to poop on our front lawn. I also witnessed a friend scrape frosting off an Oreo with her teeth and then put the cookie part back into the carton."

Cooper laughed. "That's dark stuff."

"It gets worse. My spy career ended when my mother found detailed notes from my Hollywood Vice Detective neighbor's case file. That's when I learned spies can get caught and imprisoned in their bedroom for a timeout."

I'd always been a bit of a loner, so I didn't tell Cooper that being confined to my room reading books wasn't the punishment my mother envisioned. The tragedy came when she confiscated the notebook Lydie had given me and burned it in the fireplace on a funeral pyre of newspapers and grocery-store logs. In my mind's eye, I could still see the hot, licking flames and smell the fire curling and consuming my pages. I imagined my crushed spirit mixed among the charred ashes. That began my mother's purge of all things Lydie. I didn't tell Cooper because the wounds were fresh, even after all these years.

He tilted his head and frowned. "So, you gave up spying?"

"I never give up."

After a momentary lull in the conversation, the entrees arrived, giving me time to tamp down the painful memory.

"It's amazing how Lydie encouraged your creativity," he said, "and also ironic that the curiosity skills you learned from a kid's spy game might help you find out how she died."

The truth of his comment took me aback.

A woman passed our table on the way to the restroom, engulfing me in the aroma of her strong perfume. The smell reminded me of the incense I'd found in the duffle bag from Lydie's Tibet trip. A moment later, a high-pitched ringing blocked out all ambient sounds.

The room began to spin. At first, I thought—*too much wine*. My mind glazed over. Words ricocheted in my head like a sinister spelling bee—fire, red, spy, dark. My aunt's terrified face peered from her bedroom window, staring into the abyss at a shadowy figure creeping toward her. I don't know how long I inhabited that fugue state. The next thing I remembered was Cooper's voice.

"Emma."

I sat in the chair, gripping my napkin like my life depended on it. My heart pounded. Cooper knelt on the floor beside me with wide-eyed concern.

An electric jolt surged through my body as his hand touched my face. "Are you okay?"

It took a couple of beats before I could answer. "I'm not going back to Los Angeles."

He took my cold hands in his and squeezed. "Are you sure?"

"I'm not leaving here until I find out who killed my aunt."

Chapter Twenty-Two

As soon as I got home that night, I called Walter to let him know I wouldn't be returning to Los Angeles, that I planned to stay in Justice Bay to settle my aunt's estate and to offer whatever support I could to law enforcement until they arrested Lydie's killer. I added that my job at Fortuna Cruise Lines was over because people who should have stood up for me hadn't. Another reason I wanted to stay was Cooper, but I didn't mention that. I wrapped up my monologue by asking to extend the rental agreement for Cassandra's Collectibles. He listened without comment until I finished.

"Good," he said.

I emailed a letter of resignation to my boss, Mike Woods. As a courtesy, I left Brad a message to tell him I wouldn't return to work.

The following day, I got a call from somebody from Fortuna's Human Resources department, confirming they would deposit my final paycheck directly into my bank account and asking me to return the key card to the garage as soon as possible. Brad didn't return my call, telling me everything I needed to know.

Before heading into the shop, I went for a short run, hoping to find my mojo. The fresh air solidified at least one decision. My rent wasn't due on my L.A. apartment for another couple of weeks, so I'd either have to notify the property manager or keep the place for a while. I'd probably continue paying rent until I decided what to do with the contents. Juggling another move right now would cause stress overload.

Arthur spoke with a customer as I walked into Cassandra's. He'd composed descriptions for the display cards with a charming and quirky style that delighted shoppers. Again, I realized how instrumental he'd become to the smooth running of Cassandra's.

I didn't want to tell him the shop would remain open until I calculated how much money it would take to compete with his offer from the county. My inheritance sounded like a lot of money, but it wouldn't last forever. If keeping him employed wasn't viable, I couldn't let him give up the other offer.

During a lull in customer traffic, my thoughts turned to the work I'd done compiling the database of area storage facilities and body shops where a person might store a damaged Mercedes. I assumed Walter gave the list to Greene, but I'd seen no evidence the Chief had acted on it.

"Arthur," I said. "I feel terrible abandoning you again, but I have an errand. Do you mind working alone for a while?"

"Go do your thing," he said. "I'm having a blast. Besides, I want to tell my book club about the Sue Grafton novel to see if anybody is interested."

"You're the best, Arthur."

He smiled. "I am, aren't I?"

I stopped at Pack-And-Go Moving & Storage a few miles outside Justice Bay. The manager looked middle-aged with a white Santa Claus beard and a visible paunch under his worn Grateful Dead T-shirt. I told him I wanted to store some household furniture and other items to assure him I was a serious customer. He told me no garage could accommodate the contents of an entire house, but he showed me three smaller units. They weren't together, but I estimated any of the three could hold any new collectibles I might acquire if Cassandra's continued growing. As a plus, the contract only required a month-to-month lease. It occurred to me that I could store Lydie's Beetle here if I couldn't find a buyer or didn't want to leave it in the garage.

"Is there a unit large enough for cars?" I asked.

"You'd have to give me the dimensions, but sure."

My jaw tingled. If the facility stored cars, maybe one of the units held the vehicle that killed my aunt.

"What about a Mercedes?"

He squinted. "Like I said, it depends on how big it is. You got a Mercedes to store?"

"Maybe. Could you show me a stored Mercedes as an example so I can see how it fits in the space?"

"I don't monitor what goes into the garages once money changes hands, so I have no idea what's here. Even if somebody stored a Mercedes and I could access the customer's lock, I wouldn't show it to you. That would be an invasion of privacy."

"Real estate agents show occupied houses all the time. Seems like the same thing, don't you think?"

He chuckled, causing the fat on his belly to jiggle. "Not sure what your angle is, lady, but forget it."

"No angle," I said. "Just curious."

I hesitated to ask if the police contacted him about a Mercedes with a missing side mirror. Maybe it was too soon for Chief Greene to act on the evidence I'd provided if he ever planned to do so. Back at the office, the man handed me an inventory sheet and asked me to calculate the value of the items I planned to store—for insurance purposes, he told me.

"If you leave the vehicle for over thirty days," he said, "I suggest you fill the gas tank. Maybe put in an additive. Also, get a battery tender so it doesn't go south on you. If you ignore my advice, we sell cables if you need a jump start."

I promised to get back to him soon.

Before returning to Cassandra's Collectibles, I detoured to the closest body shop on my list. I scoped out the building from the parking lot before leaving my car. There were two service bays, but neither held a Mercedes. I debated between two cover stories, pretending to be an insurance adjuster or posing as a potential customer. I chose the more straightforward customer option.

A man in his early thirties came out of the office to greet me, wiping black grease from his hands onto a coarse-blue cloth. He smelled of engine oil and cigar smoke.

"Can I help you?"

"I hope so," I said. "My mother's Mercedes got sideswiped in a parking lot. The impact ripped off the mirror. She's in a tizzy, so I offered to help her find somebody to repair the damage."

He didn't respond, so I kept talking. "My mom drove away before realizing what had happened. When she went back, the mirror had disappeared."

He frowned. "Got another request like that from a guy a few days ago. Another Mercedes."

My body tensed. He'd just confirmed the caller was a man. "Maybe that was my dad. He might have forgotten to tell me he'd already called you. What was his name?"

"I didn't bother to ask after he told me the wiring and electrical connectors on the mirror were damaged. I told him the only place nearby that does work like that is the Mercedes dealership over at Cedarbrook. I don't mess with electronics. I do good bodywork in case there's other damage to your mom's car."

"I don't suppose he left his number?"

"Why would I need that? I told you I couldn't do the work."

If this guy had hoped to discourage me with his bad humor, he'd never worked in the travel industry.

Cedarbrook was a medium-sized town about a forty-five-minute drive from Justice Bay. I wanted to visit the dealership to see if they had repaired the Mercedes that killed Lydie. But I'd already been gone almost two hours. I didn't want to leave Arthur alone despite his assurances. My trip to Cedarbrook would have to wait until tomorrow, when I'd have plenty of time to check out the dealership. If I didn't find anything there, I'd visit a few more body shops on my way home.

On the drive back to Justice Bay, I made another decision. I hoped it was the right one.

Chapter Twenty-Three

When I returned to Cassandra's, I found Arthur alone, sitting on Lydie's reading chair, holding a legal thriller from her library. He looked up and smiled. "Did you accomplish your mission?"

"Not completely, but I'm making progress." I pulled up a chair and sat next to him. "Arthur, there's something I need to tell you."

He closed the book and frowned. "If it's about a farewell party, you don't have to worry. The Literary Society is throwing a wine and cheese get-together after we close on Saturday."

I leaned toward him with my forearms on my knees. "That's wonderful, but here's the thing." My brain searched for the right words but came up short. Instead, I blurted out the news. "I quit my job last night because I'm not leaving Justice Bay until I find out who killed my aunt. The shop will stay open for now, and I'd love for you to keep working with me, but that wouldn't be fair because I know you just got a great job offer with the county, and I don't know if I can match their salary and as for benefits, those are probably off the table, at least for now."

Arthur's concerned expression slowly transformed into a smile. "Emma, I'm twenty and live with my mother in my childhood bedroom. I'm still young enough to be listed as a dependent on her health insurance policy. I don't need the county's money or their fancy-schmancy benefits. I need a job that makes me happy and gives me purpose. Cassandra's Collectibles does that. Every day I walk through that door, I feel energized. I would love to stay and help you make this place a success."

141

We reached out to hug, but abandoned the idea when a customer entered the shop. Arthur and I worked until about four before closing. I drove home, strategizing different ways to pay Arthur's salary over the long haul. When I arrived at the house, I printed a fresh list of auto body shops for my trip to Cedarbrook the following day.

Arthur arrived at the cottage on his bicycle a short time later to look for additional items to sell at the shop. When the doorbell rang, Boo raced upstairs to hide. She didn't like loud noises but generally rejoined the party as soon as calm had returned.

Arthur wandered out to the veranda and did a one-eighty turn. "I've never been here before. The view is spectacular. I don't know why Pearl can't find a buyer."

"It is puzzling." His comment reminded me to have Pearl take the house off the market.

Arthur returned to the kitchen and set his messenger bag on the island. "So much is going on, I almost forgot to tell you." He reached inside the bag and pulled out the Dzi stone. "I told John Osgood I needed an appraisal for a client of my temp service. Since he thinks you're a pill, I told him the party considered the inquiry confidential."

"What did he say?"

Arthur set the stone on the countertop. "He wanted to keep it temporarily, but I told him no. He took some photos, but warned me there are a lot of cheap lookalike stones that are just beads manufactured for the tourist trade. Some look authentic, but they aren't. He'll make some calls. If he gets any bites, he'll need to show the stone in person to the prospective buyers."

"Good work, Arthur."

He smiled. "Where shall I start looking for new inventory?"

"I stored some things in the garage," I said, "and there are more books and other possibilities upstairs in Lydie's office."

"Is anything off-limits?"

"I'll evaluate everything before we decide, but don't stifle your imagination now." I pointed to the stairs. "The office is up there. Turn right on the landing. The door is open."

While Arthur went upstairs, I decided to blow my cover and ask John Orson Osgood for more information about the Dzi stone as soon as possible. For now, I searched online and confirmed what Arthur had already told me. The Dzi stone is a semi-precious gemstone, also called a Tibetan bead. Ancient Tibetans carved unique patterns and colors onto the surface. They are rare, expensive, and thought to bring good fortune if genuine.

Thirty minutes later, Arthur walked down the creaky stairs wearing sunglasses and carrying a statue of a mottled gray horse under one arm and what looked like a boxed set of cassette tapes under the other. Boo galloped past him at warp speed, nearly knocking him over. As predicted, the cat had banished any doorbell worries and prepared for action.

Arthur set the horse and cassettes on the countertop. "I've put aside a stack of books for you to okay, but I wanted to ask about this horse."

I smiled at the memory of Lydie's trip to Xian, China. "That's a replica of a terracotta horse sculpture, one of around eight thousand pieces buried with the first emperor of China as part of an army meant to protect him in the afterlife."

"Sort of like burial art? Is it valuable?"

"It's just a souvenir. Lydie bought it at the burial site in Xian. That Shanghai panda at the shop is from that same trip."

Arthur pointed to the box of cassettes. "What about these French language tapes?"

I ran my hand over the box, remembering the story. "Lydie went on a ski vacation in Chamonix. She fell in love with France and her hunky ski instructor, who inspired her to learn the language."

Arthur took off the sunglasses and laid them on the counter. "That might explain why she bought these Vuarnets. Great for après-ski at the lodge. They're from a shop in Paris. The original receipt is still in the case." He paused for a moment to think. "Maybe I can make a French-themed gift basket to sell at the shop. The sunglasses. The tapes. The ooh-la-la story."

"Arthur, you're a marketing genius."

He beamed and took a bow. "All we need to complete the package is one of those prehistoric cassette players."

Boo jumped onto the counter and stomped across the laptop keyboard, crashing my internet connection. I brushed her tail away from my face. "Keep looking. You might get lucky."

Arthur gazed out the French doors at the moonlight shimmering on the bay. "I envy your aunt, how she traveled to all those exotic places. Don't get me wrong. It's not hostile envy, more like admiration envy."

"What's stopping you from traveling?"

Arthur's wistful expression collapsed into a frown. Boo settled on the counter near him to dispense her brand of comfort.

"I can't leave my mother alone right now."

"Why? Is she sick?"

Worry creased his forehead as he petted Boo. "She misses my dad."

I put my hand over my heart. "I'm so sorry. I lost my father at age thirteen. I know how that feels."

Arthur clicked his tongue on the roof of his mouth in an audible tsk. "He's not dead. He's living in Denver with his new wife and baby daughter."

Arthur explained his parents went through an acrimonious divorce during his senior year of high school. The University of California at Berkeley offered him admission after he graduated, but money remained tight, so he declined their offer. Instead, Arthur attended the community college in Cedarbrook. Even that became unworkable because he had to borrow his mom's car, leaving her without transportation.

"After the second quarter at Cedarbrook," he said, "I dropped out just until things got better. The only problem is they never did, at least for us."

"Arthur, it's important for you to have a college education. Can't your dad help out?"

"He's got a second family now, so no. He bought my bicycle out of guilt, but paying my tuition is a non-starter."

"At least you're all still speaking to each other."

"My dad is under the misguided impression that my mother is happy for him. Every picture he texts of that kid in her Lilliputian pink tutu is like a knife through her heart."

"Can't she just ask him to stop?"

Arthur sat motionless, staring at his hand on Boo's back. "She's too nice. I'd tell him myself, but she doesn't want me involved." His cell chirped with an incoming text. At the sound, Boo jumped from the counter and raced upstairs. Arthur glanced at the screen and stood. "Enough of my dysfunctional family saga. I should go. My mother is making crab croquettes for dinner."

I wondered how long Arthur would set aside his life to support his mother. As noble as it sounded, it could be unhealthy.

"It's dark outside," I said. "Let me drive you home."

"My helmet has a light. I'll be fine. It's only a couple of miles."

As Arthur walked out the door, I experienced a pang of unease as I pictured Lydie lying in the loamy soil at the side of the road, dying alone in the dark.

Chapter Twenty-Four

After Arthur left, I looked in the refrigerator for something to eat. A thud came from the guest room. I ran upstairs to investigate. When I noticed that Boo had batted the Tibetan prayer book off the desk and was frantically clawing at it, I shouted, "Boo! No!"

Spooked by my harsh tone, she bent low to the ground and skulked out of the room. I kneeled to assess the damage and noted that Boo's claws had damaged my birthday note from Lydie.

I rolled over on the floor and gazed at the ceiling, recalling my aunt's cryptic note. At first glance, I thought it read like a script from a hostage video. My aunt sensed danger even before leaving on her trip to Tibet. She'd said as much to Walter when she bought that red blouse. Perhaps she had a premonition of her death during her travels and left the note in the prayer book to memorialize her fears, hoping her tone would be a call to action for me. Boo might be a cat psychic, pointing me to a vital piece of evidence.

My imagination exploded with improbable thoughts. My aunt traveled the world, but why did she choose Tibet, and why now? Did that trip have anything to do with her death? Cooper had promised me a meeting with Walter to learn more about his relationship with Lydie. Either he'd forgotten to ask—unlikely—or Walter had refused to discuss his personal life with me. My bucket of unanswered questions overflowed. I couldn't wait. I had to speak to Walter.

I sensed Boo's presence, staring at me with her piercing green eyes. When I reached out to pet her, she collapsed at my side, letting me know she'd forgiven me for yelling at her. I forced myself to my feet and called Walter's number. He didn't answer, but I managed to reach Cooper.

"Where's your uncle?"

"What's wrong?" His tone acknowledged the tension in my voice.

"Everything. I need to speak with Walter. It's urgent."

"We're on my boat. Shall I hand him the phone?"

This conversation had to be face-to-face so I could show him the note. "No, I'm coming over."

"The water's a little cold for a swim. I'll pick you up in the dinghy."

Having Walter trapped in a confined space during my interrogation was perfect. "Don't bother. I've got Lydie's rowboat."

He hesitated before answering. "Your choice. I'll leave the light on for you."

The sun set as I grabbed the windbreaker from my backpack and zipped the house keys into my pocket, along with Lydie's note. Billowy charcoal clouds drifted inland. A thick mist saturated the air as I tugged the boat toward the water.

I followed the anchor light toward Cooper's sailboat. Rowing against the current turned out to be more challenging than anticipated. He leaned over the lifeline as I approached and grabbed the painter. He tied the line to a stanchion while I climbed the swim step into the cockpit. Walter slumped against a large pillow on the bench. A half-full glass of amber liquid sat on the table before him.

"What's going on, Emmaline?" He asked, his tone wary.

I pulled my aunt's shredded note from the pocket of my windbreaker and thrust it toward his face.

He straightened his spine as he read. "Where did you get this?"

"Lydie bought a prayer book in Tibet for my birthday. This note was inside. The wording sounds off. A few minutes ago, I found Boo clawing it. I know it sounds unhinged, but maybe the cat senses Lydie's message has something to do with her death. Why did my aunt travel to Tibet?"

His face remained stony. "Maybe Lydie liked hiking at high altitudes."

I ignored his flippant tone. "Should I show the note to Chief Greene? What progress has he made on the investigation?"

147

Cooper swept his gaze from me to his uncle and back to me as if trying to keep score in a fast-moving tennis match.

Walter took a sip from his drink glass. "I doubt he's interested in birthday greetings. And I told you before, I can't discuss any evidence Chief Greene has collected."

Frustrated, I sat on the bench across from him. "So, tell me something that's not classified. How did you meet Lydie?"

The creaking of the mast and the slap of waves against the hull interrupted the long silence. Cooper turned and began coiling lines.

Walter studied his drink, avoiding eye contact. "Eight years ago, I interviewed her at Spellman Polk and Kimble about a case."

I leaned toward him, invading his space. "Who were you investigating?"

"An employee," he said. "Lydie's unique insights helped me bring an indictment against the suspect."

My aunt worked in Human Resources for a company that developed top-secret weapons systems for the U.S. military, so that made sense. Cooper laid down the coiled line and joined me on the bench. The warmth of his body comforted me.

"What were the allegations against the employee?" I asked.

"He was stealing top-secret documents and selling them to the Russians."

"You mean like espionage? How did he pull that off?"

"He simply downloaded information onto a thumb drive and walked out the door. His supervisors were lax about auditing his work because he'd been at the company for ten years without incident."

"Excuse me if I find it hard to believe that nobody searched him when he left the building."

"Believe it," Walter said. "The issue with this guy was he didn't stand out in any way. The intelligence community has a name for people like him—a gray man. On the surface, he was competent but completely forgettable. Dig a little deeper, and he fits the classic profile targeted by spy recruiters. First, he'd lost a huge chunk of his savings in a bogus gas and oil investment and almost lost his home. Then he started drinking. Heavily. Bad signs for people with access to classified documents."

"How did the Russians recruit him?"

"Once they found his Achilles' heel, they sent an attractive young woman with a sexy accent to slither up to him at his favorite bar. One thing led to another."

My muscles tensed. "I wonder how many innocent people died because of his betrayal."

"Hard to say," Walter said.

"How did my aunt get involved?"

"The employee was a senior IT Systems Administrator authorized to move documents from one computer to another. Lydie sensed a dark presence surrounding him and made a point of watching his movements. She noticed his thumb drive transfers seemed repetitive and confusing, almost like a shell game. She alerted the company pooh-bahs of her concerns. They called the Bureau. The prior document thefts were damaging, but we suspected he was testing the company's security for a bigger prize. The Russian military was developing a new cruise missile but needed a workable exhaust system. Lydie's company had the crucial technology. We directed company engineers to alter the plans before the employee could download them. If he managed to smuggle the material out of the building before we arrested him, the changes were subtle but capable of making the Russian missiles even bigger duds. Fortunately, we nabbed the guy as he left work with the stolen documents on his thumb drive. Mr. IT guy was lucky we got to him before the Russians did."

"Talk about dodging a bullet," I said. "How long did Lydie continue to provide insights on your case?"

He hesitated before answering. "For a while."

"Why did she stop?"

"It got personal."

I leaned forward. "You two became an item, and you had to go elsewhere for your insights, right?"

He stared at the lights along the shore. "Something like that."

I pressed Walter for more. He told me about their mutual attraction, but a romantic relationship was a non-starter while he struggled through a contentious divorce.

Over the years, they had lunch together whenever their schedules permitted and stayed in touch by text and email. Walter visited her once in Justice Bay but slept in the guest room. He loved the area, so he bought the property next to hers when it became available.

A year ago, long divorced and retired from the FBI, Walter became a full-time resident of Justice Bay. That's when he and Lydie were finally able to be together. She hadn't yet retired, but they juggled their schedules and made it work.

"Why didn't she tell me about you?"

"We both figured our relationship should remain need-to-know."

Walter's information gave me much to process, so I let it settle and moved on. I'd already told him about the mysterious man who'd come into the shop insisting on speaking with me and the incident at the cemetery, so when he finished explaining his history with Lydie, I told him about my visit to one of the body shops on that list I'd given him.

"The owner told me a man called and asked him to repair a Mercedes side mirror," I said. "The police haven't interviewed him, or he would have mentioned it."

Walter's expression remained unreadable. "Interesting."

I blinked hard. "Is that all you have to say? What's going on? What's Greene doing? Anything?"

He stood and nodded to Cooper. "Take me back to shore."

I bolted from the bench and moved toward him. "What are you going to do?"

He untied the dinghy painter. "Make some calls."

"About what?"

Cooper slid three boards into the boat's opening and secured them with a padlock.

Walter wheeled around to face me. "Look, Emmaline, I'm going to talk to some people. Just go home and let me handle this."

I bristled at his tone. "Don't shut me out. Tell me something. Anything."

He didn't respond to my plea. "Ride in the dinghy with us. Cooper can tow the rowboat." He turned toward his nephew. "Drop me off first."

This time, I didn't bother to argue. The night had grown colder and darker. I'd struggled against the current on the way over. I didn't want to do that again. Except for the hum of the dinghy motor and the breeze rattling through the hood of my windbreaker, we rode to shore in silence. Cooper dropped his uncle off on the beach in front of his house.

"When you get home," Walter said, "make sure all your doors and windows are locked. Don't let anybody in unless you trust them."

"You think I'm in danger?"

Walter pushed the dinghy back into the water. "Just pretend you're still living in Los Angeles and act accordingly."

I hid my irritation over his L.A. bashing as we watched Walter sprint toward his cabin.

Chapter Twenty-Five

Cooper navigated the dinghy and rowboat along the shore to Lydie's house. He cut the motor and lifted the blades out of the water as the waves gently pushed us onto the pebbly beach. I scrambled onto the land while Cooper secured both boats.

Cooper brushed sand from his hands. "Maybe I should come in and check the house?"

"You think somebody's in there?"

"Did you lock the door when you left?"

I scoffed, remembering Walter's dig about my hometown. "Of course, I locked the door." I paused and added, "But it wouldn't hurt if you looked around."

Cooper smiled. "Right."

We entered the house through the French doors. I flipped on a lamp by the living room couch and listened. A loud meow interrupted the silence. Boo lumbered over to Cooper and threaded her body around his ankles. He leaned over and picked her up, massaging the space between her eyes with his thumb.

"Hey, baby," he said seductively, sparking purrs that sounded like a pigeon cooing.

"Smooth," I said. "You've practiced that move before."

He smiled. "Mm-hmm."

Cooper rested his cheek on Boo's head and stroked her back. Seeing him interact with the cat, I wanted to hear even a mundane memory from his past. He could have told me a sweet story about all the cats he'd known and loved. But he didn't.

I considered telling him my parents never allowed me to have a cat. Before I was born, my father gave my mother a kitten, which she accidentally trapped inside the refrigerator. The little guy didn't end up as a catsicle only because my father opened the door to get cream for his coffee, and the kitty tumbled out minus one of his nine lives. Before he had a name, my mother regifted him to a neighbor and forever banned felines from our lives.

"I think Boo's in love," I said. "How many others have fallen prey to your charms?"

"A few." Cooper set Boo on the floor and gave me a knowing look. "Are we still talking about cats, Emma?"

My cheeks burned with embarrassment. "Yes. Of course. Cats. But now I'd like to talk about wine. Would you like a glass?"

He studied me as if he were charting a course with celestial navigation when survival required advanced electronics. "Let me take a quick look around the house. That's why I'm here, right?"

"Right."

The hunt for intruders seemed like a silly distraction. Nobody lay in wait inside the house, but we went through the motions anyway. Together, we searched the ground-floor rooms, flipping on lights as we entered and checking that I'd locked all the windows. We repeated the process upstairs.

When we stepped into Lydie's bedroom, a strange energy overtook me. I stood motionless, clenching my jaws as I scanned the room. Something seemed out of place, disturbed. Perhaps Arthur had been in the room searching for collectibles, but I didn't think so. He would have told me. A chill crept up my spine as I considered one possibility. While I'd been on Cooper's boat, somebody had entered the house. At least one person had a key. Pearl Potts. Were there others?

Cooper's voice jarred me back to reality. "Something wrong?"

I rubbed my arms to ward off a chill. "The room seems rearranged, but I can't be sure."

"If it makes you feel safer," he said, "I can crash on your couch tonight."

"Thanks, but that's not necessary. I'll be fine."

Cooper nodded. Once we'd confirmed there were no intruders in the house and all locks were secure, I silenced my internal alarm bells and headed downstairs to the kitchen.

I poured two glasses of wine and handed him one. "There's not much to eat around here. How do you feel about canned sardines?"

"Hostile."

I laughed and walked toward the living room couch with my glass. "I trust you implicitly now."

He smiled. "Okay, then let's sit outside on the swing."

"It's cold out there."

Cooper tilted his head. "I thought you trusted me."

I grabbed Lydie's wool afghan from the back of the couch. "Okay, but we'll need this." We settled on the porch swing a moment later with the blanket spread across our laps.

"I forgot to tell you," I said. "I quit my job."

His eyes widened. "How did your boss react?"

"Let's just say he didn't offer me a gold watch and a going-away bash at the Biltmore."

Cooper eased into the next question. "What about Brad?"

I swirled the wine around in the glass as if a witty answer and the bouquet of vanilla, apples, and honeyed peaches might rise to the surface. "I left Brad a message because we work together, and he needed to know I would not be coming back. He didn't return my call. I'm guessing he's fine with it."

"You sound resolved."

"I told you we broke up over a month before I came to Justice Bay. I hoped we could still be friends, but I don't think that's possible anymore. I'm moving toward indifference."

He raised his glass. "To indifference." We clinked.

"What about you and Maddie?"

He frowned. "Maddie? If you think there's something between the two of us, you're mistaken. We're just friends."

Relieved by his clarification, I gazed at the night sky as we brainstormed the legal hurdles it might take to make Cassandra's Collectibles an official business.

"Will Walter tell you what he learns about Lydie's death?"

"Probably not."

"Would you tell me if he did?"

"Probably not."

"But probably isn't a no, right?" I asked in a teasing tone.

I remember Walter joking about Cooper's ability to keep secrets. He said he wouldn't talk even if my interrogation ended with his nephew sitting under a light bulb, handcuffed to a chair. I tended to believe that.

"In this case, it's definitely a no. If Walter has information to share, he'll tell you himself."

"As they say, it always seems impossible until it isn't."

After that, our conversation lapsed into a comfortable silence. All I could hear were the creaking sounds of the swing moving back and forth, waves lapping against the shore, and Cooper's even breathing. The serenity became so prolonged I finally glanced at him to confirm he was still awake.

His eyes were closed. A clump of Boo's fur clung to the sleeve of his flannel shirt. I inched closer, inhaling the lemony fragrance of laundry detergent. As I reached out to gently brush away the debris, Cooper opened his eyes. He caught my gaze and held it. Without breaking eye contact, he took my hand and squeezed it. Warmth radiated through my body as I leaned in, brushing my lips against his in a soft kiss.

Cooper didn't reciprocate. "It's late. I should go."

I shifted my gaze to the water so he wouldn't see the depth of my embarrassment. I didn't know why I thought Cooper would respond to the kiss. He'd never made any overt advances toward me. How could I have miscalculated so spectacularly? Now I'd ruined everything.

I let out a heavy sigh. "I shouldn't have done that. I'm sorry."

"I'm not." With his hand on my chin, he gently turned my head so we were eye to eye. "I'm glad you did. But here's the thing, Emma. You and Brad just broke up. I want to be more than just the rebound guy. I'll be here when you get to indifference."

"What if I'm already there?"

"I want you to be sure." He stood and walked toward the deck's steps.
"Cooper?"

He wheeled around, his eyes alert.

I pulled the afghan around my neck to ward off the chill. "You never told me. Did you ever have a cat?"

The moon's glow highlighted his puzzled frown. I hadn't asked the question he expected. "As a kid. Lots of them. Dogs, too. My mom loves animals. She believes they're a window into the soul."

"She sounds like a remarkable person."

"That she is."

"I'd love to meet her someday."

He smiled. "I think we can make that happen." He turned to leave and then stopped once more. "Look, if you ever feel unsafe here, call me. You can always stay on the boat."

"What about Boo?"

He winked. "Bring her. We'll turn her into a boat cat."

I waited until Cooper got into the dinghy. Then I went inside and locked the French doors. I pressed my nose against the glass, following the stern's steaming light until it disappeared into the darkness.

My skin prickled with dread as I turned toward the staircase, knowing that I had to have another look at Lydie's bedroom.

Chapter Twenty-Six

Boo crept up the stairs ahead of me, crouched low to the ground like she was stalking a gazelle. My apprehension grew hearing the creaking of the wooden treads under my weight. Halfway up, I considered asking Cooper to come back, but I rejected the idea as inadvisable after that kiss faux pas.

When I stepped into Lydie's bedroom, I sensed that same discordant energy from earlier that evening. I sat on the window seat overlooking the bay, but my attention stayed focused inside the bedroom, searching for anything odd. Finding nothing, I nearly gave up when I spotted a familiar object in an unexpected place. It was smooth and waxy to the touch. Some ancient souls had embedded ivory geometric markings on the dark surface, including circles, zig-zags, diamond shapes, and tiny cinnabar dots. The Dzi stone lay on the floor next to Lydie's nightstand, where it should not have been, which unleashed a jolt of alarm.

Arthur had removed it from his messenger bag and set it on the kitchen island earlier in the day. I considered the possibility my aunt had a housekeeper with a key. Maybe she didn't know Lydie had died. When she dropped by to vacuum, she moved the Dzi stone from the kitchen to the bedroom. Except there weren't any mysterious vacuum cleaner tracks on the rugs. I dismissed the idea as desperate theorizing.

I hadn't moved the stone and doubted Arthur or Cooper had either. Cooper and I had searched every room in the house. We'd checked all the doors and windows and found no sign of forced entry. Unless a poltergeist had taken up residence and moved the stone from the kitchen to the bedroom to freak me out, somebody had gotten inside, possibly using a key.

Pearl kept a spare after she sold the house to my aunt. I wondered if the prior owner had one, too. Some county office or other online sites would have records of the sale and possibly the former owner's name, but I doubted that would include information about their current location. I'd go directly to the person who might know the whole story—Pearl Potts.

Despite the late hour, I left a message on her cell, telling her to take the house off the market and return the key. I would ask about the former owner when I ran into her again.

Arthur had stacked the hallway with boxes of books and collectibles meant for the shop. I didn't feel like sorting through them, so I moved everything downstairs by the door for easy loading in the morning. Arthur indicated the Dzi stone might be valuable. To be safe, I put it in my backpack until we got an appraisal from antique dealer John Osgood.

After that, I went to bed but couldn't sleep, so I moved Boo's litter box upstairs to the guest room and shoved a small dresser and an armchair against the door. With us safely barricaded inside, I finally drifted off to sleep with Boo pressed against my thigh.

* * *

The following day, after Boo and I left our bedroom fortress, I contacted the locksmith who installed Lydie's safe and asked him to change the locks on all the doors. He promised to come over at around noon.

I finished loading the books and collectibles into the car as Pearl Potts motored up the driveway in her Lincoln Continental. She came dangerously close to hitting my car before slamming on the brakes so hard that her body bounced against the steering wheel. Her puffy white coat must have softened the blow because she tumbled out of the car intact, except for a slight readjustment to her wig.

"I was in the neighborhood and decided to drop by," she said.

She brushed past me, carrying a mustard yellow handbag that looked like it weighed more than she did, and made her way into the kitchen. I followed her inside.

"I got your message about the house," she said in that familiar gravelly voice.

"Sorry about the change of plans—"

She batted away my apology with a flap of her hand. "Forget it. I'm glad I won't have Walter Kestrel breathing down my neck anymore."

I blinked a couple of times, stalling to figure out what she meant. "I'm sure he just wanted to help me."

Pearl hoisted the handbag onto the countertop but did not attempt to remove her coat. "Lydie never wanted you to sell the place. I knew that. Walter knew that."

I let out a frustrated sigh. "I don't understand."

She rested her elbows on the counter and leaned toward me, lowering her voice in a conspiratorial tone. "Let me spell it out for you. Before your aunt died, she told Walter you would come to Justice Bay and move into the house."

Walter had told me as much the first time we met. "So what?"

"He considered your aunt the Oracle of Delphi," Pearl continued. "He asked me to discourage interested buyers so you'd stay."

The blatant sabotage shocked me. "Why did you go along with it?"

She shrugged. "I told Walter he should level with you, but he's sent me a lot of business over the years. I owe him."

It didn't take much for her to betray Walter's trust. I reminded myself not to share any of my secrets with her.

"Who owned the house before my aunt bought it?"

She hesitated before answering. "That would be Mildred and Dwight Banfield. Nice couple. They decided the house was too much for them, so they moved into the Pleasant Springs Retirement Community in Cedarbrook. To each his own. You'd never catch me living in a place that doesn't salt the food. Mildred died a few years ago, but Dwight still has an apartment there. Why the interest?"

"It's possible somebody broke into my house yesterday. That wasn't you, right?"

She scoffed and began rummaging around in her purse. "I've never had a client accuse me of breaking and entering." She pulled out a key and slammed it on the counter. "There, feel better?"

"I take it that's a no," I said. "Does anyone else have a key, like Mr. Banfield?"

"How would I know?" She tugged the handbag from the counter and slung it over her shoulder. "I'm done here." She stomped toward the exit but, at the last moment, turned. "By the way, I can switch the house title to your name for a small fee."

I threw up my hands in frustration. "Fine. Just do it."

"I'll be in touch." Moments later, the Lincoln roared to life and drove away.

Even if Mr. Banfield still had a key, I didn't want to accuse an older man of using it to enter the house illegally and move the Dzi stone. But if the Banfields kept a key to the house, it was plausible someone might have found it among their possessions when they moved. If Mr. Banfield had labeled it with the address, someone could have used it for years to prowl around Lydie's house whenever the spirit moved them. That was too creepy to fathom. With Pearl gone, I drove into town.

When I arrived in Justice Bay nearly two weeks ago, I'd only packed a couple of casual outfits because I didn't plan to stay long. I needed to drive back to L.A. and pack for the long haul, but that would have to wait. Bay Threadz was a lovely shop, but they had a limited selection of clothes. The closest town with a shopping mall was Cedarbrook, about a forty-five-minute drive from Justice Bay. I decided to carve out some time to buy a couple of new outfits and a warm jacket. While there, I'd stop by and chat with Mr. Banfield.

Despite Walter's warning to let law enforcement handle Lydie's death investigation, I planned to follow up on a couple of loose ends, including that tip from the garage worker who told me he'd referred a car owner with a broken side mirror to the Mercedes dealership in Cedarbrook. They might be repairing the car that killed my aunt. I'd just look around. Ask a few questions. Nothing more.

Chapter Twenty-Seven

As soon as Arthur saw me park the car, he came out of the shop to help unload the boxes of items he'd picked out the day before. As we sat on the floor to sort and separate them, I told him about the Dzi stone mysteriously appearing on Lydie's bedroom floor.

"I didn't move it," he said. "I only picked out collectibles from the garage and the upstairs office, just like you told me."

I looked up and caught his gaze. "Sorry, Arthur. I didn't mean to suggest you did. I think somebody broke into the house last night. I'm just trying to figure out who else has a key."

Arthur's voice rose in alarm. "That's scary. Did you call the police?"

"And tell them what? Nobody forced their way in, and as far as I can tell, nothing is missing."

Arthur grabbed a copy of Thurber's *The Last Flower* from a box and smoothed down the damaged paper cover. "Does Walter have a key?"

"Lydie gave him one, but he returned it when I arrived in Justice Bay. Besides, it couldn't have been him. He was on Cooper's boat with me."

"Who else could it be? Pearl?"

I shrugged. "I spoke to Pearl this morning. When I mentioned my suspicions, she got upset and returned her copy of the key."

"Maybe you should get an alarm system or a guard dog."

"I'm changing the locks at noon, so I'll have to leave early."

He put his hands together in a prayer position. "Do me a favor. Text me every hour to let me know you're okay."

"That's sweet, Arthur, but I don't think it's necessary."

161

He grabbed my hand. "Emma. Please."

I agreed, just to ease his mind. We shelved the new items and intermittently waited on customers until just before noon, when I grabbed my backpack and headed toward the door.

"I'm not sure how long it will take to change the locks. I might not be back before you leave."

Arthur looked up from writing a story card for a handmade drum Lydie had brought home from Ecuador. "Text me, okay?"

I gave him a thumbs-up. "Will do."

Changing the locks didn't take as long as I'd expected. Arthur had demonstrated he could easily handle the shop without me, so as soon as the locksmith left, I texted to let him know I would run a couple of errands. Then, I headed to Cedarbrook to visit Dwight Banfield.

When I arrived at Pleasant Springs Retirement Community, I found no springs, pleasant or otherwise, just a three-story brick building on a quiet, tree-lined street. I walked up a concrete pathway flanked by low-slung plants to the reception desk, where I signed the visitor's log before heading to Banfield's second-story apartment.

A man's voice responded to my knock. "Come in. The door's unlocked."

I stepped inside an overheated room and inhaled the aroma of cherished memories layered with old dust. A man in his eighties with wispy white hair sat in a wing chair surrounded by light streaming through the window. Age had compacted his body, leaving the impression of a snowman melting in the sun.

He squinted to see me better. "Are you the new therapist?"

I noted his crisp-white shirt and gray slacks and wondered if he'd dressed for the occasion. "No, I'm just a visitor."

"Can't have too many of those," he said. "Have a seat."

I pushed aside a newspaper open to a partially completed crossword puzzle and sat on the couch closest to him. The furniture was a relic of a bygone era, oversized, overstuffed, and shoehorned into the small living room, leaving little space to maneuver. I assumed it came from Banfield's previous home.

"Pearl Potts gave me your address."

"Boy, I haven't heard that name in over twenty years. Is she still selling real estate?"

I nodded. "I'm not sure you remember my aunt, but Pearl sold her your house in Justice Bay."

He closed his eyes as if dredging up a sad memory. "I only met your aunt once. Nice lady."

"She was."

He frowned. "Was?"

"She died almost two weeks ago. I inherited the house. That's why I wanted to meet you, to tell you the place is still in great shape."

I expected him to be pleased, but he looked pained as he stared at a photo on a nearby end table of a forty-something Dwight Banfield standing by a wedding cake with his arm around a woman I assumed was Mildred. I scanned the room, but no other photos were visible.

"I hated to sell that place," he said. "Lots of happy memories there. But my wife, Millie, developed health problems. Her son pressured us to move. Said we'd have fewer responsibilities here."

"How did that work out?"

His lips twitched into something resembling a smile. "Remember that movie about the prisoner who had a pet mouse? My takeaway? You get used to almost anything when you live with somebody you love."

Mr. Jingles, the only pet mouse I could recall, appeared in the film *The Green Mile*, but he'd come to a tragic end. I crossed my fingers, hoping Dwight wouldn't elaborate because I couldn't survive another sad story.

My heart would have been heavier, except Dwight's movie reference spawned a lively discussion about books and films, politics, and Chaucer's *The Canterbury Tales*. Before retiring to Justice Bay, Dwight had taught high school English in Peoria, Illinois.

We enjoyed each other's company, but I'd come to find out if Dwight had kept a key to Lydie's house. I didn't want to make him suspicious by asking directly, so I took the roundabout route.

"Did your stepson help you move?" I asked.

"He hired a company. We told him what we wanted to keep. He took the rest."

I cleared my throat, stalling while forming a tiny white lie. "I asked Pearl to put the house on the market. I live in Los Angeles, but can't decide whether to keep a key or leave it with Pearl. What did you do?"

"Keep it for now. What if the house doesn't sell? You never know. We left ours with Millie's son because we weren't going back no matter what."

"Does your stepson live in Justice Bay?"

"He does now. After escrow closed on our house, he bought a place and opened an antique store downtown. I suspect he sold anything of value we left behind. If so, we never got a penny of the profits. I didn't make an issue of it. That would have upset Millie."

Everything Dwight said after "antique store" became a blur. John Orson Osgood, the antique store owner down the street from Cassandra's, was Dwight Banfield's stepson. I remembered an unpleasant Osgood coming into Cassandra's on opening day. After trashing Lydie's treasures as "trinkets," he'd made a low-ball offer on her vintage decoy. Arthur had asked him to appraise the Dzi stone. My suspicions hiked a notch or two.

"I think I've met him. John Osgood, right?"

Dwight nodded. "I hope he was pleasant. That's not always the case."

At one time, Osgood had a key to Lydie's house. Maybe he still did and used it the previous night to go inside to look around. He made a quick exit when he realized Cooper and I had returned. Except it made no sense that Osgood would move the Dzi stone. If he wanted to steal it, he would put it in his pocket and leave.

I stood. "I should go."

Dwight's body slumped. "So soon?"

His words left a small tear in my heart. "I'll come back again. Maybe we can have lunch at the house."

His expression brightened. "Sort of like a prison break."

"Yes, but I have a cat, so no mice allowed."

I left Dwight chuckling and went to my car to process what I'd learned about John Orson Osgood. I calculated my next step as I drove to the mall. When I arrived, I had become obsessed with finding out if Osgood had a key to my house. I did some mindless shopping, bought a pair of jeans, long-sleeved warm T-shirts, and a metallic-bronze down jacket with a faux fur-edged hood, and then loaded the shopping bags in my trunk.

Before heading back to Justice Bay, I stopped by the Mercedes dealership. The body shop owner told me he'd referred a customer with a broken side mirror to the service department. Even if the customer followed up on the referral, mechanics might have already repaired the car and returned it to the owner. Still, I had to investigate.

I parked the Audi a block away, thinking I'd casually stroll by to check out the cars to see if any had a missing side mirror. A sales office fronted the building with a service area in the back. A slim blond man sat on his heels outside the closed garage doors, hand-feeding peanuts in the shell to a fat gray squirrel.

I stood adjacent to the sales office in a small parking lot with a half dozen new cars, plotting what to do next. A door slammed. Footsteps approached. A young man with a megawatt smile walked toward me.

He pointed at a nearby car. "She's a beauty, isn't she?"

I followed the direction of his finger to a new Mercedes-Benz E-Class convertible in deep blue, wondering why cars were always female.

"She's a honey, all right." I glanced at the manufacturer's suggested retail price sticker on the window and considered it out of my reach.

He thrust his hand toward me. "Rod. Rod Engel. And you are…"

I shook his sweaty hand. "Emma. Emma Peel." He didn't get *The Avengers* reference because his smile clicked up to high beam.

"What are you driving now, Emma?" I didn't respond, so he moved on. "Just so you know, if I ask my boss pretty please, I'm sure he'll okay a super generous trade-in allowance."

It troubled me that I'd become adept at lying but not embarrassed enough to stop doing it. "Money doesn't matter to me. What's important is the quality of your service department. I've experienced so much overcharging and underperforming I've become cynical. Once, I drove my BMW out of the service garage after mechanics finished work on the electrical system. Ten minutes later, my car caught fire in rush-hour traffic. That's why competent mechanics will determine whether or not I buy a Benz from you."

He flashed the thumbs-up sign. "Then you're going to be super happy, Emma, because our service manager trained at the Mercedes factory in Stuttgart. Can't beat that."

I searched for a phrase from my high school German class to express my super happiness, but all I could dredge up was *Wo ist der Bahnhof.* No train station existed within miles of here, so asking for directions didn't meet the moment.

"I'd like to tour the service area."

"I don't know, Emma," he said, stretching out the words. "We don't usually allow customers near the equipment. Too dangerous."

"Maybe I could just peek through the window."

His smile collapsed as he finally realized I wasn't a serious customer. "Sorry. No can do. Tell you what, I'll be inside at my desk. Let me know if you want to test drive the convertible."

I waited for the office door to close behind Rod before I tiptoed down the alley at the back of the building. A row of windows just below the garage's roofline was too high to see inside. A garbage Dumpster rested against the side of the building. If I could find something to use as a step, I could crawl on the lid and—

"Can I help you?"

Startled, I whirled around. A Nordic-looking, mid-thirties man with a slight accent towered over me. It was the squirrel whisperer. The name patch on his uniform shirt read: Karl with Service Manager printed underneath. Since he'd trained at the Mercedes factory in Stuttgart, he could have been German, Norwegian, or Swiss, but since I had a bad ear for accents, he could also be Minnesotan.

My face burned from embarrassment. "Rod showed me a Benz convertible but wouldn't let me tour the service area. Since it's important to me, I thought maybe I could just peek through the window, so I walked down the alley—"

He held up his hand to stop me. "I'm happy to answer your questions, but Rod's right. Regulations don't allow us to let customers into that area. Too dangerous. But you can stand at the door and look inside."

"*Wunderbar.*"

Given the puzzled frown on his face, I guessed he hailed from Minnesota. Maybe I should have said, Yah-you-betcha.

"Come," he said, beckoning me forward.

As promised, he opened one of the service doors and let me peek inside. The place looked spotless. A car occupied every bay. Hoods were open, and uniformed mechanics tinkered with engines. I scanned the cars as fast as I could. Not all of them were Mercedes. None of them had a missing side mirror.

I hid my disappointment but refused to give up. "My mom needs somebody to repair a broken side mirror on her Benz. A mechanic near Justice Bay told me he'd recently referred another customer to you with the same problem and thought you could help."

Karl nodded. "I remember that Benz, but I didn't do the work. The customer was in a rush and wanted me to push the job to the top of the list. That's not how we do business. He got upset and left."

"I've dealt with rude people like that," I said. "It's a pain. Did you refer him to somebody else?"

Karl closed the door and led me toward the sales office. "No, and his attitude wasn't the issue. I'm used to that. The grill and front passenger side fender had extensive damage. We prefer to farm that work out to a dedicated body shop, but we can do it in-house if a customer insists, and he did."

The squirrel sat at the base of a nearby tree, waiting for another handout.

"If he wanted a rush job," I said, "why not fix the mirror and worry about the other damage later?"

"The mirror wasn't the biggest problem. The car was a late model but not new. The paint was a custom job done by an after-market company that went out of business a year ago. It would take time to find somebody who could match the color."

"Interesting," I said. "What color was the paint?"

"An unusual shade of red."

My world began to spin.

Red.

The phantom red ball that rolled across the road in the exact spot where my aunt died. The red blouse that meant danger. Now, the red Mercedes-Benz. My visions weren't coincidental—the color was guiding me to the person who'd killed my aunt, possibly the person who drove that red car.

Karl's voice sounded thin and far away. "Miss? Miss! Are you okay?"

Chapter Twenty-Eight

S till shaken, I somehow managed to summon the energy to ask Karl what he remembered about the man driving the red Mercedes. He never created a work order, so he didn't have the guy's name or the vehicle's license number, but he remembered it was a California plate. He remembered the guy looked middle-aged and wore baggy chinos and a stocking hat, recollections too vague to be of much help. Nobody I'd encountered in Justice Bay matched that generic description, nor had I seen anybody driving a red Mercedes.

After leaving the dealership, I realized somebody had to tell Chief Greene about what I'd uncovered. Law enforcement must have searchable databases to find out who owned that car. I could ask Walter to pass along the information, but I remained annoyed with him for conspiring with Pearl to sabotage the house sale. I'd approach Greene myself.

I texted Arthur that I was okay. Rather than returning to Cassandra's, I drove directly to the Justice Bay police station. Instead of Pam at the front desk, I found a male uniformed officer entering data on the computer. He had an agile boxer's stance and looked fit enough to deliver a knockout punch. As tough as he appeared, the smile wrinkles around his eyes told me he laughed a lot and often. His nametag read: Officer Skip Kowalski. I asked to speak with Greene.

"He's not here."

"Any idea when the chief might be back?" I asked, feeling deflated.

"About as long as it takes to help Renee Masterholm wrangle her Shetland pony back into the corral. An hour, maybe less."

"Isn't it overkill for the police chief to go out on a call like that? Why didn't he send you?"

He grinned. "I'm from Brooklyn, ma'am. I can't tell a horse from a unicorn. Besides, I don't call the shots around here."

I wondered how this guy ended up as a cop in Justice Bay. "Where's the Masterholm farm?"

"A few miles east of town, just past Izzy's Diner."

Even if I asked for a callback, Greene likely wouldn't comply. A wise decision or not, I would drive out to the farm and find him. I didn't want to interfere in police business, but it was a Shetland pony, not the Brinks heist.

The route led me along a narrow road through picturesque forests and pastureland. A few miles past the diner, a hand-carved wood sign read: *The Masterholms*. I found a ranch-style house at the end of a long driveway. The front yard comprised at least a quarter-acre of pasture surrounded by a wooden fence.

Greene's police SUV wasn't parked in the driveway or anywhere nearby. I stopped on the shoulder and got out of the car, inhaling the aroma of hay and manure. A Shetland pony grazed inside the fence. Greene must have already completed his mission and left.

A woman came out of the house carrying a bucket filled with what looked like brown pellets and a scooper. She waved. I waved back and walked toward her.

"I'm just admiring your pony."

"Rosie can be a pain," she said, "but we love her."

"I understand Chief Greene came out to help you get her back inside the fence. Is he still around?"

She looked confused. "I haven't seen Chet in weeks. Rosie is a regular Houdini, but not today."

I blinked a couple of times. "I must have misunderstood. Sorry to bother you."

"No worries," she said. "If you find Chet, tell him Renee sends regards."

I sat in the car and sorted out my jumbled thoughts. I hadn't misunderstood. I heard what I heard. The fact that Pam had abandoned her post at the front desk confirmed my suspicions that Greene lied to Officer Kowalski. Chet and Pam were together.

I didn't know where they were, but I guessed Greene wouldn't be back at the station for at least an hour, so I took a detour back to town to explore a road I hadn't traveled before. It was restful to be under the shadow of decades-old Douglas fir trees, but I no longer recognized the area after a few miles. I stopped by a dirt utility road to consult the map on my cell and was relieved that the intersection back to town lay just a few miles ahead.

I glanced to my right as I set the phone on the passenger's seat. The fading sun bounced off something in the trees. Something red. Heat radiated throughout my body, anticipating another vision. Curiosity compelled me forward. I inched toward the glint until I glimpsed the large red taillight of a black-and-white police SUV hidden behind a clump of trees. It had to be Greene's. From a distance, I couldn't tell if anyone was inside.

I exited the car and walked along the path until close enough to get a better look. The hair on the back of my neck stood on end as I crept forward and peeked through the back window.

My legs felt like jelly. Chet Greene and Pam were making out in the back seat. I could almost hear the smacking sound of his sloppy kisses. I wasn't exactly shocked, just appalled. It didn't appear they knew I was watching because the kissing continued with abandon. My choices were to quietly back away or knock on the window and further expose them if that was even possible. Greene had a gun. If I startled him, he might shoot me. The wiser choice was to back off, but I got angry when I thought about him working on Pam instead of Lydie's death investigation. Gun or not, I'd make him listen to me.

I knocked on the window and prepared to duck.

Greene looked up, startled to see me. The mad dash to rearrange clothing rocked the SUV. A moment later, Greene exploded from the back seat. A vein in his temple pulsed as he fumbled to fasten his belt buckle.

"What are you doing here?" he shouted.

I struggled to sound calm even as my heart hammered in my chest. "Officer Kowalski told me you were out chasing ponies," I said, "but I see ponies isn't exactly the right word."

He glanced at Pam, still inside the car, her face hidden under a jacket. His hands trembled as he fumbled with his shirt buttons. He looked indignant but also unsure of what to do next. That ticked my confidence up a notch.

"Does your wife know you're manhandling the records clerk?"

His face blanched as he raked his hand through the stubble on his head. "Please." He whispered the word as if it were a prayer.

Greene's betrayal was reprehensible. His wife, Abby, was pregnant with their second child. She deserved better than this cheating lout. On some level, it would be satisfying to see this arrogant jerk get his comeuppance, but I didn't want to be the one to break Abby's heart.

"Don't worry," I said. "I won't tell her. I'll leave that up to you and your conscience."

His arms hung at his sides like dead weights, but his tone remained defiant. "What do you want from me?"

In Walter's counterintelligence world, what I had on Chet Greene was called kompromat. I didn't plan to extort him for money or favors or ask him to betray his country. I just wanted him to do his job.

"I'll tell you what I want," I said. "I want you to investigate my aunt's death like her life had meaning. You resent every lead I bring you. Here's another one. I just found the car that might have killed her." I thought of the plot of the last detective novel I'd read and added, "Do something. Find the registered owner and check his whereabouts that night. Impound the car and look for forensic evidence."

He glared at me. "I'm doing my best."

"Did you follow up on my aunt's missing phone? Did you check cell tower pings to find out where it is and who stole it?"

He appeared less sure of himself. "You've been watching too much TV."

"Don't insult my intelligence, Chet. It adds nothing to the conversation."

He stared at the ground. "Fine. If it makes you happy, I'll take your report. There's something I need to do first. Meet me at the station. Thirty minutes."

A half-hour later, I sat across from Greene in the back office of the police station. Pam hadn't returned to work. Greene's wet hair and aroma of soap indicated he'd gone somewhere to shower. He still wore his wrinkled uniform, so I doubted he cleaned up at home. I wondered if Pam had a hamper full of wet towels.

I told Greene about Karl and the red Mercedes. He wrote everything down without a hint of snark. He thanked me and said he'd be in touch. I didn't trust this new, improved Chet Greene. He was up to something.

The sun had set by the time I left the station. Before going home, I stopped by Cassandra's. Arthur had left for the day. I sat in Lydie's reading chair with the lights off, surrounded by shelves filled with her books and collectibles. I hoped Arthur and I could overcome the high rate of new business failures with his creativity and my networking skills, money, and marketing experience.

With my eyes closed, I let the memories wash over me. I wondered if Abby and Chet Greene's marriage would last. Chet had almost begged me not to tell his wife, which may or may not be a sign he still cared. With Brad, even if he had been dating Mindy from accounting during our brief fling, as I suspected, I couldn't imagine him begging anybody to spare me the pain of finding out. I wondered if he had any regrets, but realized I no longer cared.

I'd been lost in thought when Maddie's knock on the front door startled me back to reality.

"What are you doing sitting here alone in the dark?" She studied my expression. "You look frazzled. What's going on?"

I weighed the pros and cons of telling her about Chet Greene's liaison with the Vampire Princess in the back seat of a police cruiser. The pros won. Maddie didn't seem shocked at all.

"What a loser," she said. "A few weeks ago, a customer ran out of the store, hiding something under her coat. I checked the shelves where she'd just been and found an expensive set of barbecue tools missing. I filed a police report and even gave Greene the woman's name. He never followed up. I finally called her myself and guilted her into returning the items. Now this sleazy affair with a co-worker. Poor Abby. The City Council should fire him."

My shoulders tensed. "He spends more time cheating on his wife than finding the person who killed my aunt."

"Wait. It's been two weeks since Lydie died. Are you telling me he hasn't made any progress on the case?"

"None that I can see, even though I've given him leads to follow. It's maddening."

She walked over and hugged me. "Oh, Em, I'm so sorry. What can I do to help?"

"Nothing. Even if there was something you could do, I wouldn't want to burden you with more responsibilities. You're busy taking care of your dad and the store."

She stepped back. "Look, I'm on my way to C'est Shells. Come to dinner with me."

"It's been a rough day. I'm sort of tired."

"Nonsense," she said, pulling me toward the door. "The chef and I are back on, so dinner will be spectacular, and we can talk."

My skin tingled. "You're dating the chef again? What about Cooper?"

She herded me out on the sidewalk. "What about Cooper?"

"I got the impression you had a thing for him."

Maddie took the key from my hand and locked the door. "Look, Em, don't get me wrong. Cooper is a hottie, but he's not my type. At all. Besides, you're clueless if you don't know that he only has eyes for you." Maddie giggled. "Oh, did I just write a song?"

Cooper said he and Maddie were just friends, but men sometimes didn't pick up the cues. That's why it made me ridiculously happy to hear her confirmation.

When we arrived at the restaurant, Chef Gabriel ushered us to a prime table close enough to the open kitchen area to watch him make googly eyes at Maddie as he prepared food.

The edgy New York graphic designer and the talented French chef made an odd match. I understood Maddie's attraction to Gabriel's dreamy bedroom eyes, his lilting French accent, not to mention his inspired cooking. He looked equally besotted with her energy, spontaneity, and *joie de vivre*. Her New York plus his Paris made a perfect match, the more I thought about it.

I waved at librarian Pia Bianchi, who sat a couple of tables over, having dinner with a girl of about twelve, perhaps a relative. I spotted several other diners I recognized from the shop. Being with these people made it feel like a family dinner.

After we ordered, I told Maddie I'd gone to see Dwight Banfield. "I didn't know John Osgood was his stepson. Does he have a significant other?"

"John had a relationship with a woman from Santa Cruz," she said, "but they broke up long after I moved to New York. I suspect it's a challenge living with him. It's funny, but at one time, I thought he had a thing for your aunt."

"If so, it had to be one-sided on Osgood's part. He's not Lydie's type."

Lydie often traveled the world alone because she enjoyed interacting with interesting people. Osgood was the opposite—uptight and combative. I understood my aunt's attraction to Walter. He was too curmudgeonly for my taste but also intelligent, amusing, and easy on the eyes. Lydie had never mentioned Osgood's name, and I'd never encountered him on my childhood trips to Justice Bay. On the other hand, she didn't tell me about Walter, either. She hadn't shared everything with me, as it turned out.

A moment later, the entrees arrived, delivered by Chef Gabriel himself. My lobster à l'américaine was divine. Maddie had trout meunière. Between bites, I told her my suspicion that somebody had been in the house and that John Osgood once had a key.

I lowered my voice. "Do you think it could have been Osgood?"

"Osgood seems too straightlaced to do something like that, but I can't be sure." Maddie returned to her trout and a lighter tone. "What's happening with the house? Any offers?"

"It's off the market." I also brought her up to speed on quitting my job, my decision to stay in Justice Bay, and the plan to keep Cassandra's open for business.

"What about you?" I asked. "How long will you be in town?"

"My dad's improving," she said, "but my mom wants me to stay. And now that Gabriel and I are a thing again, I'm not in any hurry to return to my dinky sublet in New York." Maddie leaned over the table and whispered,

"I'm not sure I'll ever go back. I may be in love."

I raised my eyebrows. "What about your job?"

She shrugged. "Most of what I do is computer work. I can do that anywhere. If my boss insists on an in-person presentation, I'll fly back. If I get fired, I can work freelance. I've had many satisfied clients over the years who'd happily send projects my way."

"That sounds both exciting and scary."

A coy smile spread across her face. "Has Cooper made his move yet?"

I squirmed in my chair, remembering that unrequited kiss. "Cooper doesn't want to be the rebound guy."

"I get it," she said. "Your *Hahvid* attorney wants to make sure you're over Brad. How old-fashioned of him." She reached over with her fork and speared a chunk of lobster off my plate. "Are you over Brad?"

I scrunched up my face, thinking about the question. "Brad who?"

We both laughed, which elevated my mood.

Neither of us brought up Chet Greene or Lydie's death investigation again. After dinner, I drove home feeling optimistic for the first time since arriving in Justice Bay. I'd turned over potential evidence to Chief Greene that should reinvigorate the investigation. Arthur and I were starting a new business. The cottage doors had new locks, and I had the only keys. Maddie was in love. I had my first cat ever. Walter had sabotaged the house sale, but in a way, I felt grateful to him because I now lived in a beautiful place on the water, full of loving memories.

And there was Cooper.

When I opened the door, Boo scampered over to meet me. I picked her up and hugged her. Then, I went outside to sit on the porch swing. Billowy gray clouds blocked the stars, but I could still make out blurry street lights stretching from the main street of Justice Bay to the lighthouse beam at the entrance to the harbor. I sensed a familiar glow. I looked up to see the moon bursting through the clouds. My gaze fell on the ripples of water in the bay, now awash in shimmering light. I stopped. Stared.

In the distance, I noted the running lights of a sailboat. It passed the fuel dock and headed out to sea. I glanced at the bay in front of Walter's house and felt fireworks exploding from every nerve in my body. It wasn't because of what I saw but what I didn't see.

Cooper's boat was gone.

That late at night, I doubted he'd pulled up anchor to go for a sail. Maybe there had been a family emergency. His mother? Cooper wanted to make sure I'd banished Brad from my life before we got involved. A chill settled along my spine when I realized that perhaps he planned to wait someplace else. He wasn't obligated to share his travel itinerary with me, but it crushed me that he'd left without even saying goodbye.

Chapter Twenty-Nine

I awoke the following morning, still troubled about Cooper's sudden departure. I wanted to believe he'd call to explain, but I doubted he would. I could ask Walter, but part of me didn't want to know. In the worst-case scenario, I'd just have to take a deep breath and accept the death of possibility.

When I arrived at Cassandra's, Arthur was alone in the shop, sweeping a dust rag over items on the shelves. He wore his signature camel-colored cardigan with a dashing aqua sailboat bowtie I hadn't seen before. He turned toward me with a pensive expression.

"I need to make another trip to your house," he said. "We're running low on inventory again."

I stored my backpack and new coat in the small bathroom closet. "My aunt has a finite number of collectibles," I said. "Eventually, the entire inventory will be exhausted. We need a plan."

Arthur's hazel eyes opened wide. "Maybe we could go on a buying trip to one of those antique shows in the Midwest. Cedar Rapids is good."

"We?"

A flush spread across Arthur's cheeks. "Don't worry, Emma. I only think of you as a much older sister."

I laughed. "I know, Arthur. Besides, it would be more fun to pick out things together."

He brushed the dust off the glass case of a Japanese porcelain figurine. "My mother can watch the shop while we're gone."

"You think she'd do that?"

"I'm positive." He beckoned me toward the door. "Help me carry the wicker outside before customers wander in."

We moved the table, two chairs, and the potted forget-me-not to the sidewalk and returned inside.

"I just remembered something," he said. "There may be an alternative to Iowa. A member of the literary society told me about her friend in Los Angeles. She works for a bank. Her team does nothing but handle estate sales for dead clients. Maybe we could ask her to buy some stuff for us."

I picked up a stack of credit card receipts from the day before, totaling them in my head. "How will we know what we want until we see it ourselves?"

"She could text photos."

"Look," I said, "I have to return to L.A. sometime soon to pick up my clothes. I have too many other responsibilities to worry about moving, so I'll pay the rent for the next month or so."

"Why do you need an apartment in L.A.?"

I put the receipts in the cash box. "If we decide to shop at estate sales, it could be our base of operations. It's a two-bedroom on the Westside, close to the airport and restaurants. And it's more comfortable and cheaper than a hotel."

The color drained from Arthur's oval face halfway through my pitch. "What's wrong? You don't like the idea?"

He rested his long, thin fingers on my forearm, a protective gesture that surprised me. "Remember that man who came looking for you while you were at the cemetery?"

"The guy who looked like a hippie and got upset because you couldn't guarantee when I'd be back?" I didn't add that I suspected the mystery man followed me to the cemetery and spied on me from the woods.

Arthur's voice lowered to a whisper. "He's standing outside on the sidewalk."

My heart raced as I whirled around to see a thin, wiry man turning the doorknob. He looked too young to have gray hair, but a salt-and-pepper ponytail cascaded down the back of his rumpled tweed jacket. He personified those 1970s college students who hung out in coffee shops debating Marx and Sartre while stubbing out cigarettes in a tuna can ashtray.

"Ms. McCoy?" His tone flowed, soft and serene as a yoga master's. "I'm Seamus Murphy. I met your aunt recently."

The name meant nothing to me until a few moments later, when I remembered the boarding pass I'd found in her travel bag with Seamus and a phone number on it. As it turned out, Seamus Murphy worked as a professor of East Asian Studies at UC Berkeley, focusing on Chinese Buddhist art and Asian architecture. He said he'd boarded Lydie's Lhasa-San Francisco flight in Singapore and sat beside her.

"Something odd happened when we arrived at the San Francisco airport," he said. "And after I read Lydie's obituary in the Chronicle, it seems even more disturbing. I hoped you could make sense of it."

Intrigued, I grabbed my jacket and herded Seamus Murphy to the wicker table outside, my de facto corporate headquarters and the closest thing to privacy I could offer. It was too early for commerce, so we had Main Street primarily to ourselves.

"Lydie was beyond delightful," he said, picking up the conversation where he'd left off. "We'd both traveled extensively in Asia, but I'd never been to Tibet. She fascinated me with her stories. Before we landed in San Francisco, I gave her my contact information and asked her to keep in touch."

"Her stories inspired me, too," I said. "Was that the last time you heard from her?"

"Not exactly. I didn't want our conversation to end. After clearing customs, Lydie agreed to have a latte with me before heading to our destinations. Your aunt was about to show me the Tibetan Buddhist prayer book she got for you at the Tashi Lhunpo Monastery. Then her focus suddenly shifted to something over my shoulder. I turned to look, but all I saw were passengers filing out of the customs area."

From what I'd learned about my aunt, what she saw may not have been visible to mere mortals.

"Did she say anything?"

"No, but the look in her eyes unsettled me."

"What do you mean? What look?"

180

"Fear," he said. "A moment later, she grabbed her bags and told me she had to go."

"How strange. That's so unlike my aunt." I forced myself to stay calm, even as the hair on my arms lifted.

"She disappeared into the crowd but left one of those free on-flight publications on the seat. I planned to toss it in the recycling bin." He reached inside his jacket pocket and drew out an envelope. "But when I picked it up, this fell on the floor."

A sheen of moisture formed on my chest. Lydie had written my name and Justice Bay on the outside, but no street address.

"That's when I realized she hadn't given me her contact information," he continued. "She hadn't mentioned any Emmaline McCoy, so I put the letter in my briefcase, thinking I'd deal with it later."

"How did you find me?"

"Last week, I had to meet with a colleague near Justice Bay. I decided to take a side trip and have a look around. I stopped at the bakery for coffee and asked the owner if she recognized your name. She told me about your shop."

I stared hard at him. "Did you follow me to the cemetery?"

He offered a sheepish nod. "Once I got there, I realized I didn't even know what you looked like. The pollen in the woods triggered an asthma attack. I couldn't find my inhaler, so I returned to the car for a spare from the glove box. I felt sick and ridiculous, so I drove home."

"Why did you come back today?" I asked, still skeptical.

He lowered his gaze as he spoke. "I told you. I got a shock when I saw Lydie's obituary in the *San Francisco Chronicle*. The paper listed you as her niece. I don't know why, but I just had to give you what may have been the last letter she wrote."

Arthur watched us from behind the Cassandra sign inside the shop. I gave him the thumbs-up sign, and he resumed chatting with the female customer.

I feared what might be inside that envelope. I could have waited until later to read it privately, but I slid my finger under the flap and inched it open.

The stationery was from a hotel in Kathmandu. I was confused and disappointed when the note stated: "As glaciers move over land, they collect rock and sediment, which they embed into the ice, leaving it scarred with striations, also called striae." That mini white paper on what rock striations tell us about the direction of glacial flow included a rousing description of the soil composition at the base of the Himalayas. If I hadn't recognized Lydie's handwriting, I might have thought somebody else wrote that humdrum information.

I glanced up to see Seamus Murphy staring at me in anticipation.

"It's just a few notes from her trip," I said, "but thank you for your trouble."

His face sagged in disappointment. "Would you let me know when the memorial service is? I'd like to be there."

I hadn't planned one, which created significant guilt. I avoided answering the question and instead invited Murphy to lunch.

"Another time." His smile appeared tentative but warm. "I have to get back to the city."

After Seamus Murphy left, I remained at the table, processing this latest information. The day Seamus Murphy had come to the cemetery looking for me, my heightened senses told me my life depended on learning his identity. Now I understood that the red inhaler cover he'd dropped in the woods didn't mean Murphy was a threat to me. The real danger pointed to the information I had yet to learn.

Chapter Thirty

The overcast sky had transformed into a light mist that settled on my face, bringing with it the aroma of the sea. I went back inside to find Arthur pacing the floor.

"What did that professor guy want? And what about that envelope he handed you?"

Until I uncovered more information, I didn't want to inflict my concerns on Arthur, so I repeated what I'd told Seamus: the letter contained information about rocks and soil. No further questions were possible because Maddie bolted through the door a moment later.

"Cooper's boat is gone." She sounded breathless, as if she'd been running. "What happened?"

I wheeled around to face her. "I don't know, Maddie. He didn't tell me."

She put her arms around me. "Don't worry, Em. It's probably nothing. Maybe Cooper just went for a sail. Have you checked with Walter?"

"I called him. No answer."

"Keep trying," she said, patting my back. "Walter is in town. I walked past the garden store earlier and saw him buying white roses."

There could be a million reasons he bought those flowers, but only one that made sense to me. Walter loved my aunt and still mourned her loss. A few days ago, I'd found wilted white roses on the ground in front of Lydie's niche. I suspected Walter had left them. Perhaps he planned to do it again.

"I think I know where he is," I said.

"Good." Maddie gave me one last hug before walking toward the door. "I have to pick up my dad's prescription at the pharmacy. Let me know as soon as you hear anything."

After Maddie left, I told Arthur I had to run an errand. He acknowledged my departure with a nod.

Lydie's death had swept me into a whirlwind of chaos and grief. So much had happened since that awful day. I'd found a mysterious photo of a man in profile sitting in a parked car by an oleander bush, a broken Mercedes side mirror near the spot where a driver had run down my aunt, and a service department where the owner may have gone for repairs. I'd also learned that my aunt and Walter had been in love, probably since they'd met.

I drove to the cemetery and found Walter sitting on the stone bench. He was bent over, his forearms on his knees and his head in his hands. I stood motionless, not wanting to interrupt his meditation. A fresh bouquet of white roses lay near the columbarium niche where Lydie's ashes lay.

"What do you want, Emmaline?" His words sounded strained.

"I'm sorry to interrupt, but I have something to ask you."

He leaned back against the bench. "If you want to know why Cooper left, call him yourself."

"It's not about Cooper."

"Got it," he said. "I see you gave up on your little flirtation."

He was angry with me, but I didn't know why. "Is that what you think? A flirtation?"

"Not for him."

I pulled up my hood as the mist turned into a light rain. "My feelings for Cooper are none of your business."

He jabbed his finger at me. "That's where you're wrong. He's family. That makes it my business. You should have told him you were in a relationship."

My guilt mingled with defensiveness. "I did tell Cooper. I also told him it ended before I came to Justice Bay. Maybe you should have told me things, too, like how you and Pearl conspired to sabotage the house sale and that you and Lydie were an item. I had to drag it out of you."

He flinched as if my directness had slashed through the protective shell he'd worked so hard to cultivate. "I get the impression you're toying with Cooper. I thought you two might be good for each other, but he deserves better."

His words stung. I wondered if they were true. Maybe I sought Cooper's attention without the responsibilities of a relationship, but I didn't think it was that simple.

My fists clenched. "You're wrong."

"Fine. I'm wrong. What do you want?"

Now was not the time to argue about Cooper, so I stuffed my anger into that compartment of my brain labeled—to be continued.

Walter conceded no space as I sat on the bench next to him. I ignored his antagonism and held out the letter.

"What's that?" he asked.

"That's what I wanted to talk to you about."

He unfolded the paper. The furrows on his brow deepened as he read. "Where did you get this?"

I told him about the visit from Seamus Murphy. "Does that sound like something my aunt wrote?"

He didn't respond.

"Walter?"

Several more seconds went by before he answered. "It's possible. Lydie pursued a lot of interesting data."

Sprinkles of rain collected on Walter's head and rolled down his face. He wiped them away with the back of his hand.

I told Walter about Lydie's reaction at the San Francisco airport and that Seamus Murphy thought she'd seen something or someone that frightened her. His focus had shifted from anger over my relationship with Cooper to concern about my aunt.

"What do you think this letter means?" I asked.

"I have no idea, but I wouldn't read too much into it."

"Are you sure you're not keeping something from me?"

He rubbed his eyes with his palms. "Life doesn't come with assurances, Emmaline. You, of all people, should know that by now."

"Did Cooper tell you I kissed him," I asked, "and that he pulled away?"

He rolled his eyes. "You mean that 'rebound guy' boloney? Yeah, he told me. Look, do me a favor."

"Okay," I said, wondering what he had in mind.

"If you have feelings for Cooper, now's the time to let him know. Call him. Today."

I scoffed. "You think a call from me will make Cooper turn his boat around and head back to Justice Bay?"

His expression softened as he stood to leave. "Yes, that's what I think. If you don't do it for yourself, do it for me." A faint smile appeared on his lips. "I already miss his cooking."

Walter headed for the parking lot. Over his shoulder, he said, "Good luck."

I sat in my car with the window cracked open, inhaling the aroma of wet earth. Warmth radiated through my body as I realized that Walter was cheering for us despite all his huffing and puffing. I searched for the right words to say to Cooper, but "I hope you're coming back soon 'cause I have a hankering for chowder" didn't fit the occasion. I could leave it vague with a simple "we need to talk," but those words were conversation killers, especially for men.

Or I could simply tell him the truth. I've never cared about anybody like this before. You wowed me the first time we met at the restaurant when you stood to greet me. I love that you fixed the sticky door at the shop without being asked. I love that you stayed with me when I fell and bumped my head. I love the way your hair sticks up after a shower. I love your sunburned nose and the softness of your flannel shirts. I love that you don't have a clue how sexy you are. I love that you love your Uncle Walter as much as I love my Aunt Lydie. I love that you're intelligent and funny and that you bought Boo a cat tree. I love being with you, and I want you to come home.

That soliloquy gave me the courage to call Cooper's number. My stomach flipped at the sound of his voice. "Cooper?"

"Emma." His response sounded subdued.

I swallowed hard and forced out the words. "Where are you? When are you coming back?"

He inhaled a deep breath and let it out slowly. "I have some things to deal with first. I'll let you know."

In the background, a woman's voice asked. "Who are you talking to?"

Cooper put his hand over the phone to silence his reply, but I could hear his words nonetheless. "Just a friend."

Just a friend. Those were the words Brad said about Mindy-from-accounting. I sat immobile. My left hand gripped the phone, and my right clenched the emergency brake like I was in early-onset rigor mortis. Cooper must have ended the call, but I didn't remember when because I'd lost all mental acuity.

The rain had begun to fall in earnest now. Heavy drops pelted the windshield with a hard, staccato beat. Somehow, I pulled myself together enough to slip the key into the ignition. Moments ago, my heart had been bursting with words meant for Cooper, but now I felt empty and vulnerable, knowing he would never hear them.

Chapter Thirty-One

My mind emptied on the drive back into town, and Bette Midler stepped into the vacuum, singing that love is only for the lucky and the strong. I'd never been lucky in love; that hadn't changed. I no longer expected to have a romantic relationship with Cooper, but I didn't want to lose his friendship.

I mustered the strength to tackle a few loose ends, like who entered my house and moved the Dzi stone from the kitchen to my aunt's bedroom. I had no idea if that person had anything to do with Lydie's death, but I had to find out.

My aunt bought the cottage from Dwight Banfield over twenty years ago and used it as a getaway retreat before she retired and moved to Justice Bay full-time. John Osgood helped the Banfields move out of the house and dispose of things they couldn't take. Osgood might still have a key. If not, maybe he inadvertently left one in a drawer when he sold his mother's furniture. The locksmith changed the house locks, but I still planned to question Osgood.

I must have looked wet and fatigued when I walked into the shop because Arthur rushed over and placed his hands on my upper arms. "Are you okay?"

I nodded, not wanting to burden him with my disappointment about Cooper's "just a friend" comment. "Has John Osgood called about the Dzi stone?"

"No, I meant to follow up this afternoon."

"I need to ask him about something else," I said. "I'll drop by his store and check it out."

Arthur pressed his lips together in a straight line. "Is that a good idea? He doesn't like you."

"If I'm going to stay in Justice Bay, I have to make peace with him."

"Do you want me to ride shotgun?"

I shook my head. "I can handle this. I'll be back in a few minutes."

Osgood's antique store sat on the same side of the street as Cassandra's, but at the end of the block. When I got there, I peeked through the window. There were no customers inside. As I stepped over the threshold with the backpack slung over my shoulder and the Dzi stone inside, the aroma of lemon oil and cinnamon engulfed me.

Most antique retailers had shelves of inventory stacked to the ceiling, but not Osgood. He'd arranged the furniture in cozy groupings that made me feel like sitting down for a chat and a cup of tea. Other items on display accessorized the settings, including vases, silver trays, and candlesticks, oil paintings, and a glass-covered table with a small but exquisite selection of antique jewelry.

Osgood sat at a small desk toward the back of the store. Based on our first contentious meeting, I half expected to find him twirling a Snidely Whiplash mustache and cackling maniacally. Instead, he looked deep in thought as he hunched over a stack of invoices.

He acknowledged my presence with a frown. "May I help you?"

Haughtiness might be the birthright of a high-end antique dealer, but I wondered if humble reverence for the work of artists and woodcarvers might be more appealing to customers.

"What a great store," I said, opening the drawer of a writing armchair that begged for a sit-down with a pen and paper. "Love your furniture arrangements."

He looked bewildered by the compliment. "Despite your assistant's phony ploy, I'm guessing that Dzi stone belonged to your aunt, and you're here to check if I have a buyer. I may, but she wants to see the merchandise before she writes a check."

"That was quick," I said, running my hand over the polished surface of a Chippendale chest. "What did the buyer offer?"

Osgood grimaced as he scanned the wood for greasy fingerprints. "Five hundred dollars, minus my commission, of course."

He'd low-balled his offer on Lydie's vintage decoy. He'd also scammed his mother and stepfather out of revenue from the sale of their household goods. If he valued the stone at five hundred, I guessed it was worth far more than that. Before I decided to sell, I'd call Seamus Murphy. A professor of Far East studies must know somebody who could give me a second opinion on a Tibetan artifact.

"Great," I said. "I'll think about it."

He aimed his nose at the ceiling and frowned. "If the sale doesn't go through, I'll bill you for an appraisal fee."

"I wouldn't expect anything less from you," I said, keeping my tone pleasant. I wanted to say I assume that the bill will include a detailed report on your research, recent comparable sales, and any other information that went into the five-hundred-dollar asking price. But I didn't want to alienate him. Osgood didn't respond, so I continued. "By the way, I'm staying in town and keeping the shop open. Just curious, what's the customer mix between local and out-of-towners?"

"My customer database is none of your business. All I'll say is my clients extend far beyond Justice Bay. My store is well-known all over the country. Traffic on my website is off the charts. My ads run in high-end design magazines and on architectural websites."

John Orson Osgood came off as a braggart. I figured the way to his heart was to plump up his ego. "Maddie Balister told me about the eye-catching ads you design. She said they were brilliant. That's high praise from a New York graphic designer."

"My shop would have an even higher profile if Justice Bay had a hotel. When I had my store in San Francisco, I could fill the Fairmont ballroom with my shows. I could do the same here if buyers had a place to stay."

"Funny you should mention that." I leaned in and lowered my voice to a stage whisper. "I just spoke with Kevin Medwin. He and his mom plan to develop the old sawmill into a boutique hotel."

Osgood's face flushed with excitement. "I hope she'll preserve the flavor of the 1920s when Halyard built the place. I have a few pieces from that era that would be perfect in the lobby."

"Maybe you should call Sylvia."

He gazed into the distance, dreaming of ballrooms full of paying customers. "Maybe I will."

Now that I'd boosted Osgood's mood with visions of a new hotel, I moved on to Lydie's house key.

"I went to visit Dwight Banfield yesterday," I said, keeping my tone casual. "I had no idea you were related."

His good mood evaporated. "Only by marriage. As I'm sure you discovered, he was my mother's husband."

Osgood had never accepted the second marriage. I wondered what made him dislike a lovely man like Dwight Banfield.

"I wanted to let Dwight know the place remained in good hands. He told me you helped dispose of items from their house."

"So what? My mother couldn't take everything." He scrunched up his face as if my presence in his store was distasteful. "I sold her dining room set, dishes, several area rugs, small appliances, and other household goods. I can't remember who bought them. I kept my mother's Georg Jensen silverware because it's a simple design that fits my décor. I donated a carload of items to a charity in Cedarbrook and paid somebody to haul the rest to the dump."

"I'm sure the Banfields appreciated your help," I said. "Did you sell the items locally?"

"It was a long time ago. What difference does it make now?"

I picked up a sommelier's cup and pretended to be blasé. "I asked Pearl Potts to sell my aunt's house. I've since changed my mind, but she kept a key when my aunt bought the place from your mom and Dwight. Just curious if you realized that."

"I didn't know, but I'm not surprised. That woman is a dingbat."

"Is it possible anybody else kept a key to the house, or maybe you accidentally left one in an item you sold?"

"If you believe I still have a key, you are off base. I tagged all keys with a number and the address so I wouldn't lose track." He paused as if his mind had drifted into an unpleasant memory. "I think Pearl had Dwight's key. I had my mom's. But I can't be sure. Dwight dumped all the responsibility on me. I didn't live in Justice Bay back then. I had to sleep on a cot in their living room and prepare the house for sale. After your aunt bought the place, Pearl might have made a key for your aunt and kept the one she had. I could have given her my mom's key, or I might have thrown it away. I just don't remember."

Osgood's confusion may have caused his mind to wander because if he was lying, it was an Oscar-worthy performance.

"That's understandable. It must have been a difficult time for you."

He tapped his pen on the desk, ignoring my comment. "I just remembered something else. They left a large ornate bureau in the dining room where my mother kept table linens. Not many people these days have room for furniture like that. It sat in my store for a year before it finally sold."

"Who bought the bureau?" My pulse quickened as I waited for his answer. But a part of me had already solved that mystery.

He settled back into the chair and crossed his arms. "Sylvia Medwin."

A cold chill swirled around me as I remembered Medwin's maid removing luncheon napkins and placemats from that bureau. In the past, I'd speculated that somebody might have found Lydie's house key inside a drawer of the Banfields' discarded furniture. Osgood said he'd labeled all the keys with the address. Even if Sylvia Medwin had found a tagged key in the bureau, no magical thinking explained why she would use it to wander around inside my aunt's house. Except I'd learned over time that sometimes nothing is what it seems.

"I saw that bureau in the castle's dining room when I went there for lunch," I said. "It's lovely."

"I suppose if you're into heavy design." He picked up an invoice from the stack on his desk. "Let me know about the Dzi stone."

I left Osgood's store and headed back to the shop.

When I walked into Cassandra's, I said, "Arthur, we need a website."

"Easy-peasy," Arthur said. "I used one of those online sites to create one for my temp service. We should also ask whoever runs the city webpage to add us to their list of local businesses."

"Brilliant idea."

He smiled. "I'll get right on it."

I called Seamus Murphy and asked him about getting an appraisal for the Dzi stone. He promised to check with his friend, a museum curator of Far East artifacts. For the rest of the afternoon, Arthur used my laptop to work on our website while I helped customers. At around five, we closed for the day.

The sun had already set when I entered the driveway and observed the moon illuminating the Rapunzel turret. I'd moved most of the collectibles from the garage to Cassandra's, so I parked inside next to Lydie's Beetle. I glanced toward the front porch and saw a cardboard box marked with the Fortuna Cruise Lines logo on the front steps. I closed the garage door and walked over to investigate.

Once I got inside, I opened the container and found the personal items from my work desk. My feelings of loss over Cooper's abrupt dismissal of me as "just a friend" intensified as I stared at the remains of a ten-year career reduced to the contents of a small brown box: My gargoyle bookends. A vintage copy of *Europe on Five Dollars a Day* and *Two Years Before the Mast*, a book I'd never opened but intended to read someday. The box also included a collection of framed photos—me posing with travel agents on a familiarization AKA fam cruise to Ensenada, and me at the finish line of my first 5k run with my skinny legs and sweaty honey-colored ponytail.

Unloading all the items left me drained. Boo jumped inside the empty box and claimed it as her own. I turned the lights out and propped myself against the couch pillows, staring at the moonlight on the bay. I remembered all the strange events I'd experienced since my aunt died. I'd found no apparent connection between them. Yet, I couldn't shake the feeling that someone guided me on a paranormal scavenger hunt searching for clues associated with the color red. If I kept following the trail, it would lead me to the person who killed my aunt.

I must have dozed off because I woke up in total darkness to the sound of scratching at the front door. I bolted upright. My breathing accelerated when I realized somebody was trying to get into the house with a key that no longer fit the lock.

Chapter Thirty-Two

I'd parked my car in the garage, and the house lights were off. Whoever was outside didn't anticipate I'd be at home. If I'd been in my apartment in L.A., I would have called 911. With Chief Greene in charge of the Justice Bay Police Department, I dismissed the thought as counterproductive.

A cloud cover obscured the moon, but I could see that the intruder wore a black hooded sweatshirt. I rolled off the couch, planning my next move. All the windows on the main floor with a sightline to the landing would also expose my position. I crept upstairs to the office and peeked out the window. I doubted the new lock could be defeated, but I couldn't just stand by and wait for them to try another entry point.

I chose the only reasonable maneuver and set my phone on video mode. Startled people generally look toward the source of a threat. If I shouted something menacing, the person at the door might look up so I could see his or her face. When that happened, I'd start taping.

I banged on the window and shouted, "I changed the locks!"

Instead of looking at me, the intruder turned and ran down the driveway toward the main road and disappeared into the darkness, leaving me with a useless video.

I flooded the house with lights as random thoughts circulated through my head. I recalled that vision at the restaurant with Cooper when I saw my aunt looking out the window at a shadowy figure, similar to what I'd just experienced. I felt unnerved but relieved that I'd had the foresight to change the locks. That wouldn't be enough for someone bent on breaking into the house in the future, so I searched online for home security cameras and alarm systems. There were several that I could set up myself or with Arthur's help, but I'd need a professional installer for the more sophisticated equipment.

It boosted my confidence to take action, but I still couldn't face going to bed, so I forced myself to focus on my start-up business. Helen Marché had to file legal documents for Cassandra's Collectibles and Arthur's employee paperwork. I had to set up a business account at the bank, check into getting insurance for the shop, and do a million other things. I'd also have to buy cleaning supplies and, most importantly, a coffeemaker. I'd drop by the hardware store in the morning before work and get everything I needed.

After that, I wandered around the house until I stumbled across a black metal collapsible table perfect for holding a coffeemaker and cups. I pulled a couple of placemats from a kitchen drawer to complete the ensemble.

Nothing in the refrigerator looked appealing. C'est Shells might still be open for dinner, even this late. Maddie would likely be there. Instead, I barricaded Boo and the cat box with me behind the door to my room before turning out the light.

* * *

The following day, I loaded the collapsible table and placemats into the car and headed downtown. Balister's Hardware sat at the end of the block across the street from Osgood's antique store. I parked the Audi out front for easy loading of the supplies I planned to buy. I loved snooping through hardware stores as much as browsing through gift shops, so I looked forward to seeing what Maddie had on the shelves.

As I stepped inside, an odd swirl of anticipation and wariness overtook me. It had been a while since I'd visited the store, but not much had changed, including the familiar four rows of shelving. A self-service copy machine stood in a corner near the front cash register. Maddie worked alone at the counter. She looked up from the *New York Times* and waved.

"Hey, Em. You're out and about early this morning."

"I need a few things," I said, "like a coffeemaker for the shop and a home security system for the house."

She laughed. "You're not in Los Angeles anymore, girl. You're in Justice Bay. Most people around here don't even lock their doors." She came around the counter and hugged me. "But you're in luck with your coffeemaker problem. We have two on the shelf. Same brand. Different colors. If you take the Big Bird yellow unit off my hands, I'll give you a discount."

"I wasn't joking, Maddie. Somebody tried to break into the house last night."

Her eyes widened. "Did you call the police?"

"No, because it wouldn't do any good. Chet Greene already thinks I'm a pest. Nobody got inside. He'd just say no big deal."

A noise came from behind one of the aisles. I hadn't realized anybody else was in the store. I looked at Maddie.

"Sorry," I whispered. "I didn't mean to scare your customers."

"Nothing you say would scare this customer." She nodded toward someone standing behind me.

I turned. Cooper held a wrench and some kind of filter. I sensed that same conflicting energy I'd experienced when I walked into the store.

"Cooper," I said, aiming for nonchalance. "You're back. I didn't see your boat."

He looked as surprised to see me as I was to see him. "I got in late last night, too tired to anchor. So, I tied up Brief Encounter at the fuel dock."

"Ooh-la-la," Maddie said, batting her eyelashes. "Sounds kind of kinky."

Cooper ignored her comment. He set the tools on the counter and turned to me. "Did I hear you say you had a break-in?"

"Attempted." I walked over to the shopping carts and separated one from the herd. "Maddie, where do I find the coffeemakers?"

She glanced from Cooper's confused frown to my tight-lipped smile. "Aisle three."

Cooper's energy swirled around me as I checked out the inventory. The nearest shopping mall was in Cedarbrook, so the store had an eclectic array of items for sale to accommodate those customers who didn't like straying too far from home. Aside from the standard mom-and-pop hardware store merchandise, they also had everything from motor oil to fishing gear, boat supplies, and funky T-shirts and hoodies. I picked up a small pack of white cocktail napkins with blue anchors, thinking they'd look good on Cooper's boat. I returned them to the shelf at the last minute because he wouldn't likely invite me aboard again.

Arthur had been using a rag to dust the shelves, so when I found the perfect feather duster, I dropped it into the cart before making my way to the appliance section. The black coffeemaker seemed like a reasonable choice. The mustard yellow model struck me as the brainchild of a well-meaning product designer who failed to read the room. That made me love it all the more. I pulled the box off the shelf and loaded it into the cart, along with a pound of coffee, filters, paper cups, sugar cubes, and a pack of stir sticks. In a small cooler against the back wall, I found a pint of half-and-half. It would spoil without refrigeration, but I didn't care. Sometimes, you just have to live for the moment. I waited until Cooper left before returning to the counter.

"What in the world was that all about?" Maddie asked.

I handed her my credit card. "Not sure what you mean."

"You just gave Cooper the brush-off. Why? I thought you liked him." Maddie scanned the items in my cart.

"I don't have time to discuss this right now. I have to get to work."

"Seriously, Em, I don't know what's happening with you, but don't screw this up." She put the smaller items and the receipt in a paper bag.

The last thing I needed was a lecture. "Thanks, Maddie. Talk to you later." I grabbed my purchases but paused before leaving. "By the way, I need a basket for the Schwinn. Can you order one?"

"I'll look into it."

When I got to the car, my muscles tensed. A frowning Cooper leaned against the passenger-side door with his arms crossed.

"I'm sorry I couldn't talk when you called yesterday," he said.

"No need to explain," I said, loading the shop supplies into the trunk before returning to where he stood. "After all, I'm just a friend." I used air quotes around "just a friend," pretending to be amused.

He glanced up at the sky and sighed. "Ah, now I get why you're upset. Just so you know, I met with the managing partner of my old law firm. I don't share personal information during a business discussion."

"I guess it got too late to call me back."

"It was late," he said, "and I'd already headed home. What did you want to tell me?"

In a voice gravelly with emotion, I said, "That I'd already reached indifference way before I met you."

He uncrossed his arms, studying my expression. My confession resonated because he stepped close enough to take my hand. "I'd like to hear the details…" he said with a tentative smile, "…I think. How about tonight at dinner?"

"At Walter's?"

He pulled me closer. "No, just the two of us."

I felt hyper-aware of his body so close to mine. "We could meet at my place."

"How about you come to my boat? I'll pick you up in the dinghy. Six o'clock."

"Then I can't leave when I want to."

He flashed an amused smile. "Let's just play it by ear."

I don't recall who broke physical contact first. All I remember is my skin tingling as I stood on the sidewalk, watching Cooper disappear around a corner.

Arthur was at the shop when I arrived. He loved the collapsible table and the feather duster, but the sight of the yellow coffeemaker sent him over the moon.

"Let's fire up Colonel Mustard and celebrate."

And thus, our coffeemaker had an official name. We made a toast with our paper cups after the first brew like we were ushering in a new year—not exactly a new year, but a new era for both of us. We sat for a few minutes sipping coffee and discussing sales and pricing philosophy before Arthur returned to work on our new website.

All I could think about was my upcoming dinner with Cooper. Despite my difficulty concentrating, I called Helen Marché to get her started on the official paperwork for the business and Arthur's employment. She told me I'd need a city permit since the store had shifted from a pop-up to permanent. Arthur and I had worked nearly every day of the last two weeks, so I told him to take Monday off. For the rest of the day, I felt hopeful about the future.

At six that night, I stood on the beach holding a bottle of wine and waiting for Cooper to pick me up. I'd filled Boo's food and water bowls. Before leaving the house, I gave her extra hugs to tide her over until I returned. Since dinner was a special occasion, I'd put on one of my new outfits, jeans, and an apricot Henley-style T-shirt with tiny blue flowers. I refreshed my makeup and spritzed myself with eau de toilette from Lydie's dresser, *Un Jardin Sur La Lagune*, a light fragrance by Hermes that reminded me of a summer day. I'd also ditched the ponytail and let my honey-colored hair go wild.

Cooper had moved his boat from the fuel dock back to the anchorage in front of Walter's place. I watched the dinghy's navigation lights leave the mother ship and move toward the beach. After the bow drifted onto the pebbly shore, I handed him the wine bottle and jumped in, noticing his weathered boat shoes—the mark of a true sailor.

Once we boarded the sailboat, he gestured for me to sit on a cockpit bench decorated with teal cushions and a couple of green bean-bag pillows.

"What can I get you to drink?" he asked.

"Wine, I guess."

"How about a Dark and Stormy?"

"I have no idea what that is, but okay."

"It's a sailor's drink," he said, "dark rum, ginger beer, and a squeeze of lime. I promise you'll be a fan."

"Sounds more like a pirate's drink."

He smiled. "Maybe that, too."

He went below and returned with two highball glasses filled with dark liquid. We sat across from each other, separated by a small teak table. The clouds had dissipated. With Justice Bay so far away from big city lights, brilliant stars filled the sky, something I seldom observed in Los Angeles.

"Why were you meeting with the managing partner?" I asked.

He sipped his drink, eyeing me over the rim of the glass. "Christine called out of the blue and asked me to come to San Francisco. I told her if she'd drive to Mendocino, I would sail down to meet her."

"That's a long way to go for a meeting."

"It's about forty nautical miles, an easy one-day trip. I hadn't had the boat out in a while, so I considered it a pleasant exercise."

I zipped my coat up to my chin against the chilly air. "What did she want?"

"The firm is bleeding attorneys and staff. To reverse that trend, she knows the corporate culture has to change. That's why I left, so I agreed with her."

"And she wants you to come back and help make change happen."

He didn't waste words. "Yes."

"What did you tell her?" I held my breath and waited for his answer.

"That I'd think about it."

An involuntary shiver rocked my body, not from the chilly air but from uncertainty. "Big decision."

"You look cold." He stood and went below deck, returning with a blanket. He motioned for me to join him on the opposite bench. I sat between his legs with my head on his chest. He pulled the blanket over both of us. I felt content in his arms, even though I suspected we looked like a two-person bobsled team training for the Olympics.

While I searched for the Big Dipper, he pointed out constellations with unfamiliar names—Cepheus, Cassiopeia, and Draco. We finished our drinks, and I declared my fangirl allegiance to Dark and Stormy.

"Are you hungry?" he asked.

I hated to abandon bobsled training, but I followed him below deck to the warmth of a polished teak interior and candlelight flickering from a gimbaled brass lantern. Soft romantic music played on the stereo, including contemporary R&B, soul, and classic rock selections. The aroma of garlic and fresh basil filled the room. Cooper had set the table with placemats and cloth napkins. On a hook in the tiny galley hung a chef's apron printed with the words, *Don't be afraid to take whisks*.

I nodded toward the apron. "Cute."

He rolled his eyes. "A birthday gift from my mom. She's never met a pun she didn't like."

"The same for Lydie." I pulled the apron off its hook and placed the loop over Cooper's head. "Is your mom a good cook?"

He lifted his arms so I could reach around his waist and find the loose ends. "My mother is a terrible cook. Even she says so." He didn't take his eyes off me as I took perhaps a little too long groping with the ties behind his back.

I brought them to the front and tied them into a bow. "What do you want me to do next?"

He hesitated as if looking for subtext before removing a green salad and a bottle of dressing from the refrigerator. He handed me a set of wood-handled tongs. "Have at it."

I still worried he might choose San Francisco over Justice Bay, so I steered the conversation to more neutral subjects as we ate salad and a chicken and mushroom linguine dish that put Chef Gabriel to shame. After we finished eating, Cooper got up to collect plates while I gathered the napkins and placemats.

"There's something else I wanted to tell you when I called yesterday," I said.

He wiped his hands on a towel and turned to face me. "Shoot."

"I like you—a lot. Does that scare you?"

He handed me a dishtowel and smiled. "Only if you invent a pet name for me."

I stacked the dried plates on the counter. "Never."

I glanced into the blue eyes of a man who was a beautiful human being by every measure. I calculated our relative heights and considered burying my face in his neck to inhale the fragrance of lavender soap and fresh air. But as waves slapped against the hull and wind whistled through the rigging, reality intruded.

I thought of all my failed relationships, all the miscalculations and hasty decisions that ended in disaster. I listened to Whitney Houston singing from the stereo, and I...yi...yi...will always love yoooo-ooo-ooo and reminded myself of a painful truth—sometimes always wasn't forever. Neither experience nor intuition could predict my future with Cooper, but tonight, I would err on the side of caution because, in my heart, I understood he was worth the wait.

"I should go," I whispered.

He studied me for a long time before responding. "Whatever you want."

Cooper followed me to the cockpit and leaned over the rail, pulling the dinghy painter toward the swim step. Tan shorts exposed the golden hairs on his bare legs, luminescent in the glow from the deck lights.

The short, awkward dinghy ride back to my place ended when we reached the beach. Cooper jumped out and guided the boat onto the shore. As soon as I planted my feet on terra firma, I turned toward him, not wanting to leave with any bad feelings between us.

"When will I see you again?"

"Maybe tomorrow night. Maddie asked a few guys to come over after she closes the hardware store to help move shelves around. I can drop by after that if it's not too late. We can talk about tonight."

"It won't be too late."

I watched him return to the boat and then walked into the house with Whitney's song about "always love" playing on a loop through my head.

Cooper's absence left a void. I went inside the house and found Boo sleeping on Lydie's bed. She let out a banshee meow to show her displeasure with my absence and then left the room in a huff. Still unsettled by the attempted break-in, I inspected every room in the house to assure myself nothing had been disturbed while I visited Cooper's boat.

I'd rejected the clueless housekeeper theory for lack of evidence, but at least one alternative was possible. Lydie hid something important in her house nobody had yet found—maybe a clue that led to the driver of the murder car. If so, the burglar would likely return to look again. I shook off a chill and headed to bed.

Chapter Thirty-Three

As I made coffee the following morning, I glimpsed my reflection in the kitchen window. I'd fallen asleep without removing my makeup. The so-called waterproof mascara had smeared under my eyes. The glamorous wild hair I envisioned the night before had turned into a honey-colored mushroom cloud. Instead of a sexy beast, I looked like a radioactive raccoon.

I'd given Arthur the day off, so I had to get ready for work, but my mind kept returning to the night before with Cooper: stargazing, dinner, and Whitney Houston. While Boo ate breakfast, I showered, swept my hair into a ponytail, put on jeans and a T-shirt, and scrubbed off the old makeup and reapplied it. After replenishing Boo's food and water bowls, I cleaned her box. Then I pedaled the Schwinn into town.

I unlocked the door and rolled the bike inside the shop. After turning on the lights, I booted up the laptop to see Arthur's progress on the website. It had potential even in its barebones state. I used my cell to snap a few shots of Cassandra's exterior with Maddie's sign in the front window and took photos of the merchandise. The Shanghai panda had vanished from the shelf. Not that it mattered, but I wondered who'd bought it. I emailed the photos to Arthur to incorporate them into the site.

It was a slow Monday. People walked past the shop but didn't come in. I thought about calling Cooper, but we'd only been apart for a few hours. Contacting him so soon might be construed as clingy.

While waiting for my first customer, I used the new duster to tidy up. When I finished, I sat in Lydie's reading chair and opened the latest Harry

Bosch novel. At some point, my mind wandered. In my reading experience, detectives always solved crimes by tracking the movements of victims and killers. That could be a worthwhile idea, so I found a scratchpad and began jotting down what I'd learned about the last days of my aunt's life.

Shortly after retiring from Spellman Polk & Kimble, Lydie went to Tibet. Not unusual. She loved to travel. While there, she acquired several items, including a Dzi stone and a Tibetan Buddhist prayer book.

On her flight home, she sat next to Seamus Murphy, a professor of Far East studies. Lydie usually slept on long flights, but the two initiated a friendly conversation at some point, which continued over coffee after arriving at the San Francisco airport Friday morning. Murphy said she appeared frightened by something and left in a hurry, but nobody knew the source of that fear. It could have been a human or a psychic vision. After Lydie left, Murphy found notes she'd left behind about soil and glaciers that could have been a coded message or, in mystery novel speak, a red herring.

I assumed my aunt drove home from the airport. Justice Bay is around two hundred fifty miles north of San Francisco. Public transportation is iffy, so she always left her car in the airport parking garage for quick access when she returned from a trip. She preferred to drive home on the day of her arrival. It wouldn't have been my choice, but a four-plus-hour drive meant nothing to her. If she'd followed her usual routine, including stops for fuel and coffee, she would have arrived back in Justice Bay late Friday afternoon.

My brain needed a break. I plugged in Colonel Mustard and brewed a pot of coffee while the aroma of hot water filtering through fresh grounds made me think of better times.

I grabbed my coffee and returned to Lydie's reading chair to resume working on my timeline. According to the date stamp on the photos I'd found hidden in the music box, my aunt snapped that picture of a man in a car parked near an oleander bush at the rest stop near her house at around five o'clock Friday. How odd. She must have been exhausted by then, so stopping ten minutes short of her front door made no sense unless she'd agreed to meet somebody or spotted someone she recognized. She hid those photos. Why? The man wasn't driving a Mercedes. What did that photo have to do with her death two days later?

Out of the corner of my eye, I observed a man peering through the front window. He wore a baggy blue jacket and an olive-green cuffed watch cap pulled low on his forehead. His hand sheltered his eyes like a sun visor, so I couldn't see his face. The outfit reminded me of a Halloween commando costume.

Several people had walked by Cassandra's since I'd opened the shop that morning. None of them stopped. I considered him a potential customer. I beckoned him inside. He immediately turned and hurried down the street. Some people didn't want to engage, but at least he could have waved back or shouted "just looking."

All that coffee on an empty stomach made me feel dizzy and disoriented, so I collapsed on the chair and closed my eyes. I flashed back to that vision I'd had at Walter's dining room table of my terrified aunt running through the woods.

Disjointed thoughts pinged inside my brain until a unifying theme of my aunt's final days again emerged—red. The phantom red ball rolling across the road where my aunt died, the red blouse she told Walter signified danger, and the red Mercedes. If only those random events would lead to concrete answers.

A call from Arthur interrupted my reverie.

"What's happening?" he asked. "Need me to come in?"

"Everything is fine. Enjoy your day off."

"Okay, but call if you get slammed. I'm only a bike ride away."

"Will do," I said. "By the way, the Shanghai panda is gone."

"I sold it to an older man wearing a green watch cap. He wasn't very chatty. He just paid for the panda and left."

The buyer sounded like the guy I'd seen looking through the window. Nothing inherently suspicious about that. At least, I didn't think so. Arthur and I talked for a moment or two before ending the call. I took the notebook and went outside, hoping passersby would see we were open. I sat at the wicker table and reread my notes. Despite my best intentions, nothing I'd written led me any closer to the whereabouts of that red Mercedes or who had been behind the wheel the night they killed my aunt.

Frustrated, I searched my brain for anything I'd missed about Lydie's activities when she left Spellman Polk & Kimble. That's when I remembered her retirement party in San Francisco the day before she left for Tibet. I'd planned to be there, but a crisis at work forced me to cancel at the last minute. So much had happened since arriving in Justice Bay that I'd forgotten about Kelly Hinson from the firm's benefits department and the photos she'd taken at the event.

For reasons I couldn't explain, my hands trembled as I pulled out my phone and opened Hinson's email.

Chapter Thirty-Four

A biting onshore breeze ushered in the aroma of brine as I sat at the wicker table and opened the email Kelly Hinson had sent. I clicked on the photo attachments and studied Lydie's retirement party pictures. They showed my aunt posing with various groups of people, Lydie alone on a dais with a microphone in her hand, and one near a decorated cake that read Happy Retirement on the hors d'oeuvres table. A sharp pang of guilt reminded me of the work-related crisis that had kept me from being there, the details I couldn't even remember.

I became so distracted by a car honking at a pigeon in the road that I almost scrolled past a photo of a room packed with people. Toward a far corner, I spotted Lydie with a middle-aged man. His hollowed-out cheeks made him look gaunt, and the combover only emphasized his thinning hair. His demeanor caught my attention as he jabbed his index finger at her face. Even in profile, I could see his open mouth shouting at her. Lydie showed no reaction as he hunched over her like a vulture appraising roadkill.

Nobody witnessed the argument except a woman in her early twenties standing nearby with her arms wrapped around her body, making her look wary and uncomfortable.

If the guy had a beef with my aunt, I needed to know his name. In our previous telephone conversation, Kelly offered an unconditional promise to help. I punched in her number to test her sincerity. She took my call immediately.

"Thank you for sending the party photos," I said. "Seeing them makes me doubly sorry I couldn't be there."

"It was a lovely event."

I didn't know how she'd react to my questions, so I burnished my pretext, AKA lying skills. "I didn't know many of Lydie's work friends, but I recognize the man standing with her in the photo marked Ballroom #3. I just can't remember his name. Bob something, right?"

"Let me pull up the file." She went silent for a few moments. "Here it is. That's Howard Valdis. He's one of our software engineers."

"Yes, that's it. Howard," I said in a silly-me tone. "He looks annoyed with Lydie like she snagged the last chicken wing off his plate."

During a long silence, I sensed Kelly weigh the consequences of elaborating. "There's a history between those two, and it has nothing to do with chicken wings."

"History? Now I'm intrigued."

"I shouldn't—"

I interrupted her mid-sentence. "Look, Kelly, don't worry. Anything you say is strictly between the two of us."

"Okay," she said, hesitating for a couple of beats. "About six months ago, multiple complaints started filtering into HR that Howard had come to work intoxicated. Lydie confronted him. He agreed to get counseling. We all thought he'd cleaned up his act, but he got drunk the night of the party, making a fool of himself. None of us wanted to ruin the evening by calling out his behavior, but it became intolerable. Lydie finally pulled him aside. He didn't appreciate the intervention. He stormed out of the room right after I took that picture."

"Is that Howard's wife standing behind him?"

"Sheila didn't come. He invited that woman as his guest. One of our employees told me she'd just graduated college with an engineering degree. Howard introduced her around to help with the job search."

I took a closer look at the woman in the photo. She wore large, dark-framed glasses that made her look nerdy and a turtle-neck sweater pulled up over the lower part of her face.

"Did she leave with him?"

"I don't know."

"Do you recall her name?"

"Not offhand. I could check if the woman is on the guest list if it's important."

"Thanks, Kelly. I'd appreciate that."

"I meant it when I told you we're here to help," she said. "Hold while I pull up the file."

A few moments later, Kelly came back on the line. "Her name is Grace Chin. No other information is listed."

Kelly had been forthcoming, so I continued with the pretext. "I hope Howard had a designated driver that night. If he were as buzzed as you say, I'd hate to hear that he dinged that beautiful red Mercedes of his."

Even over the phone, I sensed her discomfort.

"I have no idea if he drove himself home," she said, "and I doubt he owns a Mercedes. He doesn't seem the type. Why are you asking all these questions?"

I remained nonchalant. "No reason. I thought I remembered seeing Howard's car once, but I may have him mixed up with somebody else."

"Yes, I'm sure that's it." Her tone confirmed she now realized she'd said too much. "Sorry, but I have to ring off."

After we ended the call, I processed this new information. Howard Valdis had a drinking problem. Lydie had retired, but she still had clout at the company. Maybe he feared my aunt would tell his bosses he'd fallen off the wagon. He could get fired. People killed for less.

Except that didn't make sense. Anybody at the party that night could have ratted out Valdis's drunken bender to company poobahs. Current employees filled the room, including Kelly in benefits. It had to be something else between Valdis and my aunt. I just had to uncover the source of the conflict.

I needed to do a deep dive into Howard Valdis's background. I stood to go inside when I observed Abby Greene heading my way. My muscles tensed, wondering if she'd discovered her husband's affair and would find a way to blame me.

"Hey, Emma. I'm on my way to the hardware store. Need anything?"

Judging by her cheery demeanor, I assumed she didn't yet know about

CHAPTER THIRTY-FOUR

Chet and the Vampire Princess.

"Thanks, Abby. I'm good for now."

"I'm planning a birthday party for Chet this Saturday afternoon. I'd love for you to be there."

"Is it a surprise?" I hoped not, for Greene's sake and mine.

She winked. "Chet knows about it. We have an announcement. Hope you can make it."

Announcement. Abby acted too upbeat to be broadcasting a divorce. I wondered what it could be. They were already expecting a second baby, so maybe they'd planned one of those over-the-top gender reveal parties.

"Can I bring Cooper?"

"Walter's nephew? Sure. The more, the merrier." She waved and continued down the sidewalk.

After she left, a few customers wandered into the shop, but only one made a purchase. Monday turned into a total bust. At three-thirty, I slipped the laptop into my backpack and pedaled the Schwinn home.

I turned into the driveway, and as I got closer to the house, I noted Walter unloading firewood from the back of the Creamsicle and stacking it against the side of the garage. He stood by the tailgate, removing a pair of dusty work gloves. I braked a few feet away.

He glanced up and gave me a hypercritical stare. "You look different." He squinted, not taking his eyes off me. "What did you and Cooper do on that boat?"

"Not what you think."

He looked at me. I looked back. He slammed the tailgate closed. "Good."

The man was incorrigible, so I gave up the fight and changed the subject. "Thanks for the firewood."

He opened the driver's door. "Winter is coming. You have to prepare."

A chill crawled down my spine. Walter meant keeping the house warm, but his words sounded like a doomsday prophecy.

"Somebody tried to break into the house last night," I said. "I think they had a key. They couldn't open the door because I changed the locks."

He'd slid halfway inside the driver's seat when he jerked to a stop. He got out and stared at me. His body looked coiled and ready to strike. "Show me."

We walked to the front door, where I pointed out the scratches on the brass plate surrounding the lock. "It happened at night," I said. "I assume the person couldn't find the keyhole."

He sat on his heels and inspected the damage. "Those don't look like key marks. They're too thin and deep. A sharp instrument like a lock pick made them."

"Who other than locksmiths carry those?"

"Lots of people." He stood. "You have to report this, Emmaline. I'll call Chet Greene and ask him to add your house to nightly patrol rounds."

"How is he going to do that? Besides Greene, the department consists of Officer Kowalski and Pam, the records clerk."

"A volunteer squad of retired law enforcement officers patrol at night. It's an excuse to get together and trade war stories, but they know what to do if something goes sideways."

"Like a Protection Squad? Are you a member?"

He arched an eyebrow. "Stay close to your cell and call 911 if something else happens."

"I'll take that as a yes." I tilted my head and smiled. "Good."

I went inside and heard the sound of an object moving over hardwood floors—Boo playing handball with a water bottle cap. If history were an indicator, she would soon disappear the thing in a place undiscoverable by humans. Years from now, some archaeologists would find a secret stash of plastic bread clips, bottle caps, and cat toys inside the floor vents.

I removed the laptop from my backpack and set it on the kitchen island near my phone. I gazed at the crystal-encrusted cell cover I'd given Lydie for her birthday. She'd always considered Machu Picchu a spiritual place, so I closed my eyes and whispered, "Lydie, please send me a sign. Where should I look next?" I'd never made a habit of talking to myself, so I was surprised by the rush of energy it produced.

Before searching for information on Howard Valdis, I ran upstairs to the office and found a magnifying glass and a stack of blank paper for note-taking. Then I logged onto my computer.

I'd done many background checks on job applicants at Fortuna Cruise Lines, so I knew the drill. The company subscribed to a database with access to all sorts of information. I tried my password, but human resources had already flushed me from the system. I'd have to do this the hard way.

I typed Howard Valdis's name into the web browser search box. He had no social media presence except for a job search site. He'd listed academic degrees and his experience developing software programs for defense contractors and the military, but it didn't mention Spellman Polk & Kimble as his current employer. With his well-documented drinking problem, he might not want prospective employers to call for references before he could spin the story.

Valdis's wife's name was Sheila, according to Kelly Hinson. I found her on Facebook and scrolled through a year's worth of posts. It amazed me what people revealed about themselves on social media. Many messages were inspirational memes, like when something goes wrong in your life, just yell "plot twist" and move on. I made a mental note to pass that along to the Justice Bay Literary Society. Sheila had posted multiple photos of trips to Las Vegas with her husband. Another meme pictured a row of slot machines with the words, In the end, the machines always win, which made me think luck wasn't always on her side.

Approximately six months ago, her messages got darker. She posted a "feeling sad" message and another that read "traveling," to which she added, "to see my attorney." After that, she didn't post at all for an extended time.

There were signs things had gotten better recently. Sheila added photos of a kitchen remodel and a new designer handbag. She also posted a video of a renewal of the wedding vows ceremony. Howard's white dinner jacket hung on this thin frame. His sunken cheeks and wild, darting eyes made him look haggard and demented. His sad combover flopped onto the frosting roses when he leaned over to cut the wedding cake.

Sheila uploaded a photo of an unusual ring on the bathroom floor. It was rose gold inlaid with blue lapis. The caption read: Howie's lost so much weight, his wedding ring keeps falling off!

Even I could connect the dots. Howard Valdis had an alcohol problem, a gambling addiction, and a turbulent marriage. With all that stress, no wonder he'd lost weight.

I wanted to confirm my suspicions about their marriage problems, so I paid a fee to an online company that allowed access to public records. The extent of data collected on private citizens without their knowledge staggered me. I searched for Howard Valdis and found that Sheila had filed for divorce about six months before and memorialized her husband's dual addictions—gambling and alcohol—in those documents. Maybe that's why she'd dropped off social media. She had nothing positive to post during that time.

Sheila and Howard had no children, so there were no custody issues. At the time of the filing, they had been deeply in debt. Assets included a house with a mortgage, two older-model cars—no Mercedes, I noted—and a joint bank account with a balance of fewer than ten thousand dollars. They were also warring over a sad list of small items like pewter candlesticks, living room curtains, and a teapot with four cups. All the effort they'd devoted to marriage only to end up bickering over teacups.

That made me think of Brad. He still had my toaster oven. I'd considered it a long-term loan, but now I had no desire to see him or it again. I sincerely wished that every future toasted cheese sandwich he made would taste of betrayal. I took that as an omen and swore never to loan Cooper any small appliances—no use courting heartbreak over a milk frother.

I went to the veranda and sat on the porch swing to absorb what I'd learned about the two known confrontations between my aunt and Valdis. He'd been so angry during that final exchange that he left the event prematurely. I wondered what Lydie had said or done to enrage him like that.

I looked out at the bay. Cooper's boat was dark except for the anchor light. He'd promised to stop by when he finished helping Maddie move shelves. I glanced at my watch with a twinge of concern. I reached for my phone to call him when I heard a knock on the door.

It would have been logical to assume Cooper stood outside on the porch, but given everything that had happened over the past two weeks, I went inside, locking the French doors behind me. Then I texted him. Is that you at the door?

No response.

I tiptoed to the window to peek outside. My heart rate accelerated. A man built like a linebacker stood in the shadows. He appeared to be in his early forties with dark, close-cropped hair sprinkled with silver. I had no idea who he was or why he stood at my door.

Chapter Thirty-Five

I'd just grabbed my cell phone to call the police when I saw Cooper approaching the house in the Creamsicle. He rolled out of the pickup, exchanged a few words with the burly guy, and shook his hand.

Stunned and relieved, I opened the door.

Cooper glanced at me and smiled. "Emma, this is Zeke Digby. He's a friend of Walter's. Zeke is a Marine who served two tours in Afghanistan and a former LAPD homicide detective. Walter asked him to look after you."

"Nice to meet you, ma'am." The handheld radio on Zeke's belt crackled.

"Impressive resume," I said. "What brought you to Justice Bay?"

He hesitated before answering. "A Crips gangbanger shot me as I left the station. After my release from the hospital, a friend suggested I come to Justice Bay to recover—fresh air and all that. He found a rental cabin for me and Tango, my chocolate lab. Anyway, I just stopped by to tell you not to worry if you see a car parked at the end of the driveway. It's just my partner and me. If you have any problems, call 911. We'll be around as a backup."

Knowing Zeke's background should have quieted my concerns, but it reminded me that he only guarded my house because somebody had attempted to break in.

"Thanks for letting me know," I said.

Zeke nodded again and walked toward the road.

Cooper stepped inside and followed me to the kitchen. "Look, I can't stay. Walter needs help with something. He said it was important."

My breath caught in my throat as I turned to face him. "Just a warning. He knows about our dinner on the boat. I didn't tell him anything, but he made assumptions."

Cooper grinned. "Sounds like Walter." His expression turned serious. "Before I go, I want to tell you something."

Despite the room's cool temperature, my skin felt hot. "That sounds ominous."

He took my hands in his. "I accepted the firm's job offer."

I pulled my hands away.

In a flat monotone, I said, "If that's what makes you happy."

"I'm not moving back to San Francisco. Kevin Medwin asked me to represent his interests in the sawmill-hotel project. It seems he doesn't completely trust his mother. I convinced the managing director that Kevin's firm could become a major client. She agreed that I could work from Justice Bay if I showed up at the office whenever she needed me."

I put my arms around him. "I'd like you to know how happy this makes me."

He rested his cheek on my head and glanced at my open laptop and the papers on the island countertop. "What are you working on?"

I told him about the retirement party photos and the bad blood between Howard Valdis and my aunt. "I thought her death might be a case of workplace violence, but I just can't make all the pieces fit."

"Can I see the photos?"

"Sure." Boo jumped on the countertop to lobby Cooper for attention while I pulled up the photos on my laptop. I gave him the details I learned about Valdis from his wife's social media accounts and public records.

He leaned over the counter and brushed Boo's tail out of his face to get a closer look at the young woman standing near Valdis at the retirement party. "Those glasses and the turtleneck hide her face. It could be she's shy or doesn't want to be recognized. It's hard to believe a person looking for an engineering job with a high-profile firm like Spellman Polk & Kimble hides her face at a meet-and-greet with company executives."

"Her name is Grace Chin. Do you think she and Valdis were having an affair and that looking-for-a-job story was a lie?"

He shrugged. "Maybe."

Boo batted my pen off the counter and then sprawled on the papers. "I paid an online search site and found dozens of women named Grace Chin."

He expanded the retirement party photo to include Valdis's left-side profile. "His face is gaunt. He looks ill."

"According to his wife's Facebook page, he's been under a lot of stress." I stared at the picture. "Hold on a minute." I ran upstairs, got the photo I'd printed of the man by the oleander bush, and slid it toward Cooper. "Take a look at this."

He used the magnifying glass to compare the two photos.

"Same hollow cheeks," he said. "Ears are the same size and shape."

Something else caught my eye. A dark blemish marred his earlobe. It couldn't have been a shadow because the spot on both photos was identical. It looked like a mole.

I grabbed Cooper's arm. "The man at the rest stop is Howard Valdis."

"Looks like it."

My muscles grew rigid. "What brought Valdis to Justice Bay two days before Lydie died?

"Good question," he said. "Look, I have to go meet Walter. I'll let him know about this. Until I return, don't answer the door unless it's Zeke, my uncle, or me."

After Cooper left, I tried but failed to find more information on Grace Chin. I needed to run to quell my frustration, but that would be tricky with Zeke and his buddy watching my every move. Instead, I returned to my computer and scoured the internet for information.

My aunt cautioned me to trust my instincts and question everything. In that light, I found it hard to fathom that Howard Valdis had brought a woman half his age to a company retirement party just to provide her with networking opportunities. An alternate scenario pointed to some sort of relationship.

Grace Chin recently graduated from college, so I assumed she'd be active on all the new social media sites favored by her generation. Again, the search brought up hundreds of women with that name. Still, of those that included a photo, none looked like her, and none matched the profile of an engineering student. I also checked professional organizations that represented engineers but found nothing.

I plugged Chin's name into the paid search site and found a woman by that name who lived in Northern California, so I added that element to the initial search. Even though the scope was limited, the outcome still produced countless hits.

I whittled down the pool until I'd reduced it to a handful of possibilities. One looked promising, a Grace Chin with an address in San Francisco not far from the headquarters of Spellman Polk & Kimble. However, I found no corroborating evidence to confirm she was my Grace Chin. The woman was a ghost.

I checked my watch, seven-forty-five. The library remained open until nine. I fed Boo and decided to drive into town and ask Pia if she could access any super-secret databases that might help me find information on Chin. I thought Zeke and his partner might be up for an adventure, but I no longer saw his car when I reached the driveway's end—so much for the Protection Squad.

Chapter Thirty-Six

I reminded myself that Zeke was a volunteer, not my hired bodyguard. He hadn't given me his cell number, or I would have told him where I'd gone. He'd likely be back after making his rounds.

Ten minutes later, I pulled the car into the library parking lot. A poster at the front door announced a book signing set to begin in five minutes, likely part of the Justice Bay Literary Society's new Authors on Tour series. I recognized the author's photo. Chaz Stone wrote bestselling spy thrillers. Justice Bay represented an unusual stop on the tour of a high-profile author. I wondered what had brought him here.

Around thirty people were sitting inside on folding chairs. Not bad for a sleepy coastal town. Arthur picked me out of the crowd and pointed to an empty seat in the front row next to him.

I joined him and whispered, "How did the library score a guy like Stone?"

"He's Renee Masterholm's second cousin. Pia lobbied for ages to get him here. Renee offered him a place to stay, but the publisher wouldn't pay for his transportation from Florida. The literary society held a bake sale to raise the money."

"Stone couldn't afford airfare?"

Arthur shrugged and held up his hands, palms up. "Maybe he's not as successful as everybody thinks he is. Have you read his books?"

"The first one, I think. Stone's main character is a rogue CIA operative, right? I can't remember much about the plot, except there's a lot of blood and body parts. And sex. Lots of sex."

"Exciting, right?"

Pia saved me from a candid book review when she joined the author at the lectern. Stone looked to be in his late thirties with a mop of tawny hair, bedroom eyes, and a crooked bad-boy smile that appealed to those of the female persuasion, given that ninety-five percent of the attendees were women. He wasn't bad-looking if you liked the type. My type was Cooper.

Pia gave him a glowing introduction. Stone milked the applause for a beat too long as he cast come-hither glances at his adoring female fans. Then, the author launched into a nail-biting narrative of how his hero, Jason Storm, saved the world from cyber terrorists while fighting off the advances of multiple beautiful women. By the time he'd finished regaling us, I didn't trust my willing suspension of disbelief.

He asked if there were any questions.

A woman I recognized from Arthur's literary society raised her hand. "Is it true you worked for the CIA?"

He flashed a cagy grin. "I can neither confirm nor deny..." His words trailed off into a chuckle.

That brought on a flurry of follow-up questions by members of the audience.

One of the few males in attendance, a man with a ponytail and a soul patch, raised his hand. "Jason uncovers a lot of spies in your novel. Do foreign governments still use them? Isn't hacking more efficient?"

Stone arched his eyebrows. "People think cybercrimes are the only tools available to foreign intelligence services. But they also use spies on the ground because they work."

A young woman wearing gaudy makeup and a rhinestone tiara raised her hand. "What country has the most spies?"

"You mean other than the United States?" Stone waited for the laughter to die down. "Everybody has spies, but Russia and China are major players in this country."

"In your book, the Russians target Jason with a honeypot," said a woman, breathless with adoration for Jason, Stone, or both. "Do other countries use them, too?"

I thought she'd keel over when he winked at her. "Good question.

221

The Chinese intelligence service prefers to gather information using businesspeople and students, especially in science and engineering. Once their spies get jobs in high-tech industries, they burrow in and steal secrets at will."

A middle-aged woman in the back row waved her hand. "You think there are real spies out there right now that nobody knows about?"

"Sure. Lots of them. Case in point, what do you know about the guy sitting next to you?"

Surprised, she glanced at the man. "He's my husband."

The man pointed his thumb at the woman. "And she's my honeypot."

More laughter.

After that, the discussion moved on to questions like Where do you get your ideas? How long does it take for you to write a book? Who do you want to play your hero in the movie?

By then, I'd stopped listening. All I could think about was Walter's story of how he'd met my aunt. Seven or eight years before, he'd interviewed her concerning the investigation of an employee at Spellman Polk & Kimble for possible espionage. That employee had been a heavy drinker and deeply in debt due to bad investments. Walter referred to him in spy parlance as a gray man, someone competent but ultimately forgettable. I realized somebody else fit that profile—Howard Valdis, a software engineer with a top-secret security clearance for his work developing weapons systems for the U.S. military.

My mind swirled with the possibility that my aunt's psychic abilities and her work at a major defense contractor might have added enough knowledge of counterintelligence tricks of the trade to identify a witting or unwitting agent of a hostile foreign power. Did she suspect the relationship between Valdis and Chin entailed more than an affair or a job search? Had she shared her suspicions with her bosses at work? What would Valdis do to protect his secret if he suspected Lydie knew everything?

I realized Valdis's Patek Philippe watch might be genuine. After facing financial ruin, the money he made from betraying his country must have been addictive. He could now pay off his debts and indulge his taste for expensive watches. His wife could afford to remodel her kitchen and buy designer handbags. He didn't want to give that up.

After Lydie discovered he might be stealing national security secrets, he had to kill her. Valdis waited until she returned from Tibet, but he didn't anticipate my aunt seeing him at the rest stop and snapping his photo.

All that seemed plausible except for why Howard Valdis needed to access the house after he'd killed Lydie. He'd taken her cell from the crime scene to delete those photos of him. He must have thought something else inside would incriminate him, but I drew a blank as to what that could be.

My theory appeared sound, but I had to tie that red Mercedes to Valdis. The divorce papers listed only two older-model cars among their assets, but Sheila's social media accounts flaunted new, expensive purchases. Maybe she'd bought the car but hadn't posted a picture yet.

I couldn't access the Department of Motor Vehicles records. Years ago, after a celebrity murder in L.A., California passed a privacy law prohibiting the average Joe Blow from getting a driver's license or vehicle registration information. There had to be another way to determine if Valdis owned a Mercedes.

Then I remembered the street view feature on my computer's maps program. I had Howard Valdis's address from the court documents I'd purchased online. The couple may not still live there, but if they did, I might be able to find the car parked in the driveway. I crossed my fingers that they used the garage for storing junk and not a Mercedes. It was a long shot, but I had to try.

Arthur waited in a long line to buy Stone's new book. I waved goodbye and drove home. Zeke hadn't returned. Once inside the cottage, I found the divorce papers and typed the address into the map's search engine. A view of a modest house popped up on the screen. My breath caught because the closed garage door revealed no vehicles parked in the driveway. I leaned back against the chair to gather my thoughts. That's when I remembered the feature that allowed a 360-degree view of the neighborhood. I navigated the camera to the right, and—BINGO—somebody had parked a red Mercedes in front of the neighbor's house. The image showed no damage to the car, so it must have been taken before the hit-and-run. I took a screenshot of the car.

Valdis must have been the person who broke into Lydie's cottage, but I didn't know why. If Lydie suspected Valdis had passed classified weapons systems to the agent of a foreign government, she wouldn't have waited until she got back from Tibet to inform the powers that be. She would have told them immediately. It also made no sense that my aunt hid that information inside her house.

I began a last-ditch push to find whatever Valdis had been searching for. I'd already been through Lydie's office files when searching for the house deed, so I started in the guest room where I'd been sleeping since I arrived. Boo insisted on helping. She jumped into every open drawer and batted items off the nightstand, including a tube of lipstick she found behind a lamp.

Maddie called a moment later.

"Em! Guess what? One of our sales catalogs has a basket that fits your Schwinn handlebars. Shall I order it?"

"Yes, that would be great."

"Okay, you have two choices: metal and wicker. The metal is more durable, but the wicker basket has Martha's Vineyard vibes."

I didn't plan to tell Maddie anything about Valdis, especially if he threatened national security and the safety of people who knew about his crimes.

"The wicker one sounds good." I removed the bureau drawers and turned them over, but found nothing taped underneath.

"Good choice," she said. "It's a bit more expensive, though."

I lifted the mattress, but Lydie hadn't hidden anything there, either. "That doesn't matter. Do you want my credit card number?"

"You can pay when you pick it up."

Maddie had an insatiable capacity for minutiae. I tried not to sound impatient as she peppered me with questions—regular mail or express, large basket or small, metal hook attachments or leather straps?

All the while, I continued to look high and low but found nothing but dust and tufts of cat hair. I gave up and hurried downstairs to check out the kitchen.

"You sound out of breath," Maddie teased. "Is Cooper there?"

I rolled my eyes. "No, I'm doing some housecleaning."

"At this time of night?"

"You're right," I said. "It's late, and I'm sort of tired. I think I'll just go to bed."

"Okaaaay." She strung out the word, trying to puzzle out what I was doing. "I'll place the order and let you know when it arrives."

After the call ended, I finished looking through the kitchen and then retired to the living room couch. Boo lay paws up next to me, sleeping.

A pervasive chill filled the house. I didn't want to start a fire this late at night, so I felt relieved when the heat clicked on. The air blasting out of the vents created an annoying clinking sound. Some critter must have made a nest inside one of the ducts. The house was old. Eventually, I'd have to get an expert to inspect the entire system. For now, I'd like to see if I could find the source of the problem.

I had no idea how to locate all the house vents, but the sound came from the main floor. I yanked the flashlight from a drawer in the kitchen island and isolated the clink to a vent near the front door. I got on my hands and knees, opened the louvers, and aimed the beam into the dark abyss. Something seemed trapped, but I couldn't tell what.

I failed to locate a screwdriver, so I used a letter opener from the kitchen to pry off the cover. Looking down that dark hole, I sensed the same squeamishness when I swam in deep water. Something might be down there. I couldn't see it, but it could see me.

Boo watched and then trotted over for a look. The cat put her nose into the opening. I nudged her aside and lowered my hand into the duct. I pulled out a paperclip and a number-two pencil stub. Boo treated both as found treasure. She swiped the pencil with her paw and raced into the kitchen, chasing after it. Removing those items represented progress, but it didn't stop the clink. Something else further down the duct remained just beyond my reach.

The heat blew in my face, so I turned down the thermostat. The sound stopped. I extended my entire arm down the duct and touched a metal object. It appeared to be caught on something. I worked with my fingertips until it finally broke free. I inched the thing toward me until I could pull it out.

My skin felt clammy as I stared in disbelief at the object in my hand—a man's ring made of rose gold inlaid with blue lapis. Sheila Valdis posted a photo of it on Facebook with the caption, Howie has lost so much weight, his wedding ring keeps falling off! I suspected it dropped off Howard Valdis's finger when he entered the house to kill my aunt. But Valdis didn't kill her there. He hit her with his car. I had to find out exactly what had happened. Ignoring my chain of custody concerns, I slipped the ring into my pocket for safekeeping until I could turn it over to Chief Greene.

Chapter Thirty-Seven

I imagined Valdis returned to the house to look for the ring after I left for Cooper's boat, but Boo had already batted it into the heating vent. I wondered if Valdis also carried the Dzi stone to Lydie's bedroom for some reason.

I tapped Walter's number on the keypad of my cell. He didn't pick up, so I called Cooper instead. He answered on the first ring. I didn't wait for his response.

"Howard Valdis killed Lydie."

"The guy in Lydie's reunion photo?"

The words came tumbling so fast that I couldn't tell if they made sense. "The red Mercedes. It's his. Or probably his wife's. It's complicated. I need to tell you in person. Can you come over?"

"Okay, sure, but Walter is on a conference call. I'm guessing he'll finish in fifteen or twenty minutes."

"Can't you interrupt him?"

"It's important, so I don't think he'd be pleased, but I'm listening."

That passed as an invitation. The words spilled out. I reviewed everything I'd discovered, including at the library's author event: facts, suppositions, and theories. He didn't interrupt, not once. When I finished, I waited for him to say something. Silence. Not even a Miss Marple comparison.

"Cooper, are you still there?"

"Whew, Emma..." His words trailed off into another period of silence.

I grew suspicious. "Hello. Cooper?"

"Look, as soon as Walter hangs up, we'll drive to your place. I promise,

227

okay?"

His edgy tone unspooled my imagination. "What's going on? Is everything okay?"

"Honestly? I'm not sure." He sighed. "Listen, stay in the house. Don't go out for any reason. Don't answer the door unless you see it's Walter or me. We'll be there as soon as we can. He'll tell you everything when we get there."

That warning sounded familiar. I ended the call feeling vulnerable and alone. I'd already locked all the doors and windows, so I went upstairs to Lydie's bedroom and lay on her bed.

I must have dozed off because I woke up groggy and disoriented in a dark room, still wearing my clothes. Boo frantically scratched at the duvet as if trying to dig me out of a grave. She'd never done that before. I pulled the comforter over my head, hoping she'd give up and let me go back to sleep. But she persisted. I peeked around the room and realized I was still lying in Lydie's bed. I sat up and tried to pet her, but she darted away and disappeared into the hallway.

That's when a noise from downstairs in the living room startled me. It sounded like furniture scraping against the hardwood floor. I bolted upright. I swept my hand over the bedside table, reaching for my cell phone to call 911, hoping Zeke and his Protection Squad partner sat in their car at the end of the driveway. My cell wasn't there. I must have left it downstairs next to my laptop. I tiptoed to the door and listened. Whoever broke into the house had moved into the kitchen. I wondered if Valdis was searching for his wedding ring.

I thought about stuffing Boo into my backpack and climbing down the trellis to safety. But the house didn't have a trellis, and Boo had disappeared. I moved toward the window to see if anything below would break my fall if I jumped. No luck. I had no idea where Boo had gone, but I had confidence in her ability to find a safe hiding place. I had to go downstairs and get my phone. Then I'd call Walter. He must be off his call by now.

Footsteps ascended the creaky stairs. My breathing stopped as the intruder turned right at the landing and creaked down the hallway toward Lydie's office. I waited for a beat before opening the bedroom door. I moved downstairs one riser at a time, flinching at every groan of the aging treads.

Through the darkness, I could just make out the kitchen island. I'd almost reached my goal when my foot collided with Boo's ceramic water dish, which produced a loud crashing sound. My mouth opened in a silent primal scream. I backed away in short, jerky steps in a futile attempt to sneak out the door. Footsteps thundered down the hallway toward the staircase. My pulse hammered in my ears as I spun around and spotted a dark figure at the top of the stairs.

I snatched my cell phone from the counter and ran. Shoes pounded down the steps. I slipped the cell into the back pocket of my jeans and headed toward the open front door. Then I ran.

The beach offered the shortest route to Walter's place. I ran toward the back of the house to the shoreline near the veranda. I pulled the phone from my back pocket to call Walter, but the intruder was close behind me. I had no time to stop and make a call.

Holding the phone, I ran along the beach with his footsteps pounding on the stones close by. The shore exposed me, so I detoured into the woods, trying again to call Walter, but couldn't connect through the Wi-Fi server. My shoes sank into the ground's damp ooze, slowing me down. The crystals on the cell phone case glinted in the moonlight. Fearing the light would give away my position, I tore the cover from the phone and tossed it into the brush.

Fear and exertion left my clothes clammy and sticking to my skin. Colliding with low-hanging fir branches left the sting of abrasions on my face. I inhaled the smell of moist soil and rot. The sound of flapping wings and the rustle of a small animal scurrying through the underbrush spiked my fear.

My adrenaline surged, propelling me forward. I had almost reached the main road when a hand landed on my back and pushed violently. I plunged to the ground, gasping for air as pain shot through my body. Moisture from the soil seeped into my clothes.

I looked up, staring in disbelief. Howard Valdis stood over me with a gun aimed at my head. He wore a baggy black jacket and his combover concealed under a cuffed olive watch cap. It took a minute to figure out where I'd seen that cap before—on the man staring at me through the shop window, who bought the Shanghai panda from Arthur.

"Get up!" His voice sounded raspy. His hand trembled, which told me he had minimal skill with the weapon. That unnerved me.

I groaned. "My back hurts."

He leaned over me with a wild glare. "I said get up." As he got closer, I could smell his acrid sweat and see the menacing calculation in his expression.

I shivered from my sodden clothes as I looked around for something to use as a weapon. A log lay nearby in the brush, big enough to do some damage. Valdis inched toward me. I kicked his left knee hard when he got close enough and heard a popping sound.

He shrieked in pain. I rose to my feet with a wince, grabbed the log, and brought it down on his head. A hollow thud ripped through the woods as he dropped onto the waterlogged soil, groaning. The gun lay under his body. It seemed inadvisable to look for it. I dropped the log and ran.

I felt terrified and out of breath when I reached the road. A dark sedan loomed on the shoulder about fifty feet away, its engine running. The headlights flipped on, and the vehicle jolted forward, aiming straight for me. I raced as fast as I could toward Walter's house, but the car overtook me. I worried the driver might be Grace Chin. I planned to dart back into the woods when the sedan slowed and the passenger window rolled down.

A man's voice yelled, "Get in!"

I didn't bother to answer. I just kept running.

"Emmaline," he yelled. "It's Zeke Digby. Get in the car. Please."

For a moment, I considered him part of some dark vision, a ruse, a trap, a lie to lure me close enough to kill. Then I recognized his face in the moonlight. My world began to spin.

I got in the car and locked the door.

"Walter told me to get over here pronto," he said. "He's on his way. You okay?"

I'd become so chilled and scared my teeth chattered. "I think so. Valdis is in the woods. I hit him with a log."

"Stay put." He bolted out of the vehicle. I could hear the crackling of conversation on his handheld radio, but couldn't make out the words.

The Creamsicle squealed to a stop. Walter spilled out of the driver's side with his Glock drawn, likely the weapon I'd seen him cleaning a few days earlier. He followed Zeke into the woods.

I sat paralyzed in the passenger's seat, too terrified to close my eyes. I recalled my vision at Walter's dinner table of a frightened Lydie running for her life through the woods. I remembered the crystals on my aunt's phone cover, sparkling in the moonlight, threatening to give away my position.

A buzzing sound filled my head. My breathing became shallow as I realized I'd dropped the cover in the exact location where I'd found it two weeks before. The place Lydie had dropped it the night Valdis chased her through the woods and then killed her with his car. My body trembled, realizing I'd just relived my aunt's final moments. Except I hadn't died.

A knock on the window diverted my attention. I looked over and glimpsed Cooper, motioning for me to unlock the door.

Chapter Thirty-Eight

Cooper's face looked ashen as he shouted, "Emma, open the door."
My hands trembled as I pulled on the handle.

"I'm taking you to Walter's cabin," he said. "He'll meet us there later."

I grabbed his arm as he guided me into the Creamsicle because figuring out the when, where, and how of anything took too much brainpower.

When we arrived at Walter's place, Cooper helped me into the cozy open-concept main floor of the cabin, with the living room to the left and the kitchen to the right. I took comfort in seeing familiar objects—the telescope, the unfinished jigsaw puzzle, and Lydie's rustic decoy on a table near the sliding glass doors. Outside, Cooper's Brief Encounter remained anchored in the bay, and just beyond were the distant lights of Justice Bay's main street.

At Cooper's urging, I removed my wet clothes and put on a gray sweatsuit he found in his uncle's closet. I set Valdis's wedding ring on the coffee table for law enforcement to book into evidence, hoping there were no chain of custody issues. Afterward, I sat on the couch with a blanket draped over me, nestled in Cooper's arms as if my life depended on preserving the connection.

"What about that urgent call of Walter's?" I asked.

"It was a conference call with the FBI."

"Were you on it, too?"

"No. My uncle will have to give you the details."

Forty-five minutes later, Walter entered the house, ushering in cold night air. He seemed wired by adrenaline as he walked over to where I sat.

"How are you holding up, kid?"

"I'm fine. What about Valdis?" Since I'd hit him over the head with a log, I worried about his condition.

Walter paced for a while before grabbing a couple of logs from the copper bucket by the fireplace hearth and throwing them onto the grate. He added kindling, struck a long match, and ignited the fire.

"I'm guessing he'll be fine. He's alert. He's also scared and talking. Zeke and Skip Kowalski took him into custody and will stay with him until paramedics load him into an ambulance. They'll watch over him at the Cedarbrook hospital until the docs evaluate him. The FBI will take over from there."

"When you told me not to worry, that investigators were looking into Lydie's death," I said. "I thought you'd finally persuaded Chief Greene to do his job. How did the FBI get involved? Is somebody going to tell me what's going on?"

Cooper stood. "I'll make coffee. He walked across the room to the kitchen and pulled a filter from the cupboard. When I'd run into Cooper at Tarts & Bars, he told me Walter's coffeemaker had broken. Somebody must have fixed it, or maybe he bought Colonel Mustard's sister from the hardware store.

Walter sat on the arm of the couch. "Greene stopped caring about his job long ago. Lydie's death matters to Kowalski. He's been working the case with my help. He's the real deal."

"And the FBI?"

"Special Agent Jim Foster called me earlier today. Before Lydie left for Tibet, she told her employer that Howard Valdis might be stealing top-secret U.S. Navy nuclear submarine plans."

"On behalf of Grace Chin," I said.

He nodded. "That's not the woman's real name, but yes. She was Valdis's handler. When Lydie saw her with Valdis at her retirement party, your aunt's psychic radar pinged off the charts. Chin claimed to be an engineering student looking for a job, but her background seemed sketchy. Lydie thought she was playing Valdis and sensed she was either an agent for a hostile foreign power or secretly working for one of SK&P's competitors."

In a monotone that masked what must have been underlying pain, Walter explained that Lydie had been returning to the office from lunch when she spotted Valdis pacing near a mailbox. He looked like he was going to mail an eight-by-ten manila envelope, but instead, he drew a circle on the mailbox in chalk and walked away, the envelope still in his hand. Your aunt was alarmed by Valdis's behavior and followed him down an alley until he disappeared behind a Dumpster. A minute later, the guy reemerged empty-handed.

My aunt was such a boss. I couldn't imagine lurking behind a trash bin, waiting to expose a modern-day Mata Hari. "That was brave of her to follow him. Not sure I would have done that."

Walter stood and walked to the fireplace to warm his hands. "I'm guessing you would have. Lydie recognized what we call in the biz a 'dead drop' from her work at SP&K. After Valdis left, she found a loose brick in the wall behind the Dumpster that contained the same type of envelope Valdis carried. It contained multiple sheets of microfiche that appeared to be proprietary pages of text and diagrams stolen from SP&K."

My eyes opened wide. "Microfiche? Sounds like a scene from a vintage spy novel. Except for librarians, who uses that anymore?"

"Government agencies like NARA, the National Archives and Records Administration, still use it." He slumped into a nearby chair before continuing. "It was a favorite tool of spies during the Cold War because they could deposit a large amount of data on small sheets. Stored under optimal temperatures, it can last for five hundred years. Lydie watched for a while, but nobody picked up the envelope, so she returned to her office and notified her bosses."

"I hope she took cell photos first."

Walter nodded. "She did, but the images were too small to decipher without a reading device. Lydie went to her retirement party that night and left the next morning on her scheduled trip to Tibet. Her bosses didn't object because she was due to return in two weeks, and law enforcement hadn't yet initiated a formal investigation of Valdis."

"SP&K must have been thrilled that Lydie solved another case for them."

Walter shrugged. "Lydie's word wasn't enough. The company conducted an internal investigation. Valdis came to work every day like always, so they assumed he didn't suspect anything."

From the kitchen, I smelled the aroma of fresh brew. "Are you sure he didn't? Valdis confronted her at the retirement party about something later that night."

Walter's adrenaline high appeared to be fading. He looked tired. "Exactly. They were wrong. Valdis knew. Their foot-dragging allowed him to make plans. After SP&K finished its internal investigation, the findings went up the company's chain of command before they contacted the Bureau, causing further delay. Foster just got the case a few days ago. He and I worked together on that old SP&K investigation I told you about. We kept in touch. He remembered Lydie and I were a couple, so he called tonight for information. He didn't know she was dead, which made Valdis a person of interest in the murder, as well as other charges."

With some effort, I kept my voice steady. "So, Valdis knew Lydie had blown his cover. The company finally passed their findings to the FBI, but not in time to save my aunt's life."

Walter stared into mid-space without comment, but I sensed his sadness and anger. I felt that, too.

My words shattered the silence. "You told me about that other document theft from SP&K from years ago. Why didn't they stiffen security? How was Valdis able to smuggle those documents out of the building?"

Walter gazed at the burning logs. "There's a joke from Soviet Russia days. An old man works in a factory. Every day when he leaves, he rolls a wheelbarrow filled with straw out of the building. Every day, the guard searches the straw for stolen goods. He's suspicious but never finds anything. On the old man's last day of work, the guard begs him to confess what he's been stealing for all those years. The old man replies—wheelbarrows."

I chuckled. "Funny, but what's your point?"

"Valdis used misdirection to steal secret documents right under SP&K's nose. Every day, Valdis brought a briefcase to work, along with a baloney and cheese sandwich and an apple in a battered black lunch pail with a thermos of decaf coffee in the lid. Everybody at the office knew the lunch pail once belonged to his father, who worked construction back in the day. They considered Valdis an odd duck but harmless. Before entering and leaving the building, he sent his briefcase and lunch pail through a metal detector. Every day, the security guard searched Valdis's briefcase. He also opened the lunch pail, inspected the sandwich, and looked for abnormalities on the apple, but never found anything. The guard continued searching the briefcase, but eventually, he ran the lunch pail through the metal detector without looking inside. Once Valdis conditioned the guard, he felt comfortable concealing the classified documents in a secret compartment at the bottom of the thermos. Grace Chin provided cameras and other gear to transfer the documents to microfiche at his home, making them easier to transport."

"Seems dicey for Valdis to pull off a dead drop across the street from his office."

"It freaked him out, but Chin insisted because she needed those documents pronto. He left the microfiche in his car until his lunch break and completed his mission as Lydie watched. His panic and odd behavior attracted your aunt's attention and sealed his fate."

I sat in silence for a moment, unpacking everything Walter had told me. "What happens now?"

"A judge approved a search warrant for Valdis's house and surrounding property," he said. "Yesterday, agents executed it while he and his wife were shopping. Not even the neighbors suspected they were there, so Valdis never knew. Agents found camera equipment and stacks of classified documents on microfiche. They also located a cell phone in his trash bin, which was smashed and inoperable. They're doing a forensics analysis, but I suspect it's Lydie's."

I glanced at Walter. "Sheila and Howard never finalized the divorce."

He shook his head. "When the Chinese money started rolling in, she gave him a second chance."

Cooper loaded a tray with mugs, sugar, and cream from the kitchen. If the lawyer thing didn't work out for him, he'd make an excellent—well, anything.

Cooper handed Walter a mug of coffee from the tray. I declined caffeine. I suffered from enough jitters.

"If Valdis feared exposure, why didn't he leave the country? I'm sure Grace Chin could find him a lovely apartment in Beijing. Why kill Lydie?"

Walter's tone sounded detached. "Valdis is a paper pusher, a flawed human being who betrayed his country, but people do desperate things when they feel threatened."

"Did Valdis tell you what happened that night?" I asked.

Walter's jaw muscles twitched as he sat with his coffee on a chair across from me. "Not everything. He did say that Grace Chin waited at the drop site to pick up the microfiche and saw Lydie following Valdis. Spies are paranoid. They don't trust anybody, and Chin already didn't trust Valdis because he was a sloppy spy. Knowing Lydie had compromised the dead drop further triggered her paranoia. Your aunt became a threat. Chin gave Valdis the gun and ordered him to neutralize her."

"So, the guy drove to Justice Bay on Friday when my aunt returned from her trip to Tibet. Lydie snapped a photo of him lurking near her house. Did he follow her from the airport? Why did he wait until Sunday to kill her?"

"He came to Justice Bay on Friday but claimed he chickened out and stayed at a motel in Cedarbrook for a couple of days, trying to work up the courage to finish his assignment. He finally broke into the house on Sunday, using his lockpicks. He didn't know squat about guns. He didn't want to confront her, so he planned to shoot her while she slept. But Lydie heard him come into the house. There was a scuffle. His wedding ring slipped off his finger before Lydie ran out of the house."

I shuddered, thinking how close I'd come to the truth. "Then Valdis got in his car and mowed her down."

That wedding ring incriminated Valdis in my aunt's death. He became desperate to reclaim it, so he used his lockpicking skills several times, including during my visit to Cooper's boat. I wondered if he recognized the Dzi stone as a Tibetan artifact and thought about stealing it, but changed his mind. If so, he'd made a careless mistake. He tried a second break-in but left when I shouted at him—the third and final time was tonight.

Walter stood and walked to the glass doors overlooking the bay. His muscles looked rigid, his voice low and gravelly. "I should have been there to protect her."

Cooper bowed his head and sighed. After that, the room went silent.

I wanted to tell Walter that Lydie's death wasn't his fault, but he wouldn't accept that, not yet. I thought about Cassandra, the woman in Greek mythology who spoke prophecies that nobody believed. Walter accompanied my aunt when she bought that red blouse. She explained that if she wore it, it meant danger. He blew that off as a joke, but Lydie must have sensed a credible threat from Howard Valdis. No one listened. Not even Walter. I walked over and put my hand on his arm. He flinched before his muscles relaxed.

"Lydie loved you," I said. "That's everything."

A deep breath expanded his chest. He patted my hand and broke physical contact. Then he slid open the glass door and disappeared into the night.

Chapter Thirty-Nine

T he FBI surveillance team searched Lydie's house the following day, looking for any evidence Valdis had left behind. They found nothing of interest, or so they said. Once I returned home, not even a dust bunny looked out of place, as if the houseful of FBI Special Agents had never been there.

Walter updated me on the investigation three weeks after my confrontation in the woods with Howard Valdis. "I just checked in with Special Agent Foster. Valdis and Chin have been indicted on conspiracy to steal trade secrets, economic espionage, and possession of stolen secrets. They're both in the clink. I know the place, and it ain't no Club Fed."

"Will they face charges for Lydie's death?"

"That's up to the State, but stay tuned."

"I'm curious," I said, "why didn't Grace Chin just kill Valdis and disappear? End of problem."

Walter paused. "I doubt Valdis was the only person she'd recruited. Usually, there are others, probably a network she had to protect, whatever the cost. Also, remember those classified documents the FBI found in Valdis's house? Chin desperately needed them. Once they were in her possession, who knows what might have happened to him."

"Will you be over later?"

He hesitated. "Yeah. I'll be there."

"Later" was a celebration-of-life brunch for Lydie. I'd used the same skills learned as a thirteen-year-old, organizing a wake for my father. I invited Lydie's friends for a potluck at the house. My mother emailed regrets from

Paris, adding that the party sounded lovely, but I should have hired a caterer. She didn't get the historical symbolism.

Everybody contributed something to the table. Pia Bianchi made cannolis filled with sweet, creamy ricotta cheese. Arthur brought his mother and lemon squares from Tarts & Bars. Chef Gabriel cooked omelets to order with eggs and organic vegetables from the restaurant, and I made a batch of Lydie's cinnamon rolls. In addition to Cooper acting as the perfect co-host—making clam chowder, collecting dirty dishes, cleaning up spills, and charming everybody—he gave me a gift, a copy of *Harriet the Spy* he'd bought online.

Maddie held court by the fireplace, flanked by her parents. Her father had recovered from his heart attack enough to work part-time in the hardware store. That freed her up to spend a few hours a day in Gabriel's restaurant as his hostess and bookkeeper. She planned to remain in Justice Bay until her dad fully recovered. Until then, she would work remotely for her New York employer with an eye to the future—her own graphics design company, perhaps based in Justice Bay. Boo appeared skeptical about all those guests but graced us with her presence nonetheless.

Kelly Hinson and a group of Lydie's former coworkers at Spellman Polk & Kimble rented a van and rolled into town. I'd arranged with a Pleasant Springs Retirement Community caregiver to drive Dwight Banfield to the event at his former home. He appeared emotional after seeing the house again and overwhelmed by all the support he got from friends, old and new.

I'd missed Chet and Abby Greene's party that Saturday but later found out their announcement wasn't a gender reveal. Instead, Greene told attendees he had accepted a position with the Fresno Police Department. That sounded like a wise move. People gossip in small towns. The Justice Bay grapevine would quickly spread the word about Chet's affair with Pam the Vampire Princess.

Pia Bianchi had said something cryptic when I first met her at the library: Sometimes answers become apparent when you rephrase the question. Testing that theory, I changed the question from—will Chet and Abby's marriage survive, to will leaving Justice Bay and Pam the Vampire Princess save Greene's marriage? Time would tell.

The city council appointed Officer Skip Kowalski as Acting Chief of Police, he with the laugh wrinkles and the arrest of a spy under his belt. So far, nobody knew the scuttlebutt about the Vampire Princess's employment status, but I made a mental note to warn Skip to watch himself if she planned to remain at her job as the records clerk.

Kowalski arrived at the house with a plate of homemade pierogi and told me he'd presented the case against Valdis to the Cedarbrook District Attorney's office. In addition to federal charges, the State had filed its own: vehicular homicide, breaking and entering, and several other felonies.

Seamus Murphy drove to the wake from San Francisco with his friend, the museum curator specializing in Far East artifacts. She told me the Dzi stone might be worth as much as ten thousand dollars, but she couldn't be sure until she examined it more thoroughly. Seamus suggested I consider loaning the stone to the museum. They could appraise it and maybe display it at an upcoming exhibition. I agreed.

I never liked the custom of pressuring people to say mushy things about the dead, but stories of Lydie came out spontaneously. To my relief, they were poignant and often funny.

Arthur's mom, not the wounded soul he made her out to be, recounted a slide-show presentation Lydie gave for a second-grade class about her trip to the Galápagos Islands. The kids loved the photos of iguanas, tortoises, and penguins. Mrs. Bromley had interrupted the presentation when a picture of a blue-footed booby flashed on the screen, cautioning the children to call it the bird that shall not be named.

The gathering reminded me of something Walter said the first time we met: that the best family isn't always the one you were born into, but the one you chose. With my father and Lydie gone and my mother living in Paris, the people in this room were my family now.

During all those heartfelt stories, I kept an eye on Walter. He was private, and I worried how he'd react to public memories of the woman he loved. Most of the time, I noticed his head bent over and his forearms on his knees in quiet reflection.

The recollections of my aunt were uplifting, but after a half dozen or so, they became too painful for me to hear. I walked out to the veranda for some fresh air. Arthur joined me.

"Thanks for inviting my mom. She's having a blast."

"She's great," I said.

His eyes widened. "After everything that's happened to you, how do you stay so positive?"

"Are you kidding? I'm a mess."

Arthur glanced out toward the bay. "I just talked to Seamus Murphy. He said you asked him about getting me into Berkeley. He's willing to write a letter of recommendation and help me reapply."

"That's great, Arthur. What did you tell him?"

He threw up his hands in frustration. "Emma, there's no way I could go to Berkeley right now. I don't have the money. I couldn't even manage Cedarbrook Community College without a car."

"I'm sure Seamus can point you to available scholarships, and about that car—" I reached into my pocket and pulled out a set of keys in anticipation of Arthur's arrival.

"What's that?"

"The keys to Lydie's VW Beetle. I don't need a second car. It's just deteriorating in the garage."

"Emma, I can't accept that. It's too much."

"You'd be doing me a favor. One less thing to sell. Besides, I think it would make Lydie happy."

He stared at the keys in my hand. "There's more to my decision than money and a car. I don't want to leave Justice Bay right now. I don't want to leave Cassandra's. I need a college degree, but can commute to Cedarbrook Community College for the first two years. Transfer to Berkeley after that."

I put my hand on his arm. "It's your decision, Arthur. I support whatever makes you happy."

After the guests had gone and the kitchen resumed normalcy, Cooper and I collapsed on the living room couch. Walter placed another log on the fire and sat on a chair across from us. For a while, we all stared at the flames without speaking.

"Are you okay, Walter?" I asked.

"I will be. But not today." He stood. "I'm going home. You sleeping here tonight, Cooper?" He paused. "Just joking. See you later."

Walter walked toward the door. Cooper leaned over and whispered to me. "I think the old man might need some company about now. Do you mind?"

I shook my head. "Go."

After they left, I sat on the couch with my hand resting on Boo's back. I gazed at her as she purred and wondered how I ever considered giving her up for adoption. I leaned over and kissed her head.

"You and me," I whispered, "we're a team, right?" She opened her eyes and yawned. I took that as a yes.

A short time later, I picked up the Tibetan prayer book from the guestroom and took it down the hall to Lydie's bedroom, feeling the same strange euphoria I experienced every time I held it. Boo followed me. I flopped on my aunt's bed and closed my eyes, inhaling the fading fragrance of her perfume on the pillows, mixed with the aroma of incense lingering on the pages of the prayer book. Boo draped herself over my arm and fell asleep.

I felt a surge of energy and a heightened sense of awareness. In my mind's eye, I saw Lydie standing in front of me, wearing that same billowy African Savannah outfit she wore in the photo with eight-year-old me.

Strange as it sounded, I believed she'd pointed me to her killer using red-themed clues. Now, she'd come back to let me know she was okay and that her spirit would always be there to guide me. I whispered, "I miss you." Lydie's smile radiated such love that it almost felt unbearable. A moment later, she disappeared into a sphere of bright white light. I reached out to pull her back, but I grabbed only air.

My aunt influenced me in countless ways. I didn't know if her death had triggered those paranormal messages or if I had indeed inherited her intuitive abilities. Regardless, I felt profoundly sad but also grateful to her.

Howard Valdis took Lydie's physical presence away from me on an isolated rural road in the dead of night, but as my aunt had once told me, I will love you until the day I die and forever after. I felt the same way.

Acknowledgments

Thank you to everyone who extended their support, cheerleading skills, and advice during the writing of this novel, especially the members of my critique group, who commiserated, laughed, and groaned with me through the pages of the manuscript—Harley Jane Kozak, Matt Witten, Bonnie MacBird, Craig Faustus Buck, Linda Burrows, Andrew Rubin, and Terry Shames. My gratitude goes to former FBI Special Agent and author George Fong for graciously guiding me through the finer points of dead drops and other spy lore and to author Keith Raffel for talking me down from more than one cliff with his wise counsel on all things book-related and beyond. As always, I'm indebted to all the fine people at Level Best Books and my agent, Sandy Harding of Spencer Hill Associates, for championing Emma and her enablers.

About the Author

Patricia Smiley is the author of eight mystery novels. Her short fiction appeared in *Ellery Queen Mystery Magazine* and *Two of the Deadliest,* an anthology edited by Elizabeth George. Patty taught writing at various writers' conferences in the U.S. and Canada. She is the former vice president of the Southern California chapter of Mystery Writers of America and served as president of Sisters in Crime Los Angeles.

Smiley earned a BA from the University of Washington in Seattle and an MBA from Pepperdine University in Malibu, California. She lives in Los Angeles with her two loyal and opinionated Siberian Forest cats, and a backyard after-hours feeding station for possums, raccoons, marauding felines, and other critters in search of a snack and a cool sip of water. Despite the distractions, work continues on her next Justice Bay novel.

AUTHOR WEBSITE:
https://patriciasmiley.com

SOCIAL MEDIA HANDLES:
Twitter: Patricia Smiley @SmileyWriter

Facebook (personal): https://www.facebook.com/patricia.smiley.758

Also by Patricia Smiley

PACIFIC HOMICIDE SERIES
Pacific Homicide
Outside the Wire
The Second Goodbye

TUCKER SINCLAIR SERIES
False Profits
Cover Your Assets
Short Change
Cool Cache

www.ingramcontent.com/pod-product-compliance
Lightning Source LLC
Chambersburg PA
CBHW020617110726
47899CB00002B/542